Tiny Carteret

Sapper

TINY CARTERET

by

SAPPER

(pseudonym of Herman Cyril McNeile)

1932

BOOKS BY
"SAPPER"

Bulldog Drummond
The Black Gang
The Third Round
The Final Count
Temple Tower
The Female of the Species
Jim Maitland
The Dinner Club
The Saving Clause
The Man in Ratcatcher
Word of Honour
Jim Brent
Out of the Blue
Shorty Bill
John Walters
The Finger of Fate
Tiny Carteret

Tiny Carteret

CHAPTER I

Tiny Carteret stretched out a hand like a leg of mutton and picked up the marmalade. On the sideboard what remained of the kidneys and bacon still sizzled cheerfully on the hot plate: by his side a cup of dimensions suitable for a baby's bath gave forth the fragrant smell of coffee. In short, Tiny Carteret, half-way through his breakfast.

The window was wide open, and from the distance came the ceaseless roar of the traffic in Piccadilly. In the street just below, a gentleman of powerful but unmelodious voice was proclaiming the merits of his strawberries: whilst from the half-way mark came the ghastly sound of a cornet solo. In short, a service flat in Curzon Street.

The marmalade stage with Tiny was always the letter-opening stage, and as usual, he ran through the pile in front of him before beginning to read any of them. A couple of obvious bills: three more in feminine hands which proclaimed invitations of sorts with the utmost certainty—and then one over which he paused. The writing was a man's: moreover, it was one which he knew well although it was many months since he had seen it. Neat: decisive: strong—it gave the character of the writer with absolute accuracy.

"Ronald, by Jove!" muttered Tiny to himself. "And a Swiss postmark. Now what the dickens is the old lad doing there?"

He slit open the envelope, propped the letter against the coffee-pot, and began to read.

MY DEAR TINY [it ran]—

I know that at this time of year Ranelagh and Lords form your happy hunting-grounds, as a general rule by day, whilst at night you are in the habit of treading on unfortunate women's feet in divers ballrooms. Nevertheless, should you care to strike out on a new line, I think I can promise you quite a bit of fun out here. At least when I say here, this will be our starting-point. Where the trail may lead to, Allah alone knows. Seriously, Tiny, I have need of you. There is not going to be any poodle faking about it: in fact, the proposition is going to be an extremely tough one. So don't let's start under false pretences. There is going to be the devil of a lot of danger in it, and I want someone with a steady nerve, who can use a revolver if necessary, who has a bit of weight behind his fists and knows how to use 'em.

If the sound of this appeals to you send me a wire at once, and I will await your arrival here.

Yours ever,
RONALD STANDISH.

P.S.—A good train leaves the Gare de Lyons at 9.10 p.m. Gives you plenty of time for dinner in Paris.

Tiny pulled out his case and thoughtfully lit a cigarette. A faint twinkle in his eyes showed that he appreciated the full significance of the postscript: Ronald Standish knew what his answer would be as well as he did himself. Even as the trout rises to the may-fly, so do the Tiny Carterets of this world rise to bait such as was contained in the body of the letter. And just because he knew he was going to swallow it whole, he played with it mentally for quite a time. He even went through the farcical performance of consulting his engagement book. For the next month he had not got a free evening—a thing he had been fully aware of long before he opened the book. In addition, such trifles as Ascot and Wimbledon loomed large during the daylight hours. In fact, he reflected, as he uncoiled his large bulk from the chair, the number of lies he would have to tell in the near future would probably fuse the telephone.

And at this period it might be well to give some slight description of him. The nickname Tiny was of course an obvious one to give a man who had been capped fifteen times for England playing in the scrum. But though he was extraordinarily bigly made, he was at the same time marvellously agile, as men who played him at squash found to their cost. He could run a much lighter man off his feet, without turning a hair himself. The last half of the war had found him in the Coldstream: then, bored with peace-time soldiering he had sent in his papers and taken to sport of every description, which, fortunately for him, the possession of five thousand a year enabled him to do with some ease.

That he was extremely popular with both men and women was not to be wondered at: he was so completely free from side of any sort. In fact, many a net had been spread in the sight of the wary old bird by girls who would have had no objection to becoming Mrs. Tiny. But so far beyond flirting outrageously with all and sundry he had refused to be caught, and now at the age of thirty he was still as far from settling down as ever.

Once again he glanced at Standish's letter. It had been sent from the Grand Hotel at Territet, a spot which he recalled as being on the Lake of Geneva. And once again he asked himself the same question—what on earth was Ronald Standish doing there of all places? Territet was associated in his mind with tourists and pretty little white steamers on the lake. Also years ago he had played in a tennis tournament there. But Ronald was a different matter altogether.

It had been said of Standish that only the Almighty and he himself knew what his job was, and that it was doubtful which of the two it would be the more difficult to find out from. If asked point blank he would stare at the speaker with a pair of innocent blue eyes and remark vaguely—"Damned if I know, old boy." For months on end he would remain in London leading the ordinary life of a man of means, then suddenly he would disappear at a moment's notice, only to reappear just as unexpectedly. And any inquiries as to where he had been would probably elucidate the illuminating answer that he had just been pottering round. But it was to be noticed that after these periodical disappearances his morning walk for a few days generally led towards that part of Whitehall where Secretaries of State live and move and have their being. It might also be noticed—if there was anyone there to see—that when Ronald Standish sent in his name he was not kept waiting.

Even with Tiny Carteret he had never been communicative, though they were members of the same clubs and the closest of friends. The farthest he had ever gone was to murmur vaguely something about intelligence. And it was significant that at the time of the Arcos raid the first question he had asked *before* opening the paper which contained the news, was the number of men who had been rounded up. Significant also that on two occasions after he had returned from these strange trips of his he had been absent from London for a day, once at Windsor and the other time at Sandringham.

At the moment he had been away for about a month. He had disappeared in his usual unexpected manner, leaving a Free Forester team one man short as a result. Which in itself was sufficient to show that the matter was important, for cricket was a mania with him. And yet Territet of all places! Tiny Carteret scratched his head and rang the bell.

"I'm leaving London, Murdoch," he said, when his valet appeared. "I'm going to Switzerland."

"Switzerland, sir?" The man looked at him as if he had taken leave of his senses. "At this time of year?"

"Even so, Murdoch," answered Tiny with a grin. "But I shan't want you."

"Very good, sir. And when will you be leaving?"

At that moment the telephone bell rang.

"See who it is, Murdoch. And then find out if I'm in."

The valet picked up the receiver, and Tiny heard a man's voice coming over the wire.

Tiny Carteret

"Yes, sir. This is Mr. Carteret's flat. I will see if he is in."

He covered the mouthpiece with his hand and turned to his master.

"A Colonel Gillson, sir, wishes to speak to you."

"Gillson," muttered Tiny. "Who the devil is Gillson?"

He took the receiver from Murdoch.

"Hullo! Carteret speaking."

"Good morning." The voice was deep and pleasant. "I am Gillson. Speaking from the Home Office. Would you be good enough to come round and see me this morning any time before noon? The matter is somewhat urgent."

Tiny's face expressed his bewilderment.

"Sure you've got the right bloke?" he said. "The Home Office is a bit out of my line."

The man at the other end laughed.

"Quite sure," he answered. "You needn't be alarmed. Ask for Room 73."

"All right," said Tiny. "I'll be round about half-past eleven."

"Now what the dickens does Colonel Gillson of the Home Office want with me, Murdoch?" he remarked thoughtfully, as he hung up the receiver. "And where is the Home Office, anyway?"

"A taxi-driver might know that, sir," said Murdoch helpfully. "But to go back, sir, for the moment: when will you be leaving?"

Tiny lit a cigarette, and blew out a great cloud of smoke.

"To-morrow," he said at length. "That will leave me to-day to tell the necessary lies in, and get my reservations."

"How long shall I pack for, sir?" inquired his man.

Tiny gave a short laugh.

"Ask me another," he said. "I'm darned if I know, Murdoch. Give me enough to last a fortnight anyway. And one other thing." He turned at the door. "Get that Colt revolver of mine oiled and cleaned, and pack it in the centre of my kit."

He went down the stairs chuckling gently at the look of scandalized horror on his valet's face. Revolvers! Switzerland in the middle of the London season! Such things were simply not done, as Murdoch explained a little later to his wife.

"Hindecent, I calls it: positively hindecent. Why we were dining out every night."

But Tiny Carteret, supremely unconscious of the regal pronoun, was strolling happily along Clarges Street. The morning was perfect: London looked her best, but no twinge of regret assailed him at leaving. There were many more mornings in the future when London would look her best, but a hunt with Ronald Standish was not a thing a man could hope for twice. And as he turned into Piccadilly he found himself trying to puzzle out what the game was going to be.

The Lake of Geneva! Could it be something to do with the League of Nations? And Bolshevism? He rather hoped not. Unwashed international Jews, plentifully covered with hair and masquerading as Russians, failed to arouse his enthusiasm.

"Hullo! Tiny. If you want to kiss me, do you mind doing it somewhere else."

He came out of his reverie to find himself towering above a delightful vision in blue.

"Vera, my angel," he said, "I eat dirt. For the moment my brain was immersed in the realms of higher philosophy."

"You mean you were wondering if it was too early for a drink at your club," she answered. "Anyway don't forget next week-end."

"Ah! next week-end. Now that's a bad affair—next week-end. For tomorrow, most ravishing of your sex, I leave for Switzerland."

"You do what?" she cried, staring at him.

"Leave for Switzerland," he grinned. "I am going to pick beautiful mountain flowers—roses, and tulips and edelweisses and all that sort of thing."

"Tiny! You must be mad! What about our party?"

"I know, my pet. My heart is as water when I think of it. But it is the doctor's orders. He says I require building up."

"There's a girl in it," she said accusingly.

"Thumbs crossed—there isn't. You are the only woman in my life. Good God! my dear—it is a quarter past eleven. I must hop it. Think of me, Vera, in the days to come—alone with chamois—yodelling from height to height in my endeavours to please the intelligent little fellows. Would you like me to yodel now?"

"For Heaven's sake don't. And I think you are a perfect beast."

Tiny took out his handkerchief and began to sob loudly.

"Jilted!" he boomed in a loud voice, to the intense delight of a crowd of people waiting close by for a motor-bus. "Jilted by a woman for whom I have given up my honour, my fortune, even my morning beer."

"You unspeakable ass," she cried, striving vainly not to laugh. "Go away at once. And I hope you get mountain sickness, and die in an avalanche."

He resumed his interrupted walk feeling rather guilty. He knew that the girl he had just left had engineered the week-end party simply and solely on his account, and he had gone and let her down. Now it would be to her even as gall and wormwood, and she really was a darling.

"In fact, young fellow," he ruminated, "you must go easier with the little pretties in future. It's a shame to raise false hopes in their sweet young hearts. And one of these days you'll get it in the neck yourself."

He hailed a passing taxi and told the man to drive to the Home Office. Vera Lethington was forgotten: the immediate and interesting problem was, What did Colonel Gillson want with him? Presumably it must be something to do with Ronald Standish, since he could think of no other possible reason for the summons.

He asked for Room 73, and on giving his name was at once shown up. Seated at the desk was a hatchet-faced man with an enormous nose, who rose as he entered. He was very tall, and his eyes, keen and steady, seemed to take in every detail of his visitor at a glance.

"Mornin', Carteret," he said, and the words were short and clipped. "Take a pew. I suppose you know why I rang you up."

"Well, since I haven't been copped in a nightclub raid, Colonel, I can hazard a pretty shrewd guess," answered Tiny with a grin.

The other man smiled faintly.

"That's a matter for Scotland Yard. Incidentally you were having a pretty good time at the Fifty-Nine last Tuesday."

Tiny gazed at him in amazement.

"How the devil do you know? You weren't there, were you?"

"I was not," laughed Gillson. "Nature has endowed me with a nasal organ which renders me somewhat conspicuous. So I do not frequent clubs of that sort."

"Then how did you know?" persisted Tiny.

"Had you been stopping in London," said the other quietly, "now that I know you are a friend of Standish, I should have given you a word of warning about that club."

"You assume I am not stopping on then," said Tiny.

"Naturally," answered Gillson. "A man with fifteen caps would hardly be likely to."

"Oh! that's rot, Colonel. But you still haven't told me how you knew I was there."

"I've got a list, my dear boy, of every single soul who was in that club that night. Your waiter gave it to me."

"Well, I wish the damned fellow had concentrated more on his waiting and less on making a list. He slopped soup all over my trousers."

"Seeing it was the first time he had waited I don't suppose he was too bad," said the other quietly. "A bad spot that, Carteret: a festering sore. I don't mean because they sell liquor out of hours: that by comparison is nothing. But it is the centre..." He paused and lit a cigarette. "Well, I wouldn't be surprised if in the course of the next few weeks you didn't find yourself back there again—shall we say professionally."

"This is all deuced intriguing, Colonel," said Tiny. "Can't you be a bit more explicit?"

"All in good time, my dear fellow. Let us first get down to the immediate future. I assume you are leaving to-morrow."

"Quite right," answered Tiny. "Provided I can get reservations."

Colonel Gillson opened a drawer in his desk.

"I've got them all here," he said calmly. "And your ticket as well."

"The devil you have," spluttered Tiny, half inclined to be annoyed. "And supposing I hadn't been going to-morrow."

The older man looked at him steadily for a moment or two.

"Then I should have made a very bad mistake in my judgment of human nature," he said quietly. "A mistake which would have disappointed me greatly."

"Thank you, sir," answered Tiny, all his irritation gone. "That's a very decent thing to say."

"Now then," said the other, "we'll get down to brass tacks. You will go by the 10.45 train from Victoria: your seat is booked in Pullman S.2. Take the Golden Arrow to Paris: then go to Philippe's Restaurant in the Rue Danou. You know it?"

"Can't say I do, Colonel."

"You will find it one of the most delightful restaurants in Paris. The *homard à la maison* is one of the wonders of the world. It is a small place, but travelling as you are by the Golden Arrow you will almost certainly be the first arrival, so that you will have no trouble over getting a table."

"If there is, I'll mention your name."

"Under no circumstances will you do anything of the sort, Carteret," said the other quietly. "Under no circumstances are you to mention to a soul that you have seen me to-day. Do you remember that French notice in the war—'Mefiez vous. Taisez vous. Les oreilles de l'ennemi vous écoutent.'"

He smiled a little at the look of astonishment on Tiny's face.

"My dear fellow," he continued, "don't think I'm being melodramatic. But in our trade the first rule, the second rule, and the last rule are all the same. Never say a word more than is necessary. And to mention my name there would not only be unnecessary, but might be suicidal. You don't suppose, do you, that I am giving you these detailed instructions merely to ensure that you have a good dinner?"

"Well—no," laughed Tiny. "I don't. But you must remember, Colonel, that this sort of work is a new one on me. Anyway what is going to happen when I've got down to the *homard à la maison*?"

"A message will be given to you either verbally or in writing: which I do not know, and exactly when I do not know. If in writing commit it to memory, and destroy the paper."

"Who will give me this message?" asked Tiny.

"A man," said the other. "Don't ask me to tell you what he will look like, for I haven't the faintest idea. Have you got it clear so far?"

"Perfectly," said Tiny.

"When you've had your dinner you will go to the Gare de Lyons in time to catch the 9.10 train for Switzerland. I have reserved you a berth in a sleeper, and it is more than probable, Carteret, that when you come to inspect that reservation and all that goes with it you will consign me to the nethermost depths of the pit."

"What do you mean, Colonel?" said the bewildered Tiny.

"You will find out in due course," answered the other with a grin. "But there is one thing, young fellow, and don't you forget it." The grin had departed. "Under no circumstances whatever are you to alter your bunk—not even if the rest of the coach is empty."

"Right you are, sir. I can't profess to understand what it is all about at the moment, but I know an order when I hear one. I sleep"—he glanced at the paper in his hand—"in Number 8 bunk. Hullo! the ticket is only as far as Lausanne."

"That is where you get out," said Gillson. "A room has been already taken for you at the Ouchy Palace Hotel. Go there, and then Standish will take over the ordering of your young life."

He rose, to show that the interview was over.

"But, dash it all, Colonel," pleaded Tiny, "can't you give me some idea as to what the game is?"

Gillson shook his head.

"You will find out all that it is good for you to know, at the time when it is good for you to know it. Believe me, my dear fellow, this reticence doesn't imply any lack of confidence on my part. But there are certain occasions when real genuine ignorance is worth untold gold. Standish is playing the hand at the moment, and you are a very important card. It must be left to him to decide when he is going to play you, and how he is going to play you. But if it is any comfort I can tell you one thing. I'd give a year's screw if some divine act of Providence would blast away a lump of my cursed nose. For with that landmark gone I could have faked my face sufficiently to go in your place."

"That sounds all right, anyway," laughed Tiny. "Any message for Ronald?"

And as he asked the question the telephone rang on the desk.

"Wait a moment," said the Colonel. "Hullo!"

Tiny watched him idly as he stood there with the receiver to his ear. The lean hatchet face seemed frozen into a mask, so expressionless was it: only the eyes were glowingly alive. At last the voice from the other end ceased, and Gillson spoke.

"Can you come up at once, Dexter? You can. Good."

He replaced the instrument, and then stood motionless for more than a minute staring out of the window.

"Any message for Ronald," he said at length. "Yes, Carteret; there will be. You can tell him that Jebson has been murdered in the same way as the others. Wait a little. Dexter is coming, and we'll hear all about it. Incidentally, you know Dexter. You'd better dun him for another pair of trousers."

"You mean he was the waiter at the Fifty-Nine?"

But the other appeared not to have heard. With his hands in his pockets he was pacing up and down the office, his head thrust forward, his chin sunk on his chest, whilst Tiny leaned against the desk smoking. He did not speak again: he was busy with his own thoughts. So there was murder in the business, was there?... And more than one at that. And almost as if it was an echo of what was passing through his mind Colonel Gillson suddenly ceased his restless pacing and spoke.

"Don't be under any delusions, young Carteret. We're up against the big stuff this time with a vengeance."

He swung round as a knock sounded on the door.

"Come," he called, and a man entered whom Tiny recognized at once as the waiter.

"Morning, Dexter," said Gillson. "Bad affair this. You know Mr. Carteret, I think. He tells me you spoilt his trousers for him."

The new-comer grinned at Tiny.

"Sorry about it, Mr. Carteret. If only you'd stuck to kippers it would have been all right." He grew serious again and turned to Gillson. "You're right, sir: it is a bad affair. Am I to..." He glanced hesitatingly at Tiny.

"Carry on, Dexter. Mr. Carteret is now one of us."

"Well, sir, Jebson as you know was our permanency at the Fifty-Nine. He's been there now for over three months, and up to yesterday he was convinced that not a soul suspected he was not a genuine waiter. I saw him myself at lunchtime and he told me so. He's been waiting on two of the private rooms upstairs, and for over a fortnight nothing of any importance has taken place. Just the usual young fool, with the usual woman. But last night he told me he was expecting something of interest. That little swine Giuseppi who owns the place had been running in and out of one of his two rooms the whole morning, cursing and swearing and saying that this was wrong and that was wrong—a thing he never did for his ordinary *clientèle*. And then Jebson, happening to pass Giuseppi's office, heard him on the telephone ordering masses of orchids. Mauve orchids," he added meaningly.

Once again he paused and glanced at Tiny, as if doubtful whether to proceed.

"Mr. Carteret understands, Dexter, that any name he may hear mentioned in this office is as inviolate as if it was in confession," said Gillson quietly.

"Very good, sir," continued Dexter. "He at once appreciated the possible significance: the flowers had been mauve orchids the time before."

"Mauve orchids," said Tiny slowly. "Mauve orchids! Good Lord! it's impossible."

"What is impossible?" asked Gillson quietly.

"Nothing, sir, nothing. It was only a wild idea that flashed through my mind. Just a strange coincidence."

"The longer you are in this job, my boy, the more will you realize that nothing is impossible," said Gillson. "Well, Dexter: was it she?"

"That's the devil of it, sir—we don't know. Jebson did—but Jebson is dead. We don't know if it was Lady Mary."

Gillson's eyes were fixed on Tiny—a faintly quizzical look in them.

"Nothing is impossible, Carteret," he repeated quietly. "So that was the idea that had flashed through your mind."

"No: no, Colonel—nothing of the sort. Heavens! Nothing would induce Mary Ridgeway to go to a private room at the Fifty-Nine."

"And yet she was there six weeks ago alone with a man," said Gillson.

"Damn it, Colonel," said Tiny angrily, "this is going beyond a joke. Mary is a great personal friend of mine."

"Do you really imagine, Carteret," said the older man coldly, "that I should take the trouble to make a statement of that sort about any woman, whether she was a friend of yours or whether she wasn't, unless I knew it to be true? Well, Dexter?"

"That's all, sir. That's the sickening part of it. Jebson, poor devil, has been done in."

Tiny took a step forward.

"Look here, sir," he said to Gillson, "I apologize for my last remark. But you *cannot* mean to tell me that even if Lady Mary was there you hold her in any way responsible for this man Jebson's death?"

"Most certainly not," answered Gillson at once. "Such an idea never crossed my brain for a second. The person who is responsible for Jebson's death, is the man with whom Lady Mary—if it was she—was having supper. And he is the man we want, or perhaps I should say—one of the many men we want."

Tiny sank into a chair, his brain whirling. The whole thing was too preposterous. And yet—was it? Statements made in this quiet office seemed to carry with them a definite conviction which shook him. And Gillson had quietly said in the most matter-of-fact voice that six weeks ago she *had* been to the Fifty-Nine alone with a man. If so—what about last night?

He had been dancing with her at a house in Berkeley Square, and it had struck him more than once during the evening that she had seemed unusually *distraite*—so much so, in fact, that he had pulled her leg about it. And then at half-past eleven she had pleaded a headache and left. Nothing much to go on so far, it was true: but it was the matter of the mauve orchids that worried him, and that—he cursed himself now for not having kept a better guard on his tongue—had made him say what he did. Mary adored mauve orchids: all her friends knew it: half the world knew it on the evidence of Aunt Tabitha in *Society Snippets*.

And yet the whole thing seemed too preposterous. She was undoubtedly an unconventional girl, but there were certain things at which she would draw a very fast line. And it seemed to Tiny that dining in a private room at a place like the Fifty-Nine alone with a man was most emphatically one of them. Unless she had to: unless she had no alternative. He lit a cigarette thoughtfully, and then conscious that Gillson was eyeing him shrewdly he pulled himself together. His sudden remark could easily be attributed to the matter of mauve orchids: for the moment at any rate he saw no necessity to mention what he knew of her movements the previous night. Dexter was speaking, and Tiny forced himself to listen.

"Just the same way, sir—the same in every detail. He was an unmarried man and he lodged in a back road off Hammersmith Broadway. The woman who keeps the house heard him come in about two o'clock—she is sure about that because she happened to be awake at the time and the clock in her room struck the hour. Then she dozed off only to be woken up about an hour later by a choking sort of cry. Half shout—half moan is how she described it to me. Then there came the sound of a heavy fall in the room above her— the room which belonged to Jebson. Thinking he might be ill she put on her dressing-gown and ran upstairs. Then apparently she threw a faint at what she saw.

"I really don't blame her, sir," went on Dexter. "I saw the poor devil this morning and he was a pretty ghastly sight. He was in his pyjamas, half in and half out of bed. One hand was thrown up as if to ward something off, and his face was contorted hideously. Just like the others. Teeth bared: and only the whites of his eyes showing."

"Was the light on or off when the woman went in?" asked Gillson.

"On, sir. He was evidently just getting into bed."

"And the window?"

"Wide open."

"Would it be possible, without great difficulty, for someone outside to get in through the window?

"Quite impossible, sir, unless a ladder was used. But the room looks out at the back of the building. And about three yards away there is a sort of outhouse place. Nothing would be easier than for an agile man to scramble up on the roof of the outhouse, from where he could see straight into Jebson's room."

"Quite." Gillson nodded thoughtfully. "And where was it this time?"

"In the chest."

"Where was what?" cried Tiny.

"This is the fourth affair of this sort that has taken place," said Gillson. "In each case the appearance of the victims has been the same—distorted features, teeth set in a rigid snarl, only the whites of the eyes showing. And in each case somewhere or other on the body there has been a small scratch. But on no occasion has the thing with which the scratch was made been found. You found nothing, did you, Dexter, this time?"

"Not a thing, sir, though I went over the room with a fine toothcomb."

"But have you no explanation, Colonel?" asked Tiny.

"I certainly have an explanation as far as it goes. Unfortunately that isn't very far. That these four men were murdered I have no doubt, and they were murdered in precisely the same way. They were killed by the introduction into their system of some form of unknown poison, probably of the snake venom variety. It was injected through the scratch, and the ghastly expression on their faces was due to the agony of the muscular contortion as they died. But how was it injected? How was the scratch made?"

"Blow-pipe and poisoned dart," suggested Tiny.

"You can blow a dart out of a pipe, Carteret," said the other, "but I have yet to hear of a person who can suck it back again. If it had been done that way we should have found the darts."

"That's true," agreed Tiny. "I suppose it couldn't have been done by actually introducing a snake into the room."

"Impossible, Mr. Carteret," said Dexter. "At least—almost impossible. I wouldn't say that anything was quite impossible in this case. But there are a number of difficulties over such a solution. How was it got into the room: how was it got away again? Besides, so far as I know there is no known brand of snake whose bite causes practically instantaneous death. Well, you aren't going to tell me that if Jebson found that he had been bitten by a snake he was going to do nothing about it until he died twenty minutes or so later."

"Surely," said Tiny, "the same objection applies to whatever it was that did it. You can't have a hole made in your chest without knowing it."

"Precisely," remarked Gillson. "To my mind that is the essence of the entire thing. And it is such an amazing feature of all the cases that there can be only one solution. Consider the facts. Four trained officers—each of them scratched by something: each of them taking some period of time—how long we do not know—to die, and yet not one of them doing anything during that period, either to call for help or even to write a message on a piece of paper. It is incredible: it is preposterous unless we assume one of two things. Either the poison is to all intents and purposes instantaneous, or they attached no importance to the initial puncture."

Dexter nodded his head thoughtfully.

"I get your meaning, sir. Though it doesn't seem to make things any easier," he added ruefully. "By what possible method could the scratch be made to seem accidental, and yet not be accidental?"

"When you have solved that, Dexter, you have solved the problem. But of one thing I am certain. None of those poor devils connected the pain they were suffering—pain which must have increased to agony at the end—with the thing that pricked them. If they had—with their training, their sense of duty—they would have left some record of it."

"Mightn't it be possible," put in Tiny, "that they did leave some message? And then, once they were dead, the murderer, who could then afford to take his time, destroyed it. From what you say, Dexter, the old lady fainted. Isn't it feasible that the murderer, who was concealed in the room the whole time, took the chance and calmly hopped it?"

"Doesn't get over my initial difficulty, Carteret," said Gillson. "What about that period of time between the puncture and death? Do you mean to tell me that Jebson was going to allow some strange man in his bedroom to stab him in the chest, and not raise Cain?"

"It's the devil," said Dexter. "Because whether it seemed an accident or whether it didn't, they had to make certain of doing it last night. I'm sure of that, though of course we've got no proof."

Tiny lit a cigarette.

"What should make you so sure of that?" he asked quietly.

"I believe he found out something whilst he was waiting," said the other. "And then perhaps he gave himself away—who knows? At any rate they did him in before he could make his report."

"Well, really, my dear fellow," remarked Tiny, "if you'll forgive my saying so, it seems a piece of the wildest guesswork. Why you should assume that there is any connection between this poor devil's death in Hammersmith, and a party in a private room at the Fifty-Nine is beyond my diminutive brain. And you, Colonel, went so far as to say that the man giving the party actually did it."

"Not so, Carteret: I said he was responsible for it. Which is rather different."

"A matter of words, sir. But I cannot forget either—going back a bit in the discussion—that the name of a great personal friend of mine was mentioned as possibly having been in that room. Well, put it how you will—though I quite realize that what is said inside these four walls is sacred—it's a pretty serious matter. Following it to its logical conclusion, Colonel, it boils down to this. That whoever the lady was who was present, she took part in some conversation with the others who were present which resulted in the murder of the man who was waiting on them. Am I right?"

Colonel Gillson took a couple of turns up and down the room: then he swung round and faced Tiny.

"I see that I shall have to alter my decision, Carteret." He glanced at his watch. "Come and have lunch with me at the Rag, and I'll put you wise."

CHAPTER II

"Now you'll understand, Carteret, that what I'm going to tell you is for your ears and your ears alone."

The two men were seated in a corner of the smoking-room with coffee and brandy on the table in front of them.

"Fire ahead, Colonel. I don't mind confessing that I'm deuced curious. And you have my promise that I shan't say a word to a soul."

"I'll make it as short as possible," began Gillson. "And you had better realize right away from the start that a great deal of what I am going to say is in the nature of conjecture or even guesswork. Certain bald facts stick out, and on those pegs we have had to build up our theory. How much of that theory is right, and how much wrong, only time will show. And reading between the lines of a letter Standish wrote me, I think the time is pretty close at hand.

"However, let's get on with it. About five years ago there was a series of extraordinary and apparently disconnected crimes. They were not confined to England: in fact some of the most remarkable of them took place abroad. To take only a few at random. The murder of Rodrigo, the Spanish millionaire banker, in his house in Madrid; the death of Steiner, the German coal magnate, in Essen; Vanderstum the Dutchman, who was shot late one night when going back from a dinner-party in Amsterdam; Leyland, one of our own millionaires who was brutally done to death in an hotel in Liverpool—there are four that spring to my mind. And as I say, at first sight there seemed no connection between them. But if you go a little deeper into it you will find one factor that is common to all. In each of the four cases I have mentioned the death of the victim was of inestimable value to certain other people. I won't bore you with the why and the wherefore, but the bald fact remains that no tears were shed by various vested interests when they died. Don't misunderstand me: I don't mean the same vested interest in each case—I mean four different ones."

"I get you perfectly, Colonel," said Tiny.

"About that time, too, strange rumours began to go round in the underworld. At first the police paid no attention to them: then it was found that the same stories were being circulated in Paris and Berlin and all over the continent. It was the rumour of a thing which has long been the subject of sensational fiction—namely the super-criminal. The Napoleon of crime had at last arrived—the man who sat at the centre of things and pulled the strings while others did the work.

"For a long time I refused to believe it, but at length the evidence became so overwhelming that I had no alternative but to agree. Somewhere or other there was a controlling influence at work, though whether it was one man or several we didn't know. Nor do we know to-day. But after having sifted all the information we could lay our hands on, and rejected every scrap which seemed in the smallest degree doubtful, we came to the definite conclusion that a new factor in crime had arisen and a damned dangerous factor too. In short, we were confronted with a central body of unscrupulous and clever men who were prepared—at a price—to do your crimes for you."

"Good Lord! Colonel—it sounds incredible."

"Nevertheless it is the truth," said the other gravely. "It is a lamentable fact, but when you come into the realms of high finance a good many standards seem to change. And though I do not say for a moment that the people who stood to be ruined by Leyland, for instance, would ever have gone to the length of murdering him themselves, they were by no means averse to somebody else doing it for them. Of course, to a certain extent all this is conjecture. Not one of the many men who, I believe, were collectively responsible for Leyland's death has ever said a word. Naturally not. Though it is possibly suggestive that one of them—a man well known and well respected—has since committed suicide for no apparent reason."

"But what I don't understand," interrupted Tiny, "is how the dickens they set about it. How did they get in touch with this central body?"

"I don't suppose they did for a moment: the central body got in touch with them. My dear Carteret, if our theory is correct we are dealing with people whose brains are quite the equivalent of our own. We are dealing with an organization which has ramifications and spies all over the place through whom it collects its information. And I believe what happened was this. Someone—some underling—cautiously approached one of the men who were up against Leyland. Probably no mention of the word murder was made. Probably all that was said was that for some large sum of money it could be guaranteed that Leyland would change his policy. Which shows, mark you, if my supposition is correct, that they are no ordinary type of criminal. Hard-headed business men don't part with their cash on vague promises, unless the man who makes them is pretty convincing. Anyway—still sticking to our theory—the fact remains that they did stump up, and Leyland was murdered."

"Have you any proof that they stumped up?" asked Tiny.

"No actual proof. But it is a significant fact that the bank account of the man who committed suicide shows that he drew out a sum of five thousand pounds about a week before Leyland was murdered—a proceeding so foreign to his usual habits that the cashier remarked on it."

"But surely something should be done about it."

"My dear fellow," said the other, with a short laugh, "one of the first things you find out in this game is the difference between knowing and proving. You won't believe it, but the police know of four men at large in London to-day—two of them members of first-class clubs—who have all committed murder. But they can't prove it, so nothing can be done. However, that is a digression: let's return to our friends. We dug and we delved: we tried channels known to us and channels unknown to us. We pieced together information received from every imaginable quarter and after a time things did begin to look a little clearer. But always did we come up against one impenetrable wall—the wall that we still haven't succeeded in climbing. Where is the big man? Who is the big man? At this minute we could lay our hands on half a dozen underlings, but where is the boss?"

"Interrupting you for a moment, Colonel," said Tiny, "did they use this poison on any of the cases you have mentioned?"

"No. That little joy is of comparative recent date. And you will be amazed when I tell you what we are now convinced was the first occasion it was used—at any rate in this country. Do you remember the sudden death of Prometheus just before the Cambridgeshire two years ago when the horse was at evens?"

"Do I not?" said Tiny grimly. "I stood to win a monkey over the double with Galloping Lad."

"Precisely. And there were a good many other people besides you who had backed Galloping Lad for the Cesarewitch. In fact if Prometheus had won, the bookies would have had the skinning of their lives."

"But, Colonel, you surely don't imply that there was foul play, do you? The horse was just found dead in his box one morning."

"Exactly. Doubled up in the most dreadful contortions—teeth bared, head a mass of bruises where the poor brute had hurled itself against the walls in his agony, and the stable-boy with a fractured skull in the corner of the box, due to the horse having kicked him in its frenzy."

"Of course," said Tiny, "the case is coming back to me. When the boy was fit to be examined he swore on his Bible oath that he hadn't heard a sound till the horse started bucking and rearing in the box. Then he had rushed in and been kicked. That was it, wasn't it?"

"That was it. And I've mentioned the case only because, though we didn't know it at the time, I am convinced now that that was the first time this poison was used. It was a new one on us then: no one thought of looking for any puncture, and anyway it would have been very hard to find in a horse's coat. The vet was completely nonplussed, but the horse was dead, and that was all there was to it. The boy was put through a searching cross-examination later, but he stuck to the same story. He said that he had been asleep as usual in front of the door of the box: that he was a very light sleeper, and that no one could possibly have got to the horse without waking him. And so after a while, though a lot of people maintained that the horse had been tampered with, the accepted verdict was that it had died of some inexplicable disease of the heart which had attacked it suddenly."

"Hold hard a minute, Colonel. Does this poison leave no trace?"

"No chemical trace. But it affects the muscles of the heart, tautening them up and in non-medical language bringing on acute cramp. Hence the agony which the victims suffer just before death."

"It sounds awfully jolly," murmured Tiny. "Do you mind if I have another spot of brandy? But the point I can't get at is this. If the boy was speaking the truth: if the door of the loose box was shut—how was the poison administered?"

"Don't ask me, Carteret: frankly I don't know. The window was open: the top half of the door consisted of bars as usual. If a poisoned dart was used on that occasion we should never have found it in the straw even if anyone had thought of looking for it. But—let's get on. It is really immaterial whether the poor brute was killed that way or not: there are other far more important things at stake. And perhaps the most important is the fact that from about that time we began to notice a subtle difference in the activities of the gang—a difference which brought Standish and me in more directly than before. Until then the matter had been essentially a police affair: now they began to interest themselves in political affairs. True only if big money was likely to be available: but it was a new departure, and one which made things even more serious."

He paused and lit a cigarette: then abruptly he turned to Tiny.

"Have you ever heard of Felton Blake?"

"Never—to the best of my knowledge," answered Tiny.

"Felton Blake is one of the most perfect examples of the criminal mind that exists to-day. From his appearance you would put him down as a successful lawyer or doctor. He is a clean-shaven, dark, distinctly good-looking man of about forty-five. He has a large house in Hampstead, where he entertains lavishly and well. He states, should the question arise, that he is a merchant broker, and he does, in fact, run an office somewhere down in the city. An absolute blind, of course: in reality the man is the most dangerous blackmailer in Europe. He is completely devoid of pity: the most usurious money-lender is a tender-hearted woman compared to him. Once his claws are into a human being, the poor wretch can say good-bye to hope. He is a member of this gang, and a very prominent one. And"—once again he paused—"he is the man with whom Lady Mary Ridgeway was having supper at the Fifty-Nine six weeks ago."

"Good God!" muttered Tiny. "Are you sure, sir?"

"Jebson—the man who was murdered last night—though not then waiting on the private room, made it his business to be hanging round when Blake left. He had seen him go in: had seen that he had a lady with him, but had not been able to see her face. He succeeded as she left: it was Lady Mary."

"But, Great Scott! Colonel—what the devil can it mean? Is he trying to blackmail her? If so, what for? I mean—she's a cheery soul: does damned fool things at times. But—blackmail Mary. I can't believe it."

"Is it any harder to believe than the mere fact that she was there?"

"Do you think she has written some letters or something like that? And he's got hold of them? Because if so I'll go and break every bone in the swine's body."

The older man smiled faintly.

"A very natural instinct, Carteret—but one which I fear you will have to repress. I gather you know Lady Mary pretty well, don't you?"

"I do," said Tiny and then hesitated. "Look here, Colonel," he burst out, "you've been pretty frank with me: I'll return the compliment. I didn't say anything in your office, but after all there is no good having half confidences. Of course—there may be nothing in it. I was dancing with her last night, and she was frightfully glum all through the evening. Not a bit her usual self—in fact I pulled her leg about it. And then at half-past eleven she suddenly coughed up something about a headache and pushed off. Moreover, she bit me good and proper when I suggested running her home."

"I am glad you told me, Carteret," said Gillson quietly. "As you say there may be nothing in it; at the same time it shows us that she might have been there."

"But, damn it—why should she be there?" exploded Tiny.

"That is what I would give a good deal to know," answered Gillson. "We can assume one thing at any rate: she did not go there because she wanted to—she went because she had to. Therefore Blake has some hold over her: or..."

"Or what?" demanded Tiny.

"She went there on behalf of somebody else."

Tiny Carteret

"That's much more likely," remarked Tiny. "She's the most kind-hearted creature in the world: do anything for a pal."

The other glanced cautiously round the room: then he bent forward, and his voice was hardly above a whisper.

"You saw a good deal of Princess Olga when she was over here three years ago, didn't you?"

For a moment or two Tiny stared at him blankly.

"I did," he said at length. "But firstly, how do you know; and secondly, what has that got to do with it?"

"My dear fellow," said Gillson shortly, "don't be dense. Do you imagine that when a Princess who is shortly to become Queen of Bessonia comes over here on a visit we don't know who she goes about with? And as to what it has to do with it—possibly a lot. I think I'm right in saying that she and Lady Mary became very great friends."

"You are," agreed Tiny. "Very great friends indeed."

"Six weeks ago Lady Mary returned from a visit to Bessonia where she had stayed with the King and Queen. A few days later she has supper with a notorious blackmailer in a private room at the Fifty-Nine—admittedly a thing which only the greatest provocation would cause her to do. Now do you see what I'm getting at?"

"I gather that your implication is that she is acting on behalf of the Queen. But I don't see that it takes us much further."

"It doesn't—and that is where you come in. Had Jebson not been murdered, it might have been a different matter. As it is, you've got to do what you can. But first of all get the points clear in your mind. As I told you the activities of the gang have of recent months tended to become political. Add to that the fact that at the present moment Bessonia is the open powder-keg of Europe. The overthrow of the

King and Queen would undoubtedly cause a grave crisis: but there are people who would pay a lot of money to bring it about. There is the major side of the case: now for the minor. Has Felton Blake got some hold over the King and Queen—or over the Queen alone—which if used in the proper quarter might bring about that overthrow? And is Lady Mary acting as an emissary of the Queen to buy off Blake, or to persuade him to hold his hand? That's what I want to find out: that's what I believe Jebson *did* find out last night. And was murdered for his pains."

He paused and lit a cigarette, while Tiny sat motionless, staring at him.

"Understand, Carteret, that only two other men in the world—on our side at any rate—know what I've been telling you. One is Ronald Standish. Dexter knows nothing save the obvious fact that Lady Mary had supper with Felton Blake. His is purely the police side of the show: this is our end of it."

"But surely, Colonel," said Tiny at length, "in a case of such gravity as this something could be done with this man Blake. Couldn't he be run in—on a faked charge if necessary?"

The other shook his head.

"You can't run a man in on a faked charge in this country, Carteret. At least not in peace-time. And as to a genuine charge against the swine—he's far too clever. Blake only deals in those cases where the consequences to the victim if he did come forward and lay information would be such that he simply daren't do it. There are probably forty people to-day, any one of whom could get that blackguard sent to prison for fifteen years. But not one of them will do it. Some day, of course, a social benefactor will come along who will murder Blake. And then he will be tried for his life and probably hanged. But until that moment arrives we have got to fight Blake with legitimate weapons."

"Exactly what do you want me to do?" asked Tiny.

"I would suggest that you call round and see Lady Mary this afternoon—ostensibly to say good-bye to her. Or to inquire if her headache is better. Then I leave it entirely to you. Find out what you can. Even the certainty that she was at the Fifty-Nine last night would be something."

"Can't say I like it much, Colonel."

"You are free to back out now, Carteret. You are not under my orders. But I think you are viewing the thing from the wrong aspect. Don't get into your head the idea that I am asking you to spy on her. We are entirely on her side—and the more we know the more we can help her. If only people who are up against the Blakes of this world would realize that—Lord! what a difference it would make."

"Yes: I quite see that. All right—I'll have a dip at it. But don't expect too much, sir. Mary is not an easy person to pump. By the way—you don't happen to know the number of the private room, do you?"

The other rose.

"Wait here. I'll telephone and find out."

He threaded his way through the now half-empty room, leaving Tiny with his brain whirling. It was the extraordinary inside knowledge about other people's movements that Gillson had which amazed him. And yet he had seemed to take it quite as a matter of course. Then his mind switched over to the immediate problem. Deep down he felt instinctively that Mary had been to the Fifty-Nine the night before. She had been so utterly unlike her usual self that there must have been something pretty drastic to account for it. And suddenly he became quite definitely aware of the fact that the thought of Mary having supper with Felton Blake affected him considerably more than if it had been Vera Lethington for example. The idea that there could be anything between them was simply laughable; and yet.... Why the Fifty-Nine? Why a private room? Surely if there was anything in this idea of Gillson's—if Mary was acting as a go-between for the Queen of Bessonia—she could have sent for Blake to come to her house.

His mind went back to the time three years ago when as Princess Olga he had seen a lot of her. Several little *partis carrés* with Mary and a cheery fellow about his own age. What the deuce was his name? He could remember him perfectly distinctly—a tall fair bloke with hair that crinkled naturally. Joe something or other. Funny now that he came to think of it, but he'd never seen him since. Seemed to have disappeared completely. Probably out in Kenya, or one of the colonies. What the devil was his name? Joe....

"Room number 7."

Tiny came out of his reverie to find Gillson standing beside him.

"Right, Colonel!" He got up. "It's a quarter past three now: I'll probably drift in to see her about half an hour before cocktail time. Best chance of finding her alone. And I'll let you know if I find out anything. Incidentally do the arrangements for to-morrow still hold?"

"They do," said the other. "And I know no more than you do what will happen afterwards. There is only one bit of advice I can give you—keep your eyes skinned. For unless I'm much mistaken the time is coming when you'll want 'em in the back of your head."

Tiny grinned cheerfully.

"Sounds good to me, sir. The only thing I'm not frantically set on is this poison stuff. Your description of the symptoms sounded most entertaining."

But there was no answering smile on the other's face.

"Take care, my boy," he said gravely. "There's no jest about this matter. And I'd like you to add to the fifteen next winter. Don't forget: *sleep* with one eye open. And ring me up to-night at eight o'clock and tell me what you've found out.... Sloane 1234 is the number."

Tiny strolled along Pall Mall still puzzling over the elusive name. At times it was on the tip of his tongue: then it was gone again. He would ask Mary when he saw her: she'd remember. Joe... Joe.... Though, after all, what the devil did it matter? There were vastly more important things to think about, not the least being the method of tackling Mary. From a fairly profound knowledge of her he realized that he would have to walk warily. If she got the impression that he was coming as a sort of emissary of the police the probability was that she would go straight off the deep end. And small blame to her: he would feel the same himself. And yet he saw quite clearly that what Gillson had said was right. Whatever was the reason of her meeting Felton Blake, it was better for her that it should be known. The point was—would she tell him?

He glanced at his watch: two hours still to put through. It was too early for tea: besides he felt as if he had only just finished lunch. And as he stood cogitating on what to do at the corner opposite the Athenaeum a magnificent Rolls-Royce swung past him and turned up towards Piccadilly Circus. Unconsciously he glanced at the people in it: then his eyes narrowed. For one of them was a clean-shaven, dark, distinctly good-looking man who might have been a successful lawyer: the other was Mary herself.

She had not seen him, but that fleeting glimpse had been enough for him to see the expression on her face. And it had been like a frozen mask: the man at her side might have been non-existent.

He felt instinctively that her companion was Felton Blake, though he had never seen the man before in his life. And he began to feel annoyed. Was Mary insane? In many ways it was more indiscreet of her to drive alone with the man than to have supper with him. Where one person might find out the latter, to drive alone with him in the middle of the season was proclaiming the thing to a hundred. Her features were far too well known: moreover, as far as he could see she was making no attempt whatever to conceal them.

He turned and strolled back the way he had come, and almost immediately ran into Gillson on his way to the Home Office.

"Has that man Felton Blake got a yellow Rolls limousine with an aluminium bonnet?" he demanded shortly.

"I should think it's more than likely," answered the other. "He's rich enough to keep a dozen. Why?"

"Because if he has he's just passed me at the corner there with Lady Mary alone in the car with him. Damn it! Colonel — the girl has gone mad. I must say she was looking at the swab as if he was something out of cheese. But fancy her doing such a thing! In May, in London, in the middle of the afternoon!"

"Don't forget one thing, Carteret, in your quite natural peevishness. Very few people except his actual victims know what Blake really is. You may not have met him, but he is a man who is received in very good society. So that it is not quite the howling indiscretion it seems to you. Where are you going?"

"White's — until it's time for me to go and see her."

"I'll find out about that question of the car and ring you up. So long."

But when twenty minutes later one of the pages told him he was wanted on the telephone he felt it was almost unnecessary to go. He *knew* the man was Felton Blake: and Gillson's voice from the other end telling him that the description fitted Blake's car only confirmed a certainty.

He went moodily back into the smoking-room and flung himself into a chair. The club was empty, a fact for which he was profoundly thankful. He felt in no mood for conversation: he wanted to try and get things straight in his head. And after a time one fact began to stand out very clearly. If Jebson had been murdered by this mysterious poison because he had overheard something the night before, it was obvious that he himself would be in danger of a similar attention, if it became known that Mary had confided in him. Not that that mattered in the slightest. Tiny was as much without fear as a man may be, and so long as he could help Mary nothing else counted. But he also was no fool, and the prospect of dying in the manner Gillson had described failed to appeal to him in the slightest degree. At the same time if four skilled police officers had all been caught, the odds were pretty strongly against his escaping.

He wished now that he had asked Gillson more details about the other three. Surely by comparing the four cases some factor common to all must emerge, from which it would be possible to deduce something. And yet the only deduction that seemed to have been made so far was that the puncture in each case must have seemed accidental to the victim. He quite saw the reasoning behind the conclusion: at the same time there seemed to be some grave difficulties in accepting such a conclusion. If it had genuinely seemed accidental, then surely in each case it must have been pure chance whether it came on or not. If, for instance, some form of poisoned spike had been fixed somewhere in the room, it would be an absolute fluke if the victim pricked himself on it. And if it was fixed in something he was bound to use—his tooth-brush say—it certainly would not seem accidental. Besides, only the most eccentric people use tooth-brushes on their stomachs. And that was where Jebson had got it.

At last he gave it up and sent for some tea. He would probably solve the mystery personally, he reflected grimly, and until then there was not much good worrying. The utmost he could hope for was that if he was cast for the part of number five he would have the time to pass on some warning for the benefit of number six.

At a quarter past five he left the club and hailed a taxi. And while he waited for the machine, mindful of Gillson's instructions, he stared fixedly at the passers-by, most of whom seemed to resent it strongly. But with the exception of a Bishop, who Tiny regarded with certainty as the murderer in disguise, they seemed comparatively harmless.

He gave the driver the address, and sat down with care. Beyond the fact, however, that the machine was obviously on the verge of complete disintegration, he could see no cause for alarm. No spikes stuck out anywhere, and though the cushion felt as if it was stuffed with tin-tacks he arrived at his destination without any perforation of the skin. And then came the first check. Her ladyship was in, but the butler was not sure if she wished to see anyone at the moment. She had come in with a headache, and had left word that she did not wish to be disturbed.

"That's a nuisance, Simmonds," said Tiny. "Because I'm leaving England to-morrow."

"Leaving England, sir! I dare say that would make a difference. I'll ask her ladyship."

"What's that, Tiny?" A door at the end of the hall opened and the girl herself put her head out. "Leaving England! Come in and tell me about it. But no one else, Simmonds."

"Very good, my lady."

Tiny followed her into her own particular sanctum, and she closed the door.

"It's sweet of you to see me, Mary dear," he said, taking both her hands. "How's the head?"

"As an excuse it serves, Tiny. I felt I couldn't bear that chattering cocktail crowd this evening. Sit down and tell me about this sudden change of plan. What are you leaving England for? You said nothing about it last night."

"I only decided this morning," he answered, sinking into a chair and pulling out his cigarette-case. "And then you very nearly altered my plans."

"I did? What *do* you mean?"

"Whilst communing with nature opposite the Athenaeum this afternoon I narrowly escaped death from a large yellow Rolls. And in that Rolls, Mary dear, I perceived you complete with gentleman friend."

He spoke lightly, but the sudden tightening of her lips did not escape him.

"I never saw you, Tiny." Her voice expressed only the most perfunctory interest. "But since you did escape death, why this strange move? And where are you going?"

"A sudden whim, my dear. I'm joining a very great pal of mine in Switzerland, and we're going on a walking tour. We might even pop over the border and go into Bessonia."

"Bessonia! Walking tour! My dear Tiny, what has come over you?" She was staring at him in genuine amazement, as if she could hardly believe her ears.

"Sounds a bit grim, doesn't it?" he laughed. "However, that's the programme. I wonder," he added carelessly, "if the Queen would remember me."

"Of course she does, Tiny," she said slowly. "She talked a lot about you when I was there, Give me a cigarette, like a dear."

He handed her the box and struck a match. But he noticed that it was quite an appreciable time before she seemed to be aware of either.

"Tiny," she said, when he had sat down again, "are you serious? Are you really going on a walking tour?"

"Like the headache, my dear—as an excuse it serves. By the way," he went on, "it's funny how little things worry one. I've been trying the whole afternoon to think of the name of that bloke who used to play about with us such a lot when she was over here. I can't get farther than Joe."

"Joe Denver," she said. "I suppose you don't know where he is, Tiny?"

Was it his imagination, or did he detect a certain eager tenseness in the question?

"Not a notion, my dear. I've never seen him since those days. I've a sort of idea he was in Kenya or something like that."

"I wonder if there is any way of getting in touch with him," she went on.

"I suppose an advertisement in the papers would do it in time. But is there any special reason for doing so?"

"Oh! no. I just wondered." She passed her hand over her forehead.

"Mary, dear, you're looking tired," he said quietly. "And worried. Is there anything I can do to help? You know you've only got to say the word."

"You're a dear, Tiny," and her voice was weary. "But there is nothing, old lad, that you or anybody else can do, I fear me."

"Then there is something the matter," he said insistently. "Can't you tell me, dear?"

"That's the devil of it: I can't. And even if I did it wouldn't do any good."

For a moment he hesitated: then he took the plunge.

"Mary, is it anything to do with that bloke you were driving with this afternoon?"

She pressed out her cigarette.

"Tiny, drop it, please. I can't tell you. Let's change the subject. What have you been doing to-day?"

"I lunched with a lad at the Rag," he said. It seemed to him that the moment had come to go at it bald-headed. "One of these mysterious sort of birds who move about behind the scenes, and appear to know everything. He was very full of a murder that took place last night. Some man down Hammersmith way—a waiter."

"It hardly seems of surpassing interest," she remarked.

"He was a waiter at the Fifty-Nine Club, and apparently... Mary dear——"

Every vestige of colour had left her face, and as he sprang towards her she swayed in her chair. Then she pulled herself together and pushed him away.

"It's all right, Tiny. Stupid of me. I suddenly felt faint. I'm not very fit these days. Tell me about this murder."

"There is very little to tell. The man was killed by some new and hitherto unknown poison. The only point of interest is that apparently he wasn't a waiter at all, but some secret service agent."

And once again every vestige of colour left her cheeks.

"Why on earth should they want a secret service agent at the Fifty-Nine?" she asked at length.

Tiny shrugged his shoulders as if the matter had already begun to bore him, though his heart was aching for her. What was the best thing to do? Should he put all his cards on the table? Should he tell her exactly what he suspected and implore her to confide in him what the trouble was? Finally he decided to temporize.

"Ask me another, my dear. I believe some pretty rum things go on in the private rooms there."

"It was a waiter for one of the private rooms, was it?"

"Number 7," he said, and stared straight at her. But by this time she had controlled her expression, and the shot missed.

"Poor fellow," she said. "Do you think that dark deeds of treason were being discussed in the room, and that he overheard them?"

"Nobody seems to know what went on in the room, or even who was there, because he never sent in a report. In fact, the only thing that seems to have come out up to date is that the table was decorated with mauve orchids."

"My dear Tiny," she said lightly, "what on earth are you looking at me like that for? Why shouldn't the table be decorated with mauve orchids?"

"Mary dear," he answered steadily, "I'm going to chance it. I must. Was it you who was having supper in that room last night?"

"You must be mad, Tiny," she cried angrily.

"I wish I was, Mary. Listen, my dear, for it's got to be told. This bloke I was lunching with to-day simply appalled me with his inside knowledge. For instance, he knows that you had supper at the Fifty-Nine Club in a private room about six weeks ago with a notorious blackmailer called Felton Blake."

"Go on, please," she remarked icily. "I was always given to understand that women's names were not bandied about in men's clubs."

"My dear," he pleaded, "for God's sake, get it right. There was no question of your name being bandied about. We were having a private talk after lunch."

"The upshot of which appears to be that you, a man whom I have always regarded as a friend, come round here to spy on me. I suppose whatever you find out will be added to this gentleman's inside knowledge."

"Mary," he cried passionately, "you can't think I'd be such a swine as that. Don't you see, my dear, that if you are in trouble—if this swab has a hold over you in any way—it's vital that someone should help you."

"What I see is the most unwarrantable interference in my private affairs. I foolishly imagined that if I did choose to have supper six weeks ago at the Fifty-Nine it was my concern and nobody else's."

"Even if the man you had supper with is a notorious blackmailer?" asked Tiny.

"Even if he is a murderer, forger and thief rolled into one. What business is it of anyone else's?" she cried passionately. "And anyway, what are you driving at now? Even if I did have supper last night at the Fifty-Nine, am I supposed to be responsible for this so-called waiter's death?"

Tiny got up a little wearily.

"Then you won't tell me, Mary dear? You won't let me help you."

For a moment her eyes softened: then she shook her head.

"I wish I could, Tiny: how I wish I could. Forgive me, old man—I've been talking out of my turn a bit. I didn't mean all that about spying on me: I do know you were trying to help. But it's useless, my dear—useless."

"Mary, my dear," he stammered, "would it be useless if I were in—well, in a position to look after you?"

"Bless his heart: he's proposing." She gave a tender little laugh. "Bend down, Tiny." For a moment or two she stared at him: then she kissed him on the lips. "Now run away, my dear, and forget all about it."

And Tiny, being a man of understanding, went away. Just once by the door he turned round and looked at her, and it seemed to him that she looked weary unto death. Then a little blindly he went out into the sunlit street.

CHAPTER III

That it had been Lady Mary Ridgeway with Felton Blake the previous night he was convinced. True, she had not actually admitted it, but her whole demeanour simply shouted the fact. And as he walked moodily back to his club he tried vainly to puzzle the thing out.

Tiny Carteret knew probably as much about Lady Mary Ridgeway as any other man, and a good deal more than most. He knew all her friends: they were both in the same set. And if anybody was likely to have heard of any undesirable entanglement in the past it was he. As he argued it to himself if she was in Felton Blake's power it must be due to his possession of something incriminating belonging to her. And that as far as he could see could only be letters.... Love letters. Further, they must be letters written either to some hopeless outsider, or to a married man. Otherwise, though possibly injudicious, there would be nothing incriminating about them.

The question of the outsider he dismissed at once: the mere thought of such a thing in connection with Mary was laughable. And the married man solution seemed almost as blank a wall. He made, of course, no pretence whatever to such an extremely intimate inside knowledge of her life, and there might have been some man ... might even be one now. And a letter might have got mislaid, or been stolen by a valet and sold to Blake. But somehow or other—rightly or wrongly—Tiny felt that if it had been so rumours of it would have got about, at any rate in her own immediate set. And there had never been such a rumour—not the suspicion or hint of one: that he knew.

He tried another line—could it be money trouble? If possible—even more absurd. Mary was very well off, and her father the Duke was an extremely wealthy man, who adored her. Besides, Gillson had said nothing about Blake being a moneylender.

At which point in his reflections he realized that he didn't seem to be making much progress. Incriminating letters and money trouble removed there didn't seem to be a great deal left. And quite naturally his thoughts turned along the other line; the line at which Gillson had hinted that morning. Was she acting as a go-between for the Queen?

If it was so he was in deeper waters than ever. Impossible though it was to arrive at any conclusion if it was Mary herself involved, it was doubly impossible if it was the Queen. And yet the more he thought of it the more likely did it seem to him. In the first place the mere fact that Gillson had suggested it as a likely solution weighed with him. Never in his life had Tiny Carteret been so impressed by a man's personality as he had been that morning. It wasn't only the fact that the fellow had seemed to know such an astounding amount about one's personal movements, he reflected: it was the indefinable atmosphere of power about him ... inscrutable to a certain extent, and yet quite prepared to throw all his cards on the table if it suited him. And a damned hard man to bluff.

But apart from Gillson having considered it a possibility, Tiny himself was inclining towards the idea. The difficulty of imagining Mary herself to be the victim, necessitated finding another. And it was a significant fact that the first time she had had supper with Felton Blake was immediately on her return from Bessonia. Odd remarks, to which he had attached no importance at the time, came back to him—remarks made casually during the last few weeks by pals of both sexes.

"Mary seems a bit off her oats." "Mary doesn't seem a bit herself these days." And one in particular. "My dear, I believe you've fallen in love with a Bessonian."

Trifles: laughed off as soon as made, but now taking on a new significance in Tiny's brain. What had happened to Mary during her visit there? He would have given all he possessed to know. In the answer to that question lay the solution.

He ordered a gin and bitters and picked up an evening paper. One of the headlines caught his eye—

Tiny Carteret

CRITICAL SITUATION IN BESSONIA.
INCREASING TENSION.

His eye travelled down the column.

"The situation in Bessonia is appreciably graver than it was twenty-four hours ago. As yet there are no visible signs of discontent and things are proceeding normally. But this state of affairs exists only on the surface. To anyone acquainted with the Bessonian temperament it is obvious that a clash must come soon between the Royalist party and the International group, and what the issue will be no one can say. At the moment the army remains loyal."

He put down the paper, and lit a cigarette. Like the majority of his fellow-countrymen, the internal affairs of remote foreign states bored him to extinction. He dimly remembered that he had heard a man at dinner a few nights ago saying something about the condition of Bessonia, but he had paid no attention. And it began to strike him now that if his surmise over Lady Mary was right, it was high time he ceased to pay no attention. He glanced round the room and saw the very man he wanted—Squire Straker, foreign editor of the *Planet*.

"Straker, old hearty," he called out, "in return for a few minutes of your valuable time I will donate you with a pink gin. Is it a bargain?"

"Hullo! Tiny." The other lounged over—a big loosely made man with a European reputation. "Don't often see you in here at this hour."

"Straker, I crave for knowledge. Knowledge about Bessonia. Get on with it."

The other looked at him curiously.

"Rather a new departure for you, isn't it? What do you want to know about it? If the shooting is good, or what?"

"I want to know briefly, old lad, what the political situation is there. I have just read in this rag—oh! it's one of yours, is it—that a clash is imminent between the Royalist party and the Industrial group. Why?"

Squire Straker sat down and began to fill an ancient pipe.

"If you are really interested, Tiny, I can give you the situation in a nutshell. It is not at all complicated: it is a situation which has occurred innumerable times in those small Latin states in the past, and which will occur innumerable times in the future. Political intrigue is as the breath of life to them, though I am bound to say that in this case the matter is rather more serious than usual. You probably don't remember that when the old king died five years ago, there was a very large party in Bessonia who were in favour of the place becoming a republic. The party was led by a gentleman named Berendosi, who is an extremely able man—possibly the ablest they've got. And had that party had its way Berendosi would undoubtedly have been the first President. Well—it didn't have its way, and the present bloke Peter became king. But Berendosi is not the type of man to let trifles of that sort deter him, and though he was defeated in the first round he was by no manner of means knocked out. He went on working and plotting behind the scenes, until he got a severe jolt in the second round too. That was when the King got married. The Queen, as you probably know, is a most divinely pretty creature, and she absolutely knocked the entire population endways. They raved about her, and Peter's stock soared sky high. Never had he been so popular: never had his position seemed more secure. And Berendosi looked on, smiling behind his hand. Only too well did he know his own countrymen: only too well did he know the rapidity with which the pendulum swings with people of their temperament. He could afford to bide his time. A word here, a hint there: a rumour spread and then contradicted—but by that time the damage was done. And so it went on, like drops of water wearing away a stone, until a new and completely unexpected development took place about three months ago. Am I boring you?"

"Very far from it," said Tiny.

"Up to that time the hints and innuendoes started by Berendosi and his group had been entirely political. You know the sort of thing I mean—that So-and-So was accepting bribes: that the King was grossly extravagant: that the people were being overtaxed in order that corrupt ministers might line their pockets. And then, as I say, came the change. It was done very gradually, and at first our correspondent out there—who by the way is an extremely able man—disregarded it. But after a time he could do so no longer: the rumours became so persistent. And though they varied in small details the main gist was the same: the Queen was being unfaithful to her husband."

Tiny Carteret sat up with a jerk: then sank back in his chair again.

"Go on," he said quietly.

"Now you can see at once," continued Straker, "the vast importance of the move. The Industrial party—which is another name in that country for the Republican party—and Berendosi do not care the snap of a finger if she is unfaithful or if she isn't. But the other party—the Royalist party—would literally be split from top to bottom if it were proved that she was. In fact Berendosi would have obtained everything he wants. The cement binding the Royalist party together, is the beauty and the home life and all the rest of it of the King and Queen. Once that cement was removed: once the rumour was proved true the party would simply disintegrate."

"And do you think it is true?" asked Tiny slowly.

The other shrugged his shoulders.

"The King is not a particularly prepossessing specimen," he answered. "And Queens are no different to ordinary women except that considerably more publicity surrounds their lives. No, Tiny: I can't tell you—I don't know. All I can tell you is that if the rumour becomes currently believed, it doesn't matter whether it's the truth or whether it isn't: the result will be the same. It may take longer— but in the end Berendosi will win. Of course, were it possible to prove such a thing—spectacularly, which as far as I can see it isn't, why then..."

Again he shrugged his shoulders.

"What then?" said Tiny.

"Well, it wouldn't be a question of in the end. The thing would be over in an hour, and one would never be surprised with people of the Bessonian temperament if the punishment awarded the erring lady was short and drastic. No, Tiny—that would be a very serious matter. We do not want Berendosi in power there for many reasons into which I haven't got time to go now. And as long as the matter remains in the region of rumour I don't think we shall have Berendosi in power. But if by some unfortunate chance that girl has been indiscreet, and Berendosi holds proof of it—proof which would carry conviction to the masses—it's all up. He is just biding his time now, and preparing the ground. Then when he's ready, he'll strike."

He finished his drink and rose.

"So long, old boy: this is the hour when my chief labour commences."

He shambled out of the room like a great bear, leaving Tiny staring thoughtfully out of the window. And such is the constitution of the human mind that it was not problems of high politics in the Near East that occupied the latter's thoughts, but something very much more personal. Why had not Gillson told him all this at lunch? That Squire Straker should be in possession of information unknown to Gillson was absurd. Gillson must have known all about these rumours, but not a word had he said. And Tiny began to feel irritated. He had all the independent man's dislike of being kept in the dark. Surely if he was a fit and proper person to play at all, the least he could expect was to be given full information. Why should he be used as a cat's paw? And then as suddenly as his irritation had arisen, it evaporated. Gillson's words in his office that morning recurred to him.

"There are certain occasions when real genuine ignorance is worth untold gold."

Presumably this had been one of them. Not only was he to be kept in the dark as to what was going to happen to himself on the other side, but also as to what was happening to other people. Yet, surely it would have been better had he known the rumours before he went round to see Mary. He could have asked her point blank: he could have...

And what would have been the result? He lit a cigarette thoughtfully, and a faint smile twitched round his lips. What would have been the result? Nothing: a flat denial. He knew Mary well enough for that, and so apparently did that darned fellow Gillson. Had he gone round there evidently bursting with official information, Mary would have shut up like an oyster. And so Gillson had deliberately sent him round to see her full of genuine ignorance, in the hope that she would turn to him for help. The problem that occupied Straker occupied Gillson too. Was there any definite proof of the rumour in existence? That is what he had been sent to find out, and that is what he had not succeeded in finding out.

At least, not for certain. That Squire Straker's information was of vital importance he realized. It provided a central peg on which the whole thing hung together connectedly. There *was* proof in existence, and Felton Blake held it. And Mary *was* acting on behalf of the Queen to get it back. The other difficulties—the private room in the Fifty-Nine, the motor drive which the two had taken together—seemed capable of explanation once that central fact was conceded. They were trifles compared with the main thing.

He glanced at his watch: five minutes to eight. What was he going to say to Gillson over the telephone? He had no proof: only a strong intuition. He might be wrong—wildly wrong. He might be jumping to the most absurd conclusion. And yet, once granted Mary herself was not the victim, which was even more absurd, what other possible conclusion was there?

He was still undecided as he called up Sloane 1234: still undecided when he heard Gillson's deep voice from the other end.

"Nothing for certain, Colonel," he said.

"We can't always deal in certainties, Carteret, in our trade. Did you find out anything at all?"

He answered with another question.

"Do you know Squire Straker by any chance?"

"Of course I do." Gillson seemed surprised. "Why do you ask?"

"I've just been having a long talk with him over the state of affairs in a certain country."

Was it Tiny's imagination, or did a very faint chuckle come from the other end of the wire?

"Have you indeed? I hope you were interested."

"I think you might have been a little more explicit, Colonel, at lunch to-day."

"Possibly, Carteret. But don't forget it is still only in the rumour stage. The point, however, now is this. What opinion, if any, have you arrived at?"

Tiny weighed his words carefully.

"I believe that your conjecture is right. I believe that the lady is acting for someone whose name I won't mention. But it's only belief: I haven't a vestige of proof."

"I see. Well, my dear fellow, we're moving in deep waters; and unless I'm much mistaken you shortly will be moving in deeper ones. Good night and good luck to you."

Tiny replaced the receiver, and went back to the smoking-room. A bunch of members hailed him as he came in, but he was in no mood for club back-chat. He wanted to get things straightened out in his mind; so making some excuses he went into the coffee-room and ordered dinner. And during his solitary meal he attempted the straightening process, though it would be idle to pretend he got very far with it.

The whole affair was such a complete upheaval, and such an extremely rapid one. In the course of twelve hours he had been transported from the even tenor of his ways and landed in the centre of an atmosphere of murder and blackmail. And one of his companions was Mary. That was the most staggering part of the whole business: Mary mixed up with such a bunch! It seemed incredible: almost as incredible as it would have seemed to him this morning if someone had told him he was going to propose to her.

There was no doubt about it; he had done so. And now he tried to think how he would be feeling if she hadn't turned him down. To depart from the habits of a lifetime and propose to a girl was clear proof of what an upheaval had taken place. And yet he wasn't at all certain that he had wanted to be turned down. Mary was unquestionably a darling, and that kiss she had given him....

"Give me my bill," he said savagely: the thought of Mary alone in a private room with any man, let alone Felton Blake, had suddenly become unspeakable.

"I'll write her," he reflected, as he strolled back to his rooms. "Write her to-night, and tell her I meant it. That it wasn't a spasm induced by a desire to help her."

And because he was very busy with his thoughts, he failed to notice a man who was lingering aimlessly not far from his front door, and who vanished rapidly as he entered. Nor could he possibly have known that shortly afterwards the man expended the sum of twopence on a telephone call to Hampstead.

He sat down at his desk, and pulled a sheet of paper towards him. From the next room came the sound of Murdoch finishing his packing, and for awhile he remained motionless, gnawing the end of his penholder. Then he began to write.

MARY DEAR—

Ever since I saw you this afternoon I've been feeling distracted. I *know* you're in trouble; I *know* I could help you if only you would let me. You pulled my leg about proposing to you, but believe me, Mary, I meant it. I know I'm every sort and condition of an ass, while you're just—Mary. No need to say more. I think I've always loved you, dear: but it was seeing you up against it to-day that made me cough it up.

However, let all that be for the time. Can't I do anything to help? Please let me. You can tell me as much or as little as you like: I'll go into it blind if it's for you. This letter should arrive first post to-morrow, and if you telephone me on its receipt I'll cancel all my arrangements with regard to Switzerland. Or a letter to the Ouchy Palace Hotel at Lausanne will bring me back at once. One can get through in a day, and if necessary I can always fly.

Mary dear, I beg of you to think very deeply. Are you being wise trying to tackle this business—whatever it is—alone? Can't I help you? I know I'm repeating myself, but, my dear, I do feel so terribly strongly about it. We've played a lot together in the past, Mary: we've always been damned good pals. And if you can't turn to a pal when you're up against it, it's a pretty hopeless state of affairs.

Yours ever, my dear one,
TINY.

He re-read it: then slipped it into an envelope and stamped it.

"Murdoch," he called out, "take this out and post it at once."

"Very good, sir: and the packing is practically finished."

Tiny Carteret

The man withdrew, and Tiny flung himself into a chair and lit a cigarette. Would the letter have any effect, or would she still go on playing the hand alone? And even as he asked himself the question there came the faint purring of an engine through the open window. He rose idly, and crossing the room, looked out. Drawn up by the kerb was a yellow Rolls limousine with an aluminium bonnet.

"Well, I'm damned," he muttered. "Things move."

The door opened behind him and he swung round. Standing in the entrance was Felton Blake.

For a moment or two they eyed one another in silence: then Tiny spoke.

"May I ask who you are, and what you are doing here?"

"I think you already know who I am, Mr. Carteret," answered the other. "But to prevent any possibility of error I will introduce myself. My name is Blake."

"How did you get in?" said Tiny curtly.

"I walked through a door which your man had considerately left open."

"Then would you be good enough to walk out again, and pretty damned quick at that."

Felton Blake put his hat and gloves on a chair.

"You disappoint me, Mr. Carteret," he said suavely. "I thought you were sufficiently a man of the world not to adopt such a foolish attitude. It can lead us nowhere, and I have come round here expressly to have a talk with you."

"I have not the slightest wish to talk to you in any place or at any time," said Tiny icily.

Tiny Carteret

"I can't say from the standard of your conversation," answered Blake, "that I have much desire to talk to you either. But sometimes these boring entertainments become regrettable necessities."

Tiny mastered his anger, which was rapidly rising: it occurred to him that up to date he had not shone in the interview.

"It would be interesting to know what possible necessity there can be for a conversation between you and me," he remarked.

"That sounds a little better," said Blake. "And since this isn't a stage melodrama—shall we sit down?"

"As you like. There is a chair. I prefer to stand."

"Now, Mr. Carteret—I must ask you for an explanation. You called on Lady Mary Ridgeway this afternoon, did you not?"

Once again Tiny began to see red.

"Give you an explanation," he cried. "Why the devil should I?"

"Assuredly there is no reason at all," said the other suavely, "if you had confined yourself to calling. But it becomes a different matter when, during your call, you slander me. I understand that you alluded to me as a notorious blackmailer."

Tiny stood very still: that Mary would pass on his remarks to Blake was a development he had not anticipated.

"I am waiting, Mr. Carteret, for an explanation—and an apology."

And suddenly it dawned on Tiny that the position was undeniably awkward. The man confronting him, as Gillson had said, might have been a successful lawyer: certainly he looked the acme of respectability.

"You have proof, of course, of your astounding statement," continued Blake.

Which was exactly what Tiny had not got.

"You seem very silent, Mr. Carteret. Come, sir, I insist on an explanation."

"No explanation is necessary for speaking the truth," said Tiny, lighting a cigarette.

"So you adhere to it," remarked the other softly. "And your proof?"

"Is there any good in prolonging this discussion, Mr. Blake," answered Tiny. "It bores me excessively. Of proof in the accepted sense of the word I have none. Nevertheless I repeat my assertion: you are a notorious blackmailer. And there is the door."

"Not quite so fast, my young friend," snarled the other. "Have you ever heard of the law of libel?"

"Cut it out, you poor fish," laughed Tiny. "As a bluff that is unworthy of a child of ten. You go into a law court to defend your lily-white character! I think not, Mr. Blake—somehow. Besides, where is your own proof? Even you would hardly ask Lady Mary to go into the witness-box, I presume."

For a moment Blake was silent: in a sudden fit of rage he had put up a bluff, and no one knew better than he that the bluff had been called successfully. Some other line would have to be adopted with this very direct young man.

"Mr. Carteret," he said, "you are perfectly right. Nothing, of course, would induce me to ask Lady Mary to do such a thing. At the same time I think you will agree that it is a little disconcerting, when I am doing my best to help her over some extremely ticklish negotiations, for me to be libelled in such a way."

"Leaving out the question of libel for the moment, Mr. Blake, may I ask the nature of these negotiations?"

"I regret that I am not at liberty to pass that on," answered Blake.

"Leaving that out too then for the moment, I would be greatly obliged if you would tell me why it is necessary to take her to such an impossible place as a private room at the Fifty-Nine Club?"

Felton Blake eyed him narrowly.

"Your information is good, Mr. Carteret."

"Damn my information," cried Tiny angrily. "What I want to know is how you dare compromise a girl in her position by doing such a thing."

Blake raised his eyebrows.

"Dare! Rather a strong word. You don't suppose, do you, that I dragged her there against her will? Nor can you really suppose that with her knowledge of the world she didn't know what she was doing."

"I refuse to believe that she went there willingly," said Tiny doggedly.

"Did she tell you so?" asked Blake quietly. "No: I see she didn't. Mr. Carteret—I am going to put my cards on the table."

"How many of them?" said Tiny with a short laugh.

"All that I can," answered the other. "As I said before, your information is good. Moreover, I can hazard a pretty shrewd guess as to its source. That, however, is neither here nor there. To be brief then, I am not acting, as you seem to suppose, against Lady Mary: I am acting on her behalf. I too have sources of information at my disposal, and it so happens that I am in a position where I may be able to render her a considerable service. But in order to do so it is essential that she and I should be left—if I may put it that way—in peace. Come, Mr. Carteret—I'm going to ask you a straight question. Your information came from Colonel Gillson, didn't it?"

"I refuse to say who it came from," said Tiny.

"And he sent you round to Lady Mary to find out what you could?"

"You seem to have everything cut and dried," remarked Tiny.

"Now I solemnly warn you and him as well that any outside interference at the moment may prove fatal. I speak in all earnestness. I am, believe me, on your side, and I therefore beg of you to remember what I say. If you don't, the consequences will be on your head—and on Lady Mary's."

Tiny stared at him thoughtfully: on the face of it the man was sincere. And yet...

"Touching the little matter of the waiter who was murdered," he remarked.

"I can assure you, Mr. Carteret, that I have never been more surprised in my life than when Lady Mary told me about it." He gave a short laugh. "I hope in addition to being a blackmailer, I am not suspected of that. Because, unfortunately for your kindly suggestion, I have a perfect alibi."

"When did Lady Mary tell you I had been to see her?"

"She rang me up as soon as you left: you had alarmed her so much. Hence my visit to you to-night. Mr. Carteret—I beg of you be guided by me in this matter. The issues are altogether too serious."

He rose, and glancing through the open door into Tiny's bedroom he saw the half-packed suitcases.

"You're going out of Town?" he asked.

"Didn't Lady Mary tell you that also?" said Tiny sarcastically.

"No," returned the other. "Her mind was too much occupied with other things."

"Yes, Mr. Blake: I'm going out of Town. I'm going for a walking tour—in Bessonia."

Just for an instant Felton Blake stood as if carved out of stone. Then he spoke.

"Bessonia," he said. "A most interesting country. I trust you will have a good time. Good night, Mr. Carteret; I have enjoyed our chat greatly."

He went down the stairs and crossed the pavement to his car. He had given his chauffeur the night off, and now he felt rather relieved that he had done so. For Felton Blake was one of those men who could concentrate better when quite alone. Why on earth had Lady Mary said nothing to him about this trip to Bessonia? And was there any special significance in it? For Gillson's knowledge of all sorts and conditions of things he had the most profound respect, and his reason for sending Carteret round to see her was clear in view of the friendship between them. But surely if he suspected anything he would not send an untried man like that to Bessonia. Anyway, what could he do? What could anyone do? The thing was fool-proof as far as he could see: moreover it was within the law.

Felton Blake smiled gently to himself. The soft purr of the engine soothed him with its hundred per cent efficiency—he liked efficiency because it engendered success. And success was his god. The means by which it was attained mattered nothing: the fact that at the moment he was engaged in driving one of the most infamous bargains a man can drive troubled him not at all. The only thing that concerned him was whether he had bluffed Tiny Carteret sufficiently.

There was no doubt that his interview with Lady Mary had caused him a distinct shock. Even he had not suspected that the information on the other side was as good as it evidently was. And one point struck him as being so important that it would have to be cleared up. Was it he personally who was being watched—or was it the Fifty-Nine Club? And since so far as he knew there was no reason why he should be honoured with such an attention, it rather pointed to the latter as being correct. Which was annoying: distinctly annoying. Almost as annoying as this extraordinary murder of the waiter. For one of the few truthful remarks he had made in his interview with Carteret had been when they talked about it.

He had been absolutely amazed when Lady Mary had told him about it. At first, in fact, he had refused to believe it—had assured her that she must be mistaken. And then when she had still persisted he could only come to the conclusion that it was an extraordinary coincidence. Unless....

He frowned slightly: the train of thought suggested by that word did not please him. For if it was not a coincidence, it could only mean one thing—the presence in England of the last man he wanted to see at the moment. And even then it was hard to understand. Why should he have murdered an inoffensive waiter?

He ran the car into his garage: then he let himself into his house. And the first thing he saw was a black Homburg hat lying on the hall table. For a moment he stood very still: that hat was the answer to the question. His "unless" had been justified.

He opened the door of his study and went in. Seated in an easy chair, smoking a cigarette, was a peculiar-looking individual. At first sight he appeared to be a man of about forty, but on closer inspection he might have been considerably more. He had a high domed forehead rendered the more noticeable because of his absolute lack of hair, and from beneath it there stared two unwinking blue eyes. And to complete the picture, on his shoulder there sat a small monkey which chattered angrily on Blake's entrance.

"Good evening, Zavier," said Blake. "This is an unexpected pleasure."

"Be quiet, Susan," said the other in a curiously gentle voice. "Don't you know our friend Felton by now?" He turned to Blake. "So you are surprised at seeing me?"

"I thought you were still at headquarters," remarked Blake. "What brings you over here?"

"A desire to see you, my dear fellow, amongst other things. All goes well?"

"Very well. Though I am bound to confess, Zavier, that the intelligence of our English police has been sadly underrated. They know too much."

"And to-day they would have known considerably more save for my presence. You're a damned fool, Blake—and I have but little use for damned fools. All I can say is—that I trust you stop short at foolishness. Otherwise...."

"What do you mean?" Blake's lips were strangely dry.

"Is it conceivable," said the other, and his voice was softer than ever, "that you did not realize that your waiter of last night was a police spy?"

"Good God!" muttered Blake. "So it was you, then?

"Who removed him? Oh! yes—it was I who did that."

"But, why?" stammered Blake. "What was the object?"

"It was nothing to do, I assure you, with your conversation with the young lady. There were one or two indiscretions, but nothing sufficient to warrant such a drastic step as that."

"What do you mean?" said Blake slowly. "What do you know of my conversation with Lady Mary?"

"My dear fellow, I listened with interest to every word." Zavier smiled faintly. "Charming! Charming! But I fear your suit does not progress as rapidly as you wish."

At last Blake found his voice.

"You listened," he shouted angrily. "You cursed spy. Where did you listen from?"

"You are exciting Susan again," remarked the other gently. "I must really beg of you to control yourself."

He pacified the excited little animal, while Blake with a great effort pulled himself together.

"There are secrets of mine, my dear Blake, that even you do not know. And one of them concerns the private room so prettily decorated with mauve orchids last night. A delightful girl, Blake—delightful. But what a fool you are! Even should she be insane enough to marry you, do you really think you would be happy? The daughter of a Duke!"

"That's my affair," said Blake sullenly. "What I want to know is how much you heard."

"It's just because your waiter happened to find out how I heard that he died. So I fear your curiosity will not be gratified. You were saying, however, that the English police know too much. What precisely did you mean?"

"For one thing, they know that I have twice given supper to Lady Mary at the Fifty-Nine."

"Well—what of it?" remarked the other. "It is not a criminal offence. Though what obscure idea was at the bottom of your mind in so doing is beyond me."

"I want to put her under a still greater obligation to me," explained Blake.

"My denseness must be pardoned," said Zavier, "but I confess I do not quite follow."

"Well—if there was a police raid, it would be a bit awkward for her."

"I see. You mean the next time you sup there, there *will* be a police raid. A remarkably local police raid staged by Felton Blake, and from the unfortunate consequences of which she will be saved by Felton Blake." He began to laugh softly. "My God! what a fool you are! However, if it amuses you that's all that matters. To return to the point: what else do they know?"

"That man Gillson is wise to the fact that there is something in the wind between Lady Mary and me."

"Somewhat naturally. My dear fellow, I don't want to be rude but the Lady Marys of English society do not have supper with people like you because they want to, but because they have to."

Felton Blake's face turned a deep red.

"Go to hell, Zavier," he snarled. "I'm sick of your damned sneers. And here's one for you. I believe he suspects the truth."

"So," said Zavier, pulling the monkey's ears, and staring at Blake. "And what makes you think that?"

"He sent a man called Carteret, who is a great friend of Lady Mary's, round to pump her this afternoon. Scared her out of her life—especially over the murder of the waiter. I've just been round to see him, and the last thing he said to me was that he was going for a walking tour in Bessonia, and was starting to-morrow."

"What sort of a man is he?"

"A great big fellow. A Rugby international."

"Size matters but little," said Zavier gently, "should it be necessary to remove him. I alluded more to his intelligence."

"Not very high, I should think." He was staring half fascinated at the other man. "You'll fail, you know, one day, Zavier. Last night was the fifth."

"One almost loses count," returned Zavier. "And as to failure, Blake, the only being who never fails is the one who never tries. But to come back to this man Carteret. If your description of him is accurate, I don't think it matters if he takes a walking tour in Bessonia or not."

"I didn't say it did," said Blake. "But it points to the fact that Gillson suspects."

"What if he does? What we propose to do is strictly constitutional." He rubbed his hands together. "Quite legal, in fact."

"Have you any further information with regard to dates?"

"I was talking to Berendosi three days ago. He thinks in two or possibly three months. By then he calculates that there will be no one in Bessonia who won't have heard the rumour. And that will be the time to spring the proof on them—or what they will regard as the proof. It will also give him time to mature his own plans." His shoulders began to shake silently. "What about yours, my friend," he murmured. "It strikes me you will have to press forward with your love-making."

"What do you mean?" demanded Blake irritably.

"Just this. What little chance you have of being united in holy matrimony to Lady Mary will assuredly vanish altogether when she finds you've sold her a pup. To put it another way. It is within the bounds of possibility that she might sacrifice herself to save her friend; but it is completely off the map to think that she would marry you once the revolution has taken place. That strikes home, doesn't it, Blake? And so while we are on the subject, my friend, I will tell you what I really came round here to say. From one or two remarks I heard last night, it seemed to me that you are in that condition of maudlin imbecility with regard to the girl that one usually associates with a boy of eighteen. And when that is combined with the passion of a man of your age the situation becomes grave. Anything might happen. You might even, to attain your desire, really do what you have told her you are going to do. In which case, believe me, Blake, the honeymoon would not be of long duration." His voice had dropped almost to a whisper. "As I said—one almost loses count."

The unwinking blue eyes were fixed on Felton Blake, who moistened his lips with his tongue.

"You needn't be afraid," he muttered. "I won't let you down."

"Somehow or other I don't think you will," agreed Zavier, with a short laugh.

He opened his case and extracted a thin Russian cigarette. It was the only brand he ever smoked, and his daily allowance of ten was as invariable as all his habits.

"By the way, Blake," he continued, "did you know that Standish is in Switzerland?"

"How did you find out?" asked the other quickly.

"Various Continental papers have as you know the custom of publishing the names of guests staying at the better hotels. He is staying at the Grand Hotel at Territet."

"Has it any significance, do you think?" demanded Blake.

"My experience of Standish is that anything he does has a certain significance. So I made a point of staying a week-end at the hotel, where I had made one or two inquiries. He seems to be just aimlessly putting through time there, and to put through time aimlessly is not a characteristic of Standish. So I at once arrived at the conclusion that he was doing nothing of the sort."

"Good God! do you think he's found out anything?"

"You mean as to where our cosy home is? To be quite frank with you, Blake, the possibility had crossed my mind. But now, after what you tell me about Gillson, I am almost inclined to think that he may be there merely on the Bessonian question."

Felton Blake heaved a sigh of relief.

"Then we needn't worry. On that point neither he nor anybody else can do anything to interfere with us. But if he had found headquarters..."

"He still has to get inside," remarked Zavier, pressing out his cigarette. "And that as you know, my dear Blake, presents certain difficulties. In fact to do it in safety without knowing how, is as nearly impossible as a thing can be." He rose to his feet. "Well, Susan—a little walk will be good for both of us."

"When do you return, Zavier?"

"To-morrow. So possibly I shall travel with your friend Carteret. Yes—I go back to-morrow. There are two or three big deals maturing, which I want to get through before the business with Berendosi. And on the Roumanian question I may require you. I think you have a little private information concerning two members of their cabinet which should prove useful. Well, good night, and may the course of your young love run smooth."

And his faint mocking laugh was still echoing in Blake's ears, long after the front door had banged behind him.

CHAPTER IV

Age cannot wither nor custom stale the incredible tedium of the journey from Calais to Paris. It is possible that for those who are about to gaze on that most delectable of cities for the first time the thrill of anticipation may suffice to tide them over those three interminable hours. But for the rest—*on s'ennui*.

Tiny was one of the rest. Normally he always flew to France, but on this occasion he was not his own master. The day had started badly, with a brief telephone message from Mary.

"My dear," she had said, "I adore your letter, and I'm not at all sure I don't adore you. But you can't do anything, really you can't. Now run along like a good boy or you'll miss your train."

At that she had rung off, and when he tried to get through to her again only her maid had answered. Then a grim visaged woman using her dressing-case as a battering-ram winded him badly at Victoria, and then glared at him furiously when he invoked Allah in his agony. In fact, everything seemed to have gone wrong.

Half-way to Dover had found him already regretting that he had ever left London. It seemed to him that if he went on badgering Mary long enough, she would be bound to tell him what the trouble was, and that therefore his place was near her and not flying about Switzerland. That momentary look on Blake's face the previous night, when he had drawn a bow at a venture and mentioned Bessonia, had confirmed his opinion. That *was* the root of the whole trouble, and he wished he had taxed her with it directly. Then she might have spoken.

The train was slowing down for Amiens, when he threw aside his paper and glanced round the Pullman. It was filled with the usual cosmopolitan crowd, and he was just picking up a magazine when the attendant handed him a note, scribbled in pencil and written evidently while the train was in motion.

Tiny Carteret

"Dear Mr. Carteret," it ran, "have you quite forgotten me? I am sitting directly behind you, two chairs away. Nada Mazarin."

His brows wrinkled: who the devil was Nada Mazarin? Then he turned round and looked at the writer who smiled, as she caught his eye, and indicated the seat opposite her own which happened to be free. Her face was small and *piquante*, and Tiny remembered having caught a glimpse of her on the boat, and wondering vaguely if he didn't know her. And the worst of it was, he couldn't place her even now.

He rose at once and took the vacant seat.

"It is incredibly *gauche* of me to admit it," he said, "but though I remember you perfectly, I cannot for the life of me think when and where I had the pleasure of meeting you."

"You didn't see much of me, Mr. Carteret," she answered, with only the faintest of foreign accents. "You and Mr. Denver made the four with Lady Mary and—you know who."

Tiny leaned back in his chair: now he had got the whole thing.

"Of course," he cried. "How infernally stupid of me not to remember."

Countess Nada Mazarin—that was who it was. She had been lady-in-waiting, or female of the bedchamber—Tiny was a bit vague on the correct nomenclature in such matters—to Princess Olga when she had been over in England three years ago. He recalled her perfectly: he'd seen her several times at Claridges with the Princess. And as she justly remarked she had been a bit left out of things: the others had formed a square party.

"Lady Mary told me you were crossing to-day, so I wondered if by chance we should go by the same service."

"And when did you see Lady Mary?" he asked, holding out his cigarette-case to her.

"No, thank you," she said. "But please smoke yourself. I've seen a lot of her during the few days I've been in London."

Tiny looked at her thoughtfully: proof seemed to be mounting on proof.

"Should I be right in assuming that it was in order to see her that you went to London?" he remarked.

Her face betrayed no surprise at his question.

"I wonder how much you know, Mr. Carteret," she said quietly.

"If what I knew depended on what Mary had told me," he remarked a little bitterly, "it would be mighty little. To be truthful, Countess, I *know* nothing. But I've guessed a good deal. Come: won't you be frank with me. You know I'm to be trusted."

"It's not a question of that, my dear man," she answered wearily. "Tell me—what have you guessed? From what Mary said to me last night you seem to know a good deal about her doings."

"I know," said Tiny grimly, "that she has been doing the most amazingly injudicious things with a man who is a blackguard of the first water."

"He's not as bad as that surely," she protested, her eyes dilating.

"My dear Countess, personally I know nothing about the swine except what I've been told. But, believe me, there are no flies on my informant. You don't suppose, do you, that I even knew Mary had been to the Fifty-Nine with the blighter. I was told it, and it was the man who told me that, and a lot of other things too, who put me wise as to Felton Blake's character."

"But, Mr. Carteret, he's doing all he can for Mary."

Tiny gave a short laugh.

"Countess, your look belies you. You don't trust the blighter any more than I do. If he's doing all he can for Mary, he's also doing it for himself at the same time. And that's what I can't get the hang of—having guessed, shall we put it, as much as I have." He leaned across the table towards her. "Let's quit this beating about the bush. Mary is acting for someone whose name we won't mention, isn't she?"

She gave an almost imperceptible nod.

"I thought so." Tiny sat back in his chair; it was a relief to have absolute confirmation at last. "I was sure of it. But why the dickens Mary couldn't tell me herself is what beats me."

"Mr. Blake is doing all he can for her," said the Countess alter a pause.

"That's one point in the gentleman's favour anyway. Though from what I've heard of him, I should never have expected him to be so altruistic."

For perhaps half a minute she stared out of the window in silence: then she suddenly turned to him.

"Why should you assume that he is being altruistic?" she said slowly.

"You mean he's going to make her pay? Well, it's quite in keeping with the blighter's character. And if Mary is in want of money, there are stacks of her pals who will rally round the old flag."

"You're dense, my friend," said his companion. "Money isn't the only method of paying."

For a moment or two Tiny stared at her blankly: then, as her meaning got home he half rose from his chair.

"But, good God!" he stuttered, "you're mad. It's impossible. It's ... it's ... an outrage on decency. You mean that Mary might—might marry that—that excrescence! You're joking."

"I don't say she will, Mr. Carteret," she said gently. "But, if I'm any judge of human nature, that is what he is working for."

"Ah! that's a different matter." Tiny sat back relieved. "Jove! but you gave me a shock, Countess. And why should you think that's his game?"

"I've seen them together," she answered. "I've seen him looking at her when he thought he was unobserved, and a score of little things like that."

"The insolent blackguard," fumed Tiny. "Of course she knows nothing about it?"

"If you mean by that, that he hasn't said anything to her—quite right. But Mary is very much a woman, my friend."

"You mean, she's guessed what he's up to?"

"Is there any woman in the world who doesn't guess a thing like that? Though, mind you, she's said nothing to me about it."

"But you aren't hinting, are you, that there's a possibility of Mary agreeing?" he cried, aghast.

And once again she stared out of the window before she replied.

"Supposing that was the only price he would accept," she said at length.

"Surely there is no man living who could be such a swine," he muttered. "And surely," he went on slowly, "there is no one living who could ask such a sacrifice of another person."

"I know what you mean," she answered quietly. "And if things were quite as obvious as they seem to us, there would be a great deal of justification in your remark. The someone whose name we won't mention has no inkling of that side of the case. Nor had I till I came over this time."

"Then you must tell that someone, Countess," said Tiny gravely. "At once: the instant you get back."

"Tell her what, my friend? Believe me, it isn't quite so easy as it appears to you. As I told you, Mary has said nothing to me. All I have to go on is my own intuition. And supposing Mary laughed the whole idea to scorn. She's loyal to the core, you know, and she loves that someone dearly."

"You mean she might deliberately sacrifice herself," said Tiny, and his voice was low. "Good God! There must be some other way out. Can't you tell me, Countess, what the trouble is? Damn it! I might think of some alternative: I'm not an absolute fool."

She shook her head wearily.

"Believe me, Mr. Carteret, there is absolutely nothing you or anyone else can do. Except this man Blake. He is literally our only hope. You see it's not a question of brawn and muscle, or even of brain. It's a question of being in touch with certain people, of having certain inside information. And only he possesses it. *Mon Dieu!*" she put her hand to her forehead. "I think I shall go distracted at times. One feels so utterly helpless—like a fly in a spider's web. And the spider is sitting there, just biding its time."

"Ah! Countess, what a delightful surprise. I had no idea that you were on the train."

A thick-set man with an aquiline nose had paused beside their table.

"Nor I, that you were, Signor."

The new-comer turned a pair of shrewd eyes on Tiny, and deliberately studied him before replying.

"You have had a good time in London, I trust?" he said suavely.

"Thank you," she answered. "London at this time of the year is always delightful."

He lingered for a few moments shooting little quick glances at Tiny between each platitude: then he moved on into his own coach.

"How very funny, *mon ami*," said the Countess, "that I should have been speaking about the spider just then. For that man is the spider himself."

"Indeed," cried Tiny. "Who is he?"

"A man called Berendosi," she answered. "The most implacable enemy of our someone that exists. But I don't suppose you have ever heard of him."

"On the contrary, Countess: I have. You know," he added with a smile, "I am not quite so ignorant of affairs in other countries as the average Englishman is always reputed to be."

"I would give a good deal to know what he's been doing in England," she said thoughtfully. "I suppose," she gave a little laugh, "you wouldn't like to perform a thoroughly meritorious action and drop the brute out of the window!"

"He looks the irrepressible type who would bounce back," he answered with a smile. "Hullo! we're nearly there. Now, look here, Countess, will you promise me one thing? If you should find that I can be of the smallest assistance—and you never know, I might be—

will you drop me a line to the Ouchy Palace Hotel, Lausanne. I'll make arrangements to get it with a minimum of delay whether I'm in Lausanne or not."

"I promise," she said. "And don't take what I said about Mary too seriously. I may be completely wrong."

But that was just what it was impossible for him to do. As he drove to Philippes it rang in his brain: as he sat in the empty restaurant the thought kept dancing through his mind till it almost seemed to be written on the cloth in front of him. Mary married to Blake! Mary married to Blake!

It was inconceivable: hideous: monstrous. And yet as he forced himself to think it over dispassionately he had to admit that even stranger *mésalliances* had taken place. The man at any rate looked a gentleman, and he had plenty of money. And then he recalled the expression on her face when she had passed him in the Rolls.

He ordered another Martini and lit a cigarette. That settled it. There could be no willingness on the part of a girl who looked like that. Quite obviously she disliked the man intensely. And that being the case she was not going to marry him even if it necessitated killing Blake with his own hands.

He shook himself angrily: what the devil was the use of thinking along those lines? You can't go running round London murdering people whose proposed nuptials you disapprove of. And if Mary had made up her mind, he knew the futility of trying to dissuade her. Besides, she would probably do it at a registrar's office and no one would know anything about it till it was all over.

The room was beginning to fill up, but Tiny hardly noticed it, so engrossed was he in his own thoughts. He ordered dinner automatically, and ate it scarcely conscious of what the dishes were. Which was manifestly unfair to superlative cooking. And it was not until the coffee and brandy were in front of him that he suddenly remembered that someone was to meet him there. This ghastly question of Mary had driven everything else out of his head.

He glanced round the restaurant: every table was full. And certainly no one that he could see looked in the very slightest degree like the possible bearer of a message. He was the only solitary diner present: all the other tables had parties. He looked at his watch: half-past eight. In a few minutes he would have to start for the station.

"Monsieur Carteret?"

A waiter was standing by his table, and Tiny nodded.

"A note for M'sieur."

He took the envelope from the tray, and for a moment or two he hesitated. Should he open it at once, or wait till he got in the taxi? And then he realized that if by any chance he was being spied on it would seem far more natural to do the former.

Inside was a sheet of paper on which was scrawled a single sentence.

"Tell R.S. that D. is being shadowed."

He looked round the neighbouring tables: no one seemed to be paying any attention to him. Then he beckoned the waiter.

"Who gave you this note?" he demanded.

"A gentleman who came to the door, M'sieur. He just looked in and when he saw you he gave me the note."

"Right, thank you. Give me my bill, please."

He tore the message into tiny pieces and dropped them in his coffee cup. The R.S. obviously referred to Ronald Standish, but who D. was he had no idea. Presumably Ronald would, however, and having poured some more coffee over the scraps of paper to obliterate them still further, he rose and left.

It was in the taxi that he suddenly remembered Gillson's remark about the sleeper, and he began to wonder why the temporary possession of Number 8 bunk was going to fill him with gloom and despondency. Presumably it must have something to do with the occupant of Number 7, and he groaned mentally. The night was hot, and the thought of being cooped up with some odoriferous male was not pleasant. Still his orders were quite definite, though as it happened they proved to be unnecessary. For when he got to the station he found that the train was crowded and every other berth in the coach was full. But of the possessor of Number 7 there was no sign.

He tipped the porter, and then got out and stood on the platform. The usual bunches of people seeing off others stood chattering in little groups under the glare of the arc lights, and Tiny watched them idly. There were two or three obvious English people, but for the most part they consisted of French or Italians. Two monks in brown cowls paced gravely up and down, and he wondered what their particular order was. And then just as he was beginning to hope that for once Gillson's arrangements had miscarried, and that he was going to have the compartment to himself, a strange trio advanced along the platform.

The centre one of the three was being, if not supported, at any rate helped by the other two, and a terrible premonition of impending doom assailed Tiny. And the next moment it ceased to be a premonition—it became a certainty: the trio had stopped at the entrance to the sleeper. Then one man pushed and another pulled, and the centre one shot inside. The occupant of Number 7 had arrived.

Breathing a short invocation to Heaven to give him strength to bear his cross, Tiny entered the carriage and walked along the corridor to his compartment. And what he saw shook him to the marrow. The gentleman reclining on Number 7 would have shaken anyone to the marrow.

He was a fat puffy-looking individual of about forty, with a greasy unhealthy complexion. At the moment he was breathing hard, and his eyes were roving wildly from side to side like those of a frightened rabbit. He was making periodical remarks in a language unknown to Tiny, and one of his companions was answering him in the same tongue. The third man looked and evidently was an Englishman.

It was he who first saw Tiny, and he grinned slightly.

"Had to make him a bit screwed, or we'd never have got him here," he said, joining Tiny in the corridor. "Still, he'll sleep all the better."

"Thank Heaven for that, anyway," Tiny grunted.

"He's scared out of his life," muttered the man. "And I don't wonder. Not sorry to be shot of this show myself."

"I suppose you realize that I haven't the slightest idea what you are talking about," said Tiny.

The man stared at him in amazement.

"Good God!" he cried. "Ain't you... Hullo! Train's off. Hop it, Jim."

They scrambled on to the platform, leaving Tiny gazing moodily at his bedfellow. And the more he gazed the less he liked it. So far as he could see the gentleman had no redeeming feature. At the same time, in view of what Gillson had said, he was evidently one of the pawns in the game, though where he fitted in it was impossible to say.

The arrival of the attendant settled one point: he, too, was going to Lausanne. Moreover, he was going in his own fashion. Not for him the comparative comfort of pyjamas and sheets, but something far more primitive. He did, it is true, remove his shoes, having first, with great difficulty, shut the window. Then, swaying slightly, he turned a rather glazed eye on Tiny and pointed to the top bunk.

Assuming that he was asking a question Tiny shook his head and pointed to the lower. But that apparently was not what he wanted. Still continuing to point at the bunk with one hand, he beckoned to Tiny with the other.

"Come," he ejaculated solemnly. "Come."

"Oh! you want me to turn in, do you," said Tiny. "Well, laddie, we're going to have the window open whether you like it or not."

He entered the compartment, and the instant he was inside the man shut and bolted the door. Then he bolted the door into the washing-place, made a strange grunting noise which Tiny took to mean good-night, collapsed on the lower berth and began to breathe stertorously.

But not for long: the sound of Tiny opening the window galvanized him into frenzied activity. He sprang off the bed pouring out a flood of unintelligible words, and shut it again. Then gesticulating wildly he turned to Tiny, and said "No" with great distinctness six times. After which effort he fell down.

"Yes, but look here," said Tiny, when he'd helped him to his feet, "there's not an atom of air in the carriage. *Pas de l'air. Fenêtre. Ouvrir. Insanitaire. Oui. Non.*"

"No. No. No," answered the man. "Danger."

"Rot," cried Tiny angrily. "You can't have the window shut on a hot night like this."

But the man had collapsed on his bunk again, still repeating No at intervals, and Tiny stared at him nonplussed. He knew that by the regulations for all railways abroad, the man was within his rights in insisting on having the window shut. He also knew that despite all those regulations he was going to have it open. Already the carriage was becoming stuffy and airless, and to go all through the night in such an atmosphere was a physical impossibility.

And then he had an idea. The man was half tight: once he was asleep nothing would be likely to wake him. So he hoisted himself carefully into the top bunk, and began to undress. From below came the gentle music of the sleeper, but he decided to give it a little longer. So he lit a cigarette, and opened a magazine. But after ten minutes he felt he could stand it no more. He carefully inspected his companion in the mirror, and having listened to his snores for a while he decided the time was ripe. With great caution he descended to the floor: in a moment the window was open. And—the sleeper still slept.

Tiny returned to his berth, and shortly began to yawn himself. And being one of those fortunate individuals who can sleep soundly in a train, he soon switched out the lights, leaving only the dim blue one in the centre of the roof just above him burning.

Now, as has been said, Tiny Carteret was a man whose nerves were just about as strong as a man's nerves may be. He had, like many of us, suffered moments of intense fright during the war, and again like most of us those moments had passed into the limbo of forgotten things. But it is to be doubted if the thing that happened in that sleeper some two hours afterwards will ever fade from his mind.

At first he thought he was having a nightmare: in fact, such a peculiar thing is the human brain that during the few seconds in which it happened he very distinctly said to himself—"It's that lobster." For suddenly a hand clutched his arm, and as he opened his eyes he saw not six inches away the face of the man below. Only the whites of his eyes were showing: his lips were drawn back from his teeth in a hideous snarl. And in the eerie blue light it seemed to him that he was looking at a skull.

Suddenly the man uttered a dreadful cry, which sounded to Tiny like "Bazana." Then the face disappeared.

For what seemed an eternity Tiny lay there, with the sweat pouring off him as if he was in a Turkish bath. Then with a great effort he forced himself to switch on the lights. He leaned over the edge of his bunk: the man was sprawling face downwards on the floor. And instinctively Tiny knew he was dead.

He got down and turned him over. There was no doubt about it: that strange word "Bazana" was the last he would ever utter. His face was contorted with agony: his arms and legs were rigid. And for a space Tiny stood looking at him dully, hardly able to realize what had happened.

The whole thing was so astoundingly sudden, and Tiny's brain was not at its best at the moment of waking. But at last he pulled himself together and rang the bell for the attendant, who came after a slight delay and tried the door.

"Come in," called Tiny. "*Entrez.*"

"*C'est fermé, M'sieur.*"

Of course: the door had been locked. Tiny remembered now: the dead man had locked it himself. He opened it and the conductor came in.

"*Mon Dieu!*" he cried, as he noticed the body. Then he drew back with a cry of horror as he saw that terrible distorted face.

"*Qu'est-ce-que y est arrivé?*"

And Tiny could only shrug his shoulders helplessly. What was there to say? Every symptom seemed to tally with Gillson's description of the mysterious murders, but how was it possible in this case? How could a man be murdered in a train travelling at sixty miles an hour when he was locked into a sleeper? The thing was incredible; preposterous.

The *chef du train* had arrived by this time, and after one look at the body had departed rapidly to see if there was a doctor on the train. As luck would have it there was, and two minutes later he returned with a young Englishman.

"Good God!" he cried, "the poor devil must have been in absolute torture before he died. What happened, sir?" He turned to Tiny.

"I can tell you nothing," answered Tiny. "I was in the top bunk and I was suddenly awakened by feeling his hand on my arm. His face was convulsed with agony, and then he crashed to the floor. I realized at once, of course, that he was dead. So I rang for the attendant."

"You know him? Was he a friend of yours?"

"I've never seen him before in my life," said Tiny.

Once more the doctor stooped over the dead man, and suddenly he gave a little exclamation.

"Hullo! I wonder what that mark is on his hand? It's been made fairly recently."

Tiny bent down to look: sure enough on the back of the man's right hand was a small puncture that looked as if it had been made by a thorn. Further evidence: and yet—how could it be so? Vaguely he heard the others talking: realized that the doctor in a mixture of English and French was telling the *chef du train* that nothing could be done: that the man was dead and that his body had better be removed from the train at the next stop.

"Dijon," said the worried official, and then with the attendant he lifted the body back on to the bunk and covered the ghastly face with a blanket.

"What was the cause of it, do you think, doctor?" asked Tiny.

"Without a post-mortem it is impossible to say," replied the other. "But from what you tell me, taking into account the rapidity of the thing and the contortion of the features, I should say that almost certainly it is a case of advanced disease of the heart. Look here," he went on, "I've got a carriage to myself, and I have also got a spot of Scotch. You'd better come along with me, at any rate as far as Dijon."

"I think I will," said Tiny. "It's shaken me a bit, I confess. I'll put some clothes on."

"Right you are," cried the doctor. "I'll wait in the corridor."

"Is it true that a poor fellow is dead?"

A deep voice from the doorway made them both swing round: standing there was one of the monks Tiny had noticed on the platform in Paris. His hands were clasped in front of him: the brown cowl still covered his head.

"I regret to say that it is," said the doctor. "But, reverend Father, he is not a pretty sight to look at."

"My son," answered the other, "one must learn to disregard the outer shell, and pay attention only to the inner spirit."

He drew back the blanket, and for a while his lips moved silently. Then having made the sign of the cross, as abruptly as he had come, he vanished.

"I suppose it's grossly materialistic of me," said the doctor, "but I'm blowed if I see what good that has done. However—doubtless I'm wrong."

"Look here," said Tiny, getting into his coat, "do you think the French authorities are likely to detain me at Dijon?"

He took his watch down from the hook: ten minutes to twelve—not three hours since they had left. Dijon, so far as he remembered, was about four and a half hours from Paris, and to be shot out there in the middle of the night was not a pleasant thought.

"I really don't see why they should," said the doctor. "You can do no earthly good. Of course they may keep you there on some formality. At the same time I should say the cause of death is obvious. Heart, as I told you. Come along, if you're ready. A drink will do us both good."

Tiny shut the door, and the attendant locked it at once. Then he followed the doctor along the train, his brain buzzing with the problem. What had happened? What could have happened? Had it not been for the mark on the dead man's hand, he would have been inclined to think that the doctor was right, and that death had been due to natural causes. But now the coincidence was too extraordinary. And yet how in Heaven's name had the poor devil been got at?

A possibility struck him. Had he got up and gone along the corridor for some reason? That would presuppose that the murderer was lurking outside on the bare chance that such a thing would happen. Unlikely—but at any rate it did present a solution.

Another idea. Was it conceivable that this man had been one of the users of the poison himself, and had been carrying with him whatever it was that they employed to commit their murders. Then, accidentally while he was asleep, he had run it into his own hand, and being half drunk had not awakened when he did so? If so, the implement would still be in the dead man's berth, or in one of his pockets.

For awhile he debated whether he should say anything about it to the doctor. And then it occurred to him that to suggest the possibility of foul play could do no good, and might involve him in extremely awkward complications. For on the face of it to the ordinary outsider the only person who could have murdered the man was himself.

No: it was impossible to say anything. All he could do was to hope that the French authorities would come to the same conclusion as the doctor, and attribute the man's death to natural causes. If they didn't, and detained him for a post-mortem, he would have to grin and bear it. As he reflected a little cynically, it would only be in keeping with the whole state of affairs at the moment.

But luck proved to be in at Dijon. Fortunately for Tiny one of the station officials spoke fluent English, and helped by the doctor's professional opinion, they merely asked his name and destination and then allowed him to proceed. But one thing of interest did come to light. The dead man was a Russian named Demeroff. And as Tiny got back into the train he wondered if he was the man referred to as D. in the letter he had received at Philippes. If so, the shadowing was pretty efficient...

There was no sign of Ronald Standish on the platform at Lausanne, so he chartered a car and drove to the Ouchy Palace Hotel. And there, as Gillson had said, he found that a room had been reserved for him.

"There is a letter for you, sir," said the clerk. "Delivered by hand."

It was from Ronald and was as terse as the one he had received in Paris.

"Do not let Demeroff out of your sight. Mid-day—the bar."

Tiny smiled grimly: it struck him that the writer would require more than one cocktail when he heard the news.

"There was another gentleman coming, sir, I believe," said the clerk inquiringly. "A Russian."

"I fear that he has been unavoidably detained," answered Tiny quietly.

The morning passed slowly: try as he would he couldn't get the thought of that ghastly distorted face out of his mind. And try as he would he couldn't get any nearer to solving the problem of how it had been done. Ronald's note knocked the bottom out of his theory that the thing was accidentally self-administered, because it seemed to show that the dead man had been on their side.

At twelve o'clock precisely Ronald Standish came into the bar. His face was expressionless, but Tiny knew by the way he walked that his nerves were a little on edge.

"What's this, Tiny, I hear at the office? Demeroff not come?"

"And I'm afraid he never will, Ronald. He died in the train last night: his body is at Dijon."

For a moment or two Standish said nothing: then he spoke — very deliberately.

"If," he remarked, "I ever did lose my temper, I would now swear without repeating myself for five minutes. How did they get him? Tell me exactly what happened."

He listened in silence while Tiny ran through everything from the receipt of the note in Paris to the examination at Dijon.

"You assume they got him, Ronald," he said in conclusion. "So do I, because of the mark in his hand. But if you can tell me how the devil they did it I'll be much obliged."

"What time did you say it was when you looked at your watch?" asked the other.

"Ten to twelve," said Tiny. "But what's that got to do with it?"

"Everything," answered Standish quietly. "Oh! Tiny, Tiny, if only we as a race, didn't like fresh air so much! Still, it can't be helped."

"What can't be helped?" said Tiny peevishly. "You're not going to tell me that he was murdered through the open window of a train travelling at sixty miles an hour."

"No, old lad, I'm not. He was murdered through the open window of a train standing stationary by a platform. All the fast expresses on that line stop at Laroche half-way between Paris and Dijon to change engines. It was then they got him. You were asleep and so was he. And that's when the poison was inserted. He was a bit drunk so the prick never woke him. And it wasn't until after the train had started that the poison began to work."

"Good God!" muttered Tiny. "Then I'm responsible for the poor devil's death. He said it was dangerous to open the window, but I never dreamt he meant that."

"How should you?" answered Standish. "You needn't worry, Tiny: he was a nasty piece of work, and it was only a question of time before they got him. But, if only I could have seen him for five minutes! You see, to put the matter in a nutshell, he was blowing the gaff. I don't know how much Gillson has told you; anyway I'll fill in the gaps later, but the man who was murdered last night was a member of the gang we are after. And our people had got at him in Paris. His journey here was simply and solely to split on his former pals. From the note you got at Philippes our people realized the danger. But naturally no one thought of the damned window."

"How did they get at him, Ronald? How was it done?"

"If I could tell you that, Tiny, I should have solved one problem that is worrying us all. Obviously the man who did it got out of his carriage at Laroche, saw his opportunity and seized it. If the window had been shut, of course he couldn't have done it."

He lit a cigarette thoughtfully.

"Bazana. I wonder if there's any significance. Was he trying to tell you something?"

"Quite possibly," said Tiny. "And don't forget that's only what it sounded like to me. The poor blighter's teeth were clenched, and with the noise of the train it may not have been that at all."

"Let's have another spot, Tiny. Because we've got to decide what we're going to do. I hear incidentally that you agree with Gillson and me that Lady Mary is acting as go-between."

"How do you know that?" said Tiny with some surprise.

"I got a cable in code from Gillson yesterday."

"Well, if we wanted any further confirmation I got it in the Golden Arrow yesterday," said Tiny. "Do you by any chance know a Countess Mazarin?"

"I know who you mean, though I don't know the lady personally."

"Well, she admitted it to me. By God! Ronald," he went on savagely, "something has got to be done to get Mary out of the clutches of that excrescence Felton Blake. The Countess actually told me that she thought he was in love with her."

Standish raised his eyebrows.

"He aims high," he remarked. "Still, I wouldn't be surprised if you aren't right."

"Berendosi was on the train too," said Tiny.

"I heard he'd been in England. Lord! Tiny, I'm at a dead end." He got up and started pacing up and down, his hands deep in his trouser pockets. "If only Lady Mary or the Mazarin woman would tell us what the mystery was! Though, to be perfectly frank, I don't know that it would do us much good. They've got some form of proof—faked or otherwise, it matters not—which they are going to spring at the last moment."

"And Mary thinks Blake can get it back for her?"

"Presumably. Otherwise why should she be mixed up in it at all. That's where the devil of it comes in. Of course he is double-crossing her."

"Why should you think that?" said Tiny slowly.

"My dear fellow, it's obvious. If this proof lies out here in the hands of Berendosi's crowd, you don't suppose they are going to give it up to help Blake's love affair. But as a matter of fact, I don't think for a moment it is out here. It's locked up in Felton Blake's safe. Otherwise why should he have come into it at all? He was no good to them: they didn't want him if they held it themselves. No: he started the hare himself. He holds the trump card, though he is probably pretending to Lady Mary that he is moving heaven and earth to help her."

"I'd like to wring the blighter's neck," grunted Tiny.

"So would a good many other people," said Standish with a short laugh. "But it's hardly worth while being hanged for exterminating vermin. No: it's the other one that I want, Tiny: the big man. And I hoped to get on his trail through Demeroff. You see, one of the most extraordinary things about this gang is the elusiveness of its members. It sounds fantastic, but I can assure you that sometimes I have been tempted to think that they hold the secret of becoming invisible. Not once, but a dozen times have people we wanted vanished from practically under our noses. It is incredible."

"Disguise of some sort, I suppose."

"You can take it from me that it's got to be a pretty useful disguise to deceive our fellows. And yet—they've done it. Why only a week ago in Paris, we hunted two of them to ground in a smallish hotel in the Rue Tivoli. Men were posted at every entrance, but they got away—slipped clean through our fingers. It's positively uncanny."

"Ana have you no idea of the whereabouts of their headquarters?"

"I believe it to be somewhere in this country. In fact, I'm almost sure it is."

"Well, old lad, you're the commanding officer for this expedition," said Tiny. "What does A do, beyond lighting an Abdullah?"

And at that moment a page boy entered the bar with a telegram.

"Monsieur Carteret?"

"That's me," said Tiny, taking the envelope.

He glanced through the message: then with a laugh he handed it to Standish.

"That would seem to give us a pointer, Ronald."

For the wire which had been handed in in Paris ran as follows:

"Can you go Hôtel Royal Dalzburg at once. Mazarin."

"As you say, Tiny," said Standish, "it seems to give us a pointer. Well—the capital of Bessonia is a delightful spot. And since Demeroff's removal prevents us getting direct at their headquarters, perhaps we'll do it through the side track of Berendosi's little scheme. But I wonder what the lady can have discovered in Paris to cause her to send that."

CHAPTER V

Dalzburg, as Ronald Standish had said, was a delightful place, and when they arrived there the next day it was looking its loveliest. The picturesque old town, dominated by the Palace standing on the wooded heights behind it, was bathed in the early-morning sunshine, as they rattled over the cobbled bridge which spans the river. But at the moment their thoughts were centred on the mundane questions of baths and food, and it was not until eleven o'clock that they sauntered forth from the hotel for a stroll round.

It was Tiny's first visit to the place, though Standish knew it well. And since they had found nothing further at the hotel to explain the Countess's telegram in any way, there seemed to be nothing to do except kick their heels and wait. Presumably in time its reason would become clear.

"I seem to remember," said Standish after a while, "that they make a not indifferent brand of beer. What about it, Tiny?"

"Lead me to it, old boy. These damned continental sleepers give me a mouth like a lime kiln."

They found a vacant table at a shady café on the main boulevard and sat down. The place was full of people bent on the same errand, and as luck would have it, their immediate neighbours were not tourists but natives of the place.

"You'll often get more reliable information from the apparently idle chatter in a place like this," said Standish, "than from a score of agents. But you must be able to speak the lingo."

"How many can you speak, Ronald?" asked Tiny curiously.

"About fifteen, old boy," laughed the other. "They seem to come naturally to me."

He half closed his eyes, and leaning back in his chair he relapsed into silence. To the casual observer he seemed almost asleep: in reality every sense was alert. Times out of number had he played this same game, and even if it was only once in twenty that anything tangible rewarded his efforts, it was at any rate good practice in the language.

The first essential was to shut out as far as possible the people who were obviously useless to him, and long practice had enabled him to do this in the most amazing way. He could deliberately, as it were, shut down parts of his brain, till only one particular conversation came through, while the rest seemed merely an aimless buzz. And now, having cut out a nursemaid with children on his right, and a loving couple on his left, he concentrated on two men sitting at the table just behind him as being the only possible source of interest.

At first he drew blank: they were discussing some recent reconstruction scheme in the business belonging to one of them. The other he gathered was interested financially: the matter of a mortgage cropped up. Influential men evidently: men of substance. And he was just preparing to relax and get on with his beer, when a name caught his attention. One of them mentioned Berendosi.

But luck was out: both at once lowered their voices, and strain his ears as much as he could he was unable to catch more than an odd word here and there. Suddenly, however, one of them made a remark which he heard perfectly and which riveted his attention.

"There. That man the other side of the street. The tall Englishman. I tell you it's obvious."

He opened his eyes and looked across the road. There was no mistaking whom they were alluding to: there was only one man who could possibly be an Englishman. And even as he was idly speculating as to what was obvious, he heard a sudden exclamation from beside him. He glanced round: Tiny Carteret had half risen from his seat and was staring at the Englishman himself.

Now Standish was a man who thought quickly, and though he was completely in the dark himself as to why two prominent Bessonians and Tiny should both be interested in the same man, his brain reacted instinctively.

"Sit down, Tiny," he said curtly. "Don't pay any attention to that man across the road. I'll explain later."

A little bewildered, Tiny obeyed, and once again Standish leaned back in his chair. Had the two men behind him noticed Tiny's movement? If so, good-bye to any chance of hearing any more. Apparently they had not, and stray snatches of their conversation came to him.

"Undoubted... Gregoroff saw him... Hotel Royal.... Must be the same man.... There won't be much trouble... Berendosi must see him..."

And then their voices became mere whispers, and not another word could he hear, during the remaining ten minutes they sat at their table.

"I will now have another beer," said Standish, as he watched their retreating backs.

"What was the great idea, Ronald?"

"Well, old boy, it was obvious that you knew or thought you knew the Englishman on the other side of the street. It was equally obvious that the two men who have just left were interested in him too, as they were talking about him. And I thought I might hear a good deal more if your mutual interest wasn't paraded too obviously."

"What did you hear?"

"Only snatches of conversation. He is stopping at the Royal, and he is obviously the same man. Same as what I can't tell you. They also are anxious for Berendosi to see him. Not much, I admit, but one often finds that little clues like that help one later. Now—your turn. Who did you think he was?"

"Three years ago when Princess Olga, as she then was, was over in London, there were four of us who used to get about a good bit together. She, Mary, myself, and a fellow called Joe Denver. And unless I'm very much mistaken that was Joe Denver himself. A bit more tanned, but I'm almost certain it was him—same walk and everything. And if it was him, it is the most extraordinary coincidence, because Mary and I were only talking about him the other afternoon, and wondering where he was. And here he is apparently stopping at the same hotel."

Ronald Standish lit a cigarette, and stared thoughtfully across the sunny street.

"That's interesting, Tiny—very interesting. I wonder if at last something tangible is in sight."

"What do you mean?" asked the other.

"I wonder if the thing isn't a coincidence at all—except that you and Lady Mary should have been talking about him. But is it his presence here that was the cause of the wire you got yesterday?"

"By Jove!" cried Tiny, "that's possible."

"It's more than possible, old boy—it's probable. But we must not go too fast. Let's take the points. Something must have inspired that wire. And when we find a man staying at the hotel we are told to come to, who was a friend of the Queen's in days gone by and is now an object of great interest to Berendosi and his lot, surely there must be some connection. It's stretching coincidence too far altogether to imagine there isn't. I wonder, Tiny: I wonder. Are we on the verge of something that isn't merely guess-work?"

"Mark you, I won't swear that it was Joe Denver," said Tiny.

Tiny Carteret

Standish glanced at his watch.

"Well, it's about time for tiffin. Let's go back to the pub and see."

They found him in the corner of the lounge, and all doubts were set at rest immediately. For the instant he saw Tiny he jumped to his feet.

"Carteret—by all that's wonderful. What brings you here?"

"I might almost ask the same," said Tiny. "By the way, Denver, let me introduce you. This is Standish. Well, old boy, how goes it? It's a long time since we met."

"Over three years. I've been in the back of beyond since then. This is my first leave."

"Are you spending it all here?" asked Standish casually.

"I don't know," said Denver a little curtly. "It depends."

He turned to Tiny, and asked after Lady Mary, while Standish studied him covertly with shrewd blue eyes. An expert in sizing up a man, he preferred to listen rather than to talk. And it soon became obvious to his trained observation that this good-looking youngster's nerves were on edge. There was an air of unrest about him, and once or twice he glanced round the lounge almost nervously.

That there was something the matter with him was clear: that he was not inclined to be communicative was also clear—his curt answer to Standish's question proved that. But being a past master in the art of getting things out of uncommunicative people, he was content to bide his time. That this youngster was involved in the matter in some way he was convinced: as he had said to Tiny, the coincidence if it were not so would be too amazing. Besides, his whole demeanour simply shouted the fact that something was up.

Suddenly Denver started to his feet angrily. He was glaring across the lounge, and Standish followed the direction of his glance. Two men were sitting at a small table, who looked away immediately they saw they were observed.

"I'll give that damned fellow a thick ear soon," said Denver furiously.

"Steady, old lad," said Tiny, pulling him back into his chair. "What's all the worry?"

"You see that pasty-faced swab over there with a dial like a suet pudding? Well, that fellow he's with is the fourth man he's brought in here for the express purpose of looking at me." He grinned a little sheepishly as if ashamed of his temper. "I don't resemble any blinking Prince, do I, travelling incognito?"

"Are you sure you're not imagining it?" said Standish quietly.

"Absolutely certain. It started the very morning I arrived. That's three days ago. I was sitting in here, when pasty face arrived on the scene, and sat down at the next table. At first he took no notice of me: he certainly hadn't looked at me as he sat down. And then just as I was lighting a cigarette I found him staring at me. He turned away at once, but for the next ten minutes he did nothing but study my face when he thought I wasn't looking. After that I got a bit fed up, so I wandered to the bar. And the first thing he did—I could see it reflected in the mirror—was to go over to the reception clerk and ask who I was. I'm certain it was that because the fellow opened the visitors' book. I didn't think much more about it at the time, but since then he's led in four different blokes, with the express purpose of letting them see me. Damn it! I may not be a prize beauty, but I'm not a bally freak, am I?"

"You've never been here before, have you, Denver?" said Standish thoughtfully.

"Never in my life," said the other. "Anyway, what's that got to do with it?"

"I was only wondering. At any rate it seems perfectly clear that your pasty-faced friend is interested in you for some reason or other. Perhaps you bear a strong resemblance to some local celebrity. By Jove!"—he paused as if struck with a sudden idea—"I wonder if that can be the reason. You don't know von Emmerling, by any chance?"

"Never heard of him in my life. Why?"

"I wondered if he had written and asked you to come here."

"Nobody wrote and asked me to come here. I only decided at the very last moment and got off the boat at Brindisi. Who is von Emmerling, anyway?"

But Standish seemed to have lost interest in the matter.

"It doesn't matter," he said. "Evidently as you don't know him, that can't be the reason."

"But," persisted the other, "if there was any reason why this bloke should ask me here, that may account for the other thing."

"Von Emmerling," said Standish, "is one of the big German film magnates. And I believe he is going to stage one of his productions here. Moreover I know he is on the look-out for a tall fair Englishman, and it occurred to me as a possibility that he might have approached you on the matter."

Tiny glanced at Standish out of the corner of his eye, but his face was expressionless.

"Afraid it doesn't fit," said Denver. "Still it's possible you may be right. These blokes may be sizing me up from that point of view, though I fear they'll be disappointed. And incidentally that reminds me." He leaned forward in his chair. "By Jove! Standish, I wonder if you have hit it. Yesterday morning, when I was on the other side of the river strolling along the bank, a most persistent merchant with a camera came badgering me. Wanted to take my photo: no need to pay if I wasn't satisfied with the result. You know—all the usual palaver. I told him to go to hell, but for all that he took a couple. And it was only when I threatened to fling his cursed machine in the river and him after it that he vamoosed."

Once again Tiny glanced at Standish: in his eyes there was the faintest perceptible gleam of satisfaction. But his voice when he answered was as expressionless as ever.

"It certainly looks as if I might be right," he said. "Anyway, I wouldn't let the matter worry you. Well, I don't know about you fellows but I'm going to have a bite of lunch. See you afterwards, Denver."

"The plot thickens a little, Tiny," he went on as they sat down to lunch.

"Who on earth is von Emmerling?" demanded the other.

"He wasn't too bad, was he?" laughed Standish. "Realizing our young friend was a bit nervy and touchy when asked a direct question I invented the gentleman on the spur of the moment. And I must say he justified his birth, even if he has complicated things. Because if Denver is speaking the truth it was a sheer fluke that he came here."

"I don't quite follow," said Tiny.

"My dear fellow, it's obvious. Had someone—I don't care who, asked him here, it would presuppose that that someone knew him. But if he came absolutely by chance, it's damned difficult to understand. Why should anyone be concerned with the arrival of an unknown Englishman who has never been here before? Unless..."

"Unless what?" demanded the other.

"And why bother about his photograph?" went on Standish, disregarding the question. "It's puzzling. Unless..."

Once again he paused, and this time Tiny did not interrupt.

"Tell me, Tiny"—he lowered his voice and leaned over the table—"when you and he and Lady Mary used to go about, was there anything between him and the fourth member of the party?"

"I see what you're driving at," said Tiny slowly. "Not as far as I know, Ronald. We played round a bit, and he may have been a bit keen on her. But that's all. Only, of course, I'm the world's most almighty mutt at spotting anything of that sort."

"Then I can't understand it," said Standish. "It beats me. I suppose Gillson put you wise to the state of affairs out here."

"Squire Straker did."

"Same thing. Well, what had occurred to me was that young Denver might have been indiscreet with a certain lady—written a letter or something of that sort—and these blokes have found out about it. I admit that there are a lot of difficulties—not the least of them being, how they know him. I mean if there is some letter that has fallen into the wrong hands—if, in other words, that is where Mr. Felton Blake comes in—you can't recognize a man through his handwriting. So why this excitement over him?"

"Assuming for the moment, Ronald, that you're right, and that there was more in it than I thought, mightn't it be possible that the indiscretion has been committed since he came here? That a certain lady has met him on the quiet and been spotted."

"Possible," agreed the other, "but it won't account for everything. He has only been here three days, and this song and dance started two months ago. No, Tiny: there's the deuce of a lot more in this than meets the eye. And as far as I can see our only hope is to persuade someone to talk. At present we're working in the dark. Lead Denver on after lunch, if you can. Mention of the lady in question will come quite naturally from you. And this is no time for half measures. I've got a feeling in my bones that things will shortly come to a head. By Jove! don't look round, but do you know who has just come in? Berendosi himself."

"Do you know him?" said Tiny.

"Only by sight."

"I was introduced to him in the train to Paris. It may prove useful."

"He's coming this way. If he doesn't recognize you, you recognize him. As you say, he may be useful."

As luck would have it he went to the next table. Preceded by the *maître d'hôtel*, and surrounded by other lesser minions, the great man was piloted to his seat, and having ordered his meal he glanced round the room. And the first person his eyes fell on was Tiny.

For a moment he stared at him with a puzzled look: then he came across.

"Surely we met in the Golden Arrow?" he said courteously.

"Quite right, Signor," said Tiny, "though I hardly expected you to remember me."

"You were with our charming Countess Nada," remarked the other. "I had no idea you were proposing to honour us with a visit."

"I'm just wandering at random," said Tiny carelessly. "By the way, may I introduce Mr. Standish—Signor Berendosi."

"Your first visit, Mr. Standish?" said Berendosi politely.

"No: I have been here several times. I love Dalzburg."

"It is indeed a beautiful spot," agreed Berendosi. "A little unhealthy sometimes, but one cannot have everything."

"How true," said Standish. "And one can always take suitable precautions against—er—ill health."

For a moment the eyes of the two met and measured: then with a murmured banality Berendosi resumed his seat. And even as he did so Joe Denver passed the table.

"Have you finished, you fellows?" he remarked. "If so, come and have some coffee with me outside. Who was the bird who was talking to you?" he went on as they left the room. "The method of his entry seemed to indicate he was a big noise."

"That was Signor Berendosi," said Standish quietly. "Probably the most influential man in this country. And the most dangerous."

"Oh! What's he up against?"

"The existing system, Denver," said Standish. "The Royal House, the King and—the Queen."

Denver paused with a cigarette half-way to his mouth, and stared at him.

"What's that you say?" he raid. "Up against the King and the Queen. Why?"

"Because he wants to turn this country into a republic of which he will be the President."

"But has he any chance of succeeding?" demanded Denver.

Standish shrugged his shoulders.

"You never can tell, my dear fellow, in spots like this. These people are not as we are, you know. And a small thing, such as say some bit of gossip or scandal against the Queen, might prove very dangerous."

"What the hell are you talking about?" said Denver angrily. "Scandal against the Queen! Such a thing is impossible. Ask Carteret. He knows her."

"My dear fellow," said Standish soothingly, "you are surely man enough of the world to know that it isn't the truth that counts, but what people believe is the truth. I should be the last person to believe anything against such a very charming lady: nevertheless, the bald fact remains that Berendosi and the very influential group who are backing him have started insidious rumours about the Queen."

"I'll break the damned swine's neck for him," said the youngster through clenched teeth.

"Don't be such an ass, boy," said Standish sternly but not unkindly. "You're in a country now, where if they wish, you go into prison first and the charge comes on in a year or two. You've got to keep your head and your temper, or you'll be for it. Now I'm going to ask you an absolutely straight question. Why are you so very upset over what I've told you?"

"Wouldn't any decent fellow be?" answered the other.

"That's not good enough," said Standish. "I don't wish to probe into your private affairs, but there are times when it is necessary. And this is one of them. There are international questions at stake which render it essential. Now what are the facts? You, returning from the back of beyond, as you said yourself, after three years, decide suddenly to come here. Why?"

"I suppose I can please myself, can't I?" said the youngster angrily.

"For God's sake, Denver," said Standish gravely, "don't take it that way. Try and understand that I am not being gratuitously offensive and impertinent: try and understand that there are far bigger questions at stake than your feelings or mine."

"But how on earth can my movements have anything to do with them?" demanded Denver.

"I'm damned if I know, and that's what I'm trying to find out. I don't mind confessing to you now that there is no such person as von Emmerling. I invented him to find out one thing from you, and I succeeded. Your coming here was a sudden decision: no one had asked you. Very well then—what am I as an outside observer confronted with? The very significant fact, that the group of men who are at the bottom of the conspiracy against the Queen, are also keenly interested in an unknown Englishman arriving in Dalzburg for the first time. And I ask myself: Why?"

"What possible connection can there be between the two things?" said Denver.

"None—but for one other fact. The Englishman in question at one time knew the Queen very well. Steady now: don't lose your temper. As I told you before—it's not the truth that counts, and these people are capable of faking anything. Can you think of any letter which has passed between you and the lady concerned, and which by some wild stretch of imagination might be construed into something compromising?"

For a moment Denver hesitated: then he shook his head.

"I've never written to the lady in my life," he said.

"Well, do you think it possible," persisted Standish, "that the lady in question might have written to you and the letter has gone astray?"

"That, of course, is possible," answered Denver in a low voice. "Good God! Standish, you don't think, do you, that I may have caused her any harm?"

"Not wittingly, my dear fellow, but we've got to try and find a solution to certain facts. And I tell you frankly that I cannot help thinking that the Berendosi crowd are in the possession of some definite piece of evidence which they propose to use against the Queen. And further, I cannot help thinking that you by coming here have played straight into their hands, because I believe that evidence concerns you."

"But how could they possibly know me? I've never been here before."

"That is not an insuperable difficulty," said Standish. "Berendosi's machinations have been going on for years. What more likely then, than that, when the future consort of the King was in London he had her watched? And it was there that you were seen by someone who recognized you again here."

For a moment or two he stared at the youngster, with eyes that were full of understanding, for Joe Denver's expression was plain to read.

"We are all out for one thing, young Denver," he went on gravely: "to protect the honour of a lady. And I've been very frank with you. Will you be equally frank with me?"

"What do you want to know?" said the other.

"Just this. Assuming for the moment that I am right: assuming for the moment that a letter from the lady to you had gone astray, can you give me any idea as to the terms it would have been couched in. I mean," he went on with a smile, "would it have started 'Dear Mr. Denver'?"

For a while Joe Denver stared in front of him: then he got up suddenly.

"I loved her," he said quietly, "as I didn't believe it was possible for a man to love a woman. And I think—I know, she felt the same about me. And I came here in the hopes that perhaps I might catch a glimpse of her, now and then, as she drove through the streets. I shall be in my room if you want me: this has got to be talked over. And understand one thing, Standish. I am prepared to do anything—anything to help."

"Well, I'm damned," said Tiny as Denver disappeared. "He kept mighty dark about it."

"You didn't expect him to put it in the papers, did you?" Standish gave a short laugh. "You may be a darned fine player of Rugby football, old lad, but as an observer of human nature you are not in the international class. Hell, Tiny, and once again Hell. This is a devilish serious matter."

"We're not certain yet, Ronald."

"If by that you mean we've no absolute proof, you're right. But short of that, I'm as certain of it as I ever could be of anything. You take my word for it, Tiny—a letter was written and it's fallen into the wrong hands. Lord! It's as plain as a pike-staff. That accounts for the photographer taking snapshots of him. When the time is ripe they will publish the letter in one of their rotten rags—probably in the original handwriting, and on the page opposite the snapshots of the man to whom the letter was sent. Strengthens their case enormously: just the sort of thing the public eats. They'll pretend, of course, to take some action against the editor, but the mischief will have been done. I wish to Heaven the youngster had never come here, though it's too late to worry about that now."

Tiny lit a cigarette thoughtfully.

"So you think Felton Blake in some way got hold of a compromising letter written to young Denver," he said after a while. "Bit difficult to account for, Ronald. If Denver had received one, and had then mislaid it, it wouldn't be so hard. But it's almost incredible to believe that the lady would have left it lying about, and the only other alternative is that it was tampered with in the post."

"Blotting-paper," said Standish. "An unscrupulous floor waiter or chambermaid reads the letter in a looking-glass. Then realizing who the writer is he at once sees the financial value of the thing, and in the fullness of time it finds its way into Felton Blake's hands."

He drained his coffee and began to fill a pipe.

"Don't think that I'm not fully alive to the difficulties, Tiny," he went on. "There are many. If my blotting-paper theory is right, why didn't Denver get the letter? An answer to that is that possibly the lady on second thoughts tore the letter up and never sent it. Then there's another point: how does the lady in question know anything about it? Has Berendosi told her? Has he already held it over her head? If so, it seems a very unnecessary thing to do. The one thing I should have thought he would not do is to give his victim any warning until he is ready to strike. And yet even with all the difficulties — it must be the solution; it must be."

"Look here, Ronald, would it do any good if I went and saw the Queen. I don't know how it's done, as I've never been in the habit of calling on Queens. But if we can find out the correct procedure I'm sure she'd see me, and I might be able to find out something."

"A darned good idea, Tiny: darned good. Here's Berendosi: ask him. He'll know the ropes. And you can make the request without arousing any suspicion."

"Are you making a long stay, Mr. Carteret?"

Berendosi paused by their table, and glancing up Tiny saw that his eyes were fixed on the chair just vacated by Joe Denver.

"It depends, Signor," he answered. "By the way, I wonder if you could help me over something?"

"I shall be delighted," said the other. "In what way can I assist you?"

"Won't you sit down and join us in some coffee?"

"You are very kind."

He seated himself, and leaned forward attentively.

"Two or three years ago in London," said Tiny, "I had the honour of seeing a good deal of Her Majesty the Queen before she was married. And if it is not presumption on my part I would so like to renew my acquaintance. I was wondering if perhaps you could tell me whether such a thing is possible; and if so, how I should set about it."

For a moment or two Berendosi sat as if carved in stone, his eyes fixed on Tiny's face.

"Certainly such a thing is possible," he said quietly. "And equally certainly I can help you. I feel sure Her Majesty would be delighted to see you again. As a matter of fact I am going to the Palace this afternoon, and if you would care to come with me I am sure I can arrange an audience. It will of course only be an informal one."

"That is more than good of you," said Tiny.

"And would Mr. Standish care to come as well?"

"I fear I cannot," said Standish. "I have very urgent letters to write."

"And your other friend—the good-looking boy?"

With a wave of his hand he indicated the empty coffee cup.

"He unfortunately has fulfilled your warning to me, Signor, concerning bad health," said Standish gravely. "He's got a very sharp attack of fever: I'm going up to him now."

"I would," said Berendosi suavely. "It would be a pity if in spite of his fever he suddenly appeared."

Ronald Standish's eyes twinkled: though he disliked the man his quickness appealed to him.

"He is far too well brought up a patient for that," he answered. "Well, Tiny, I shall see you later. Adieu, Signor."

Berendosi watched him in silence as he went up the stairs: then he turned to Tiny.

"So that is the celebrated Ronald Standish, is it?" he remarked. "I am glad to have met him."

"Celebrated!" Tiny raised his eyebrows. "I should hardly have thought he was that."

"His reputation is European. Not perhaps amongst the *hoi polloi*, but in those circles that count." An enigmatic smile twitched round his lips. "Well, I trust your young friend's fever will have abated: these sudden attacks are most disconcerting, aren't they?"

"A sort of malaria he got in Africa," said Tiny carelessly.

"Then, of course, it would be unwise for him to meet Her Majesty," agreed Berendosi. "One should always be careful in cases of malaria to avoid anything which might send the patient's temperature up."

"I hardly see why meeting the Queen should do that, Signor," said Tiny, staring him straight in the face.

"No? Well, well, perhaps you're right. Anyway the situation does not arise—this afternoon."

He rose from his chair.

"Well, Mr. Carteret, if you are ready, we might start. My car is waiting outside the hotel."

He relapsed into silence as soon as they moved off and Tiny was not sorry: he wanted to think. It was the personal side of the thing that hit him considerably more than it did Ronald Standish. To him the fact that these two had been in love with one another merely complicated the practical difficulties of the situation: they were just two strangers. But to Tiny they were two old friends.

He found himself wondering if Mary had known at the time. Of course she had: trust a woman for spotting anything of that sort. And now that he too looked back he began to remember little things which should have told him the condition of affairs: small pointers he had ignored at the time but which now seemed ridiculously obvious.

"I loved her, as I didn't believe it was possible for a man to love a woman."

Joe Denver's words rang in his brain, and suddenly he looked at the man sitting beside him. And a great desire took possession of him to hit that man's face and continue hitting it hard and often and then again some. For the full swinishness of the thing had struck him for the first time. Not only was he going to exploit a big love for his own ends, but he was going to do it in such a way that the woman would be held up to shame and obloquy. And his great desire grew even greater.

"Have you ever played rugger, Signor?" he asked as the car swung through the Palace gates.

"Rugger, Mr. Carteret? I am afraid I don't quite understand."

"Football, Signor," said Tiny dreamily. "And sometimes a man goes down on the ball when there are eight large forwards who want that ball."

"It sounds most unpleasant," said Berendosi politely.

"It is: most unpleasant." A gentle smile spread over Tiny's face. "You should play rugger, Signor: I am sure you would enjoy it."

"Presumably you play forward yourself, Mr. Carteret."

"I do," said Tiny.

"Then when I am next in England I must come and watch you. I should like to see what happens to the man who goes down on the ball before I start playing myself."

"They have an open grave ready dug for him," murmured Tiny.

"I think then that I will be one of the eight forwards," said Berendosi.

"You aren't a big enough man, Signor," remarked Tiny quietly, and at that moment the car stopped.

If Berendosi appreciated the insult he showed no sign beyond a faint smile. He gave a curt order to his chauffeur and then led the way past a sentry who saluted. And the first thing that struck Tiny was that even among members of the household itself, his companion was evidently, as Joe Denver put it, the big noise. Footmen and underlings of all descriptions sprang up and bowed obsequiously as he passed, and Berendosi took not the slightest notice of any of them.

"Now if you wait in there, Mr. Carteret"—he indicated a small ante-room—"I will see what I can do."

Left to himself, Tiny studied his surroundings. The room looked out over the town and river towards the snow-capped mountains away to the north. Just in front lay the garden, and beyond it came the woods which covered the lower part of the hill. Much like an ordinary English country house, he reflected, set in beautiful surroundings. And he was just wondering if he dared to smoke, when a girl appeared in the doorway.

"Her Majesty will be delighted to see you, Mr. Carteret," she said with a smile. "Come along this way."

He followed her down a corridor, until they reached a room at the end.

"Signor Berendosi is with her," said the girl as she opened the door.

They were standing by the window as he entered, and the Queen greeted him with a charming smile.

"This is a real pleasure, Mr. Carteret," she said as he bent and kissed her hand. "I could hardly believe my ears when Signor Berendosi told me you were here."

"It is more than good of Your Majesty to remember me," said Tiny.

"One doesn't forget old friends like that," she answered. "Mary was out here with me a few weeks ago."

"A pity that your visit and hers did not coincide, Mr. Carteret," said Berendosi suavely. "It would have been quite a reunion for Her Majesty."

"Where are you staying, Mr. Carteret?" asked the Queen.

"At the Royal Hotel, ma'am," said Tiny.

"With a very well-known compatriot of his, Your Majesty," remarked Berendosi. "Ronald Standish. And another friend who has gone down with fever. I didn't catch his name, Mr. Carteret."

Tiny had realized it would come sooner or later: had realized indeed that the main reason why Berendosi had taken the trouble he had was to see what effect Joe Denver's name would have on the Queen. And there was no way out of it. Manifestly he couldn't pretend not to know.

"Someone else you knew in London, Your Majesty," he said quietly. "A great friend of Mary's—Joe Denver."

Just for a moment her eyes dilated—her body grew rigid: just for a moment she gave herself away to the lynx-eyed man who was watching her. Then she recovered herself.

"Of course. I remember him perfectly," she answered. "I do hope he's not bad."

"No, no," said Tiny. "Just a sudden return of malaria."

"Should he not be better to-night, Mr. Carteret," remarked Berendosi with a faintly mocking smile, "I can give you the name of my own doctor. And now if Your Majesty will graciously excuse me I have some important papers to attend to. My car, Mr. Carteret, will be waiting for you."

He backed from the room, and the door had barely closed behind him before her whole demeanour changed.

"Drop the Queen business, Tiny," she cried. "Let's go back three years. Tell me about—about Joe Denver. Is he really ill?"

"He's not ill at all," said Tiny with a smile. "But I think it was better, don't you, that he shouldn't meet you before the extremely astute eyes of the gentleman who has just left us."

"You guessed, did you," she said softly. "Or did Mary tell you?"

And then somewhat to his relief she went on without waiting for an answer.

"I must see him again, Tiny: I simply must."

"But, Olga," he cried, "such a thing would be madness just now."

"Why?" she demanded. "Nobody else knows. It's no different to my seeing you."

For a moment he stared at her in amazement: what on earth was she talking about?

"But with Berendosi on the look out," he stammered, "it would be dangerous to a degree."

"That pig of a man is always on the look out," she cried. "And I can easily fool him. I must, Tiny: I must see him."

"Perhaps it could be arranged," he said at length, more to gain time than anything else. Was it possible that she was in ignorance of the whole plot? Certainly from the way she was talking it looked like it.

"It must be: it must be. I've never seen him, Tiny, since those days in London."

"But you've written to him," he said.

She shook her head.

"Never," she said, and he looked at her blankly.

"Not even in those days in London?" he persisted.

And once again she shook her head.

"I've never written to him in my life," she repeated.

"Are you sure you didn't and then tear the letter up?"

He saw her give a little frown of annoyance, and he realized that it must seem to her he was being *gauche*. But it was imperative to find out the truth: if the answer to the last question was again in the negative Ronald's theory fell to pieces. And it was—emphatically.

"I've never put pen to paper to him, Tiny," she said. "Why do you ask? You're mysterious, you know," she went on a little petulantly. "Like Mary when she was out here. And Nada—do you remember her? She has just been over to England."

"I travelled back to Paris with her," he said.

And then she switched back to Joe Denver. How was he? What did he look like? How long was he going to stay? And Tiny answered almost mechanically, so dumbfounded was he at the new turn of events.

At length she dismissed him, having first extracted a half promise that somehow or other he was to bring Joe Denver to see her. He had not the heart to refuse point blank; she was so desperately in earnest and so wistfully pretty.

"I will do what I can," he said gently, and just for a moment her mouth trembled.

"Half an hour is not much in a lifetime, Tiny," she whispered.

He left her standing by the window—a slim girlish figure in white—and went in search of the car. He found it waiting for him, with Berendosi inside perusing some papers.

"It was good of you to wait, Signor," he remarked as he got in.

"Not at all, Mr. Carteret. And I hope your audience with Her Majesty was a pleasant one."

"Very, thank you."

"With two such old acquaintances it was bound to be," murmured the other. "By the way, the mention of your young friend's name seemed to upset the Queen a little."

"I didn't notice it," said Tiny curtly.

"Indeed!" A faint smile flickered round the other's lips. "Perhaps it was my imagination." He turned suddenly and faced Tiny. "Mr. Carteret: it might be as well if we all understood one another. I am not under the delusion that you have come to Dalzburg to gaze upon our charming scenery. And therefore I would be glad if you would convey a message from me to the excellent Standish. So long as you confine yourselves to our scenery we shall be delighted and honoured to have you with us. But should other activities begin to take place—well, then, Mr. Carteret, I am convinced we should discover some irregularity in both your passports. Do I make myself clear?"

"I don't know about Standish, but my passport is in perfect order," said Tiny.

"Mr. Carteret! Really! Your lack of intelligence pains me. Ah! here we are. Well—you won't forget my little message. Adieu!"

The car rolled off, and Tiny entered the hotel, where he found Standish waiting for him in the lounge.

"Come into the bar, Ronald," he said. "I need a drink."

"Did you see her?" asked the other as they crossed the lounge.

"I did. And alone. She swears that she never wrote a line to him—not even one that she subsequently tore up. So unless she's forgotten, your blotting-paper theory goes down the drain. Moreover, she seems to be in complete ignorance that there is anything in the air at all."

Standish stared at him nonplussed. "That makes things a bit harder, doesn't it? And did you enlighten her?"

"I thought it better not to," said Tiny. "There's another thing also," he went on, "our friend Berendosi was kind enough to tell me that should the spirit move him he will fake up some irregularity on our passports, presumably with the idea of making us leave the country."

"That possibility—like the poor—has always been with us," said Standish with a short laugh. "And, 'pon my soul, Tiny, I don't know that we're doing much good here. I've got half a mind to go back to England and try from the Felton Blake end. I don't remember ever having felt so completely up against a blank wall. And of course we must get young Denver out of the country. I've told him that already. Hullo! there is a lady who seems to know you just entered."

Tiny swung round: Countess Nada was coming towards them.

"Mr. Carteret," she said a little breathlessly, "where is Mr. Denver?"

"I left him up in his room about half an hour ago," said Standish.

"Go and see if he's still there," she cried. "And then don't let him out of your sight."

The barman was looking at them curiously, though he could not have heard the actual words.

"Countess," said Tiny, "may I introduce Mr. Standish—Countess Mazarin."

"Go, please—go," she said urgently. "It is vital."

"Give the Countess a cocktail, Tiny," said Standish, and left the bar.

"It was because of Denver you sent me that wire?" said Tiny when he had ordered the drinks.

"Yes, of course," she cried. "I'll tell you everything in a moment. Oh! he couldn't tell, but nothing more cruel could have happened than that he should come here."

She put her hand suddenly on his arm.

"It's too late," she whispered. "They've got him."

Ronald Standish was crossing the lounge, and his face was grave.

"His room is empty," he said as he sat down, "and the floor waiter tells me he dashed out wildly about twenty minutes ago after receiving a note. Here is the envelope: I found it in the paper basket."

He held it out to the Countess, who studied the writing for a moment.

"I thought as much," she said wearily. "Sonia Gregoroff. One of the ladies-in-waiting and in Berendosi's pay. Oh! how cruel. You see, I got back from Paris a few moments after you left the Queen, Mr. Carteret. And she told me he was here. And she told me that she could not understand...." She passed her hand over her forehead. "I'm going distracted. I flew down here...."

"Don't let us lose our heads, Countess," said Standish quietly. "You are certain about the writing on the envelope?"

"Absolutely," she cried. "I'd know it anywhere."

"That settles it then. There are many questions I'd like to ask you, but they must wait. The first vital necessity is for you to get back to the Queen. Stay with her: remain glued to her side. Above all things see that those two don't meet alone. And if you find out anything telephone me here, or send a message. But—*keep them apart.*"

With a little nod she rose at once.

"I understand perfectly," she said. "I'll go now."

"A stout-hearted girl, that," remarked Standish as she left the hotel. "By Jove! Tiny, we're up against some pretty useful odds. Still it's not the first time."

He started to fill his pipe, staring idly at the cosmopolitan crowd that thronged the lounge outside.

"What's our next move, Ronald?" said Tiny after awhile.

"It's a bit difficult to decide, old boy. Beyond the fact that he has been decoyed out of the hotel by a note written by Gregoroff's daughter, we don't know anything. He may be up at the Palace now: he may be anywhere. Until we can get some further information there is nothing to be done as far as I can see."

"Do you think they've kidnapped him?"

"I wouldn't put it a bit beyond them. And if so, the proverbial needle in the bundle of hay would be easier to find. Unless somebody blows the gaff. You see, Tiny, we're at a hopeless disadvantage. In England one could go to the police: here it would be absolutely useless. We can't even go to the embassy. On the first hint of our doing anything like that Berendosi's threat would be put into execution, and our passports would be found irregular. So we've got to play a lone hand, in which the first vital trick is to get Denver out of the country."

He gave a short laugh.

"Nice easy hurdle for the kick off, isn't it? Still I've got faith in the Countess. She's loyal to the core, and she's got her head screwed on the right way. If anyone can find things out, she will."

A prophecy which was duly fulfilled twenty minutes later when a page boy brought Tiny a note. It was short and to the point.

"Mr. Denver was seen with Sonia Gregoroff driving in closed car towards Gregoroff's castle. Queen knows nothing as yet. Fear some devilry. Get him out of the country."

"On the face of it a somewhat tall order," said Standish with a grin. "However, we may as well have a dip at it."

"Sure thing," agreed Tiny. "How do you propose we should set about dipping?"

"Well, as I see it, it's like this," said Standish. "Whatever the communication was that the lady wrote him, he evidently smelt no rat. He left the hotel without any suspicions. Moreover, he took no kit with him. One of two things therefore is going to happen. Either they will keep him unsuspicious by means of some plausible story, in which case he will probably be allowed the run of the grounds: or having got him there they will drop the pretence and he will find himself a virtual prisoner. In the first event there should be no difficulty in communicating with him."

"And in the second?" murmured Tiny.

Ronald Standish knocked out his pipe.

"It will be considerably harder," he remarked shortly.

CHAPTER VI

"My dear Gregoroff, you seem absurdly jumpy. What on earth is the matter with you?"

Berendosi, his cigar drawing evenly between his teeth, surveyed his companion with amused contempt.

"It's this fellow Standish coming here," said the other uneasily. "It looks as if he must know something."

"He can know the lot for all I care," remarked Berendosi with a short laugh. "What does it matter? You know," he went on after a pause, "I'm really rather sorry for Standish. It's pathetic to see a man of his ability endeavouring to make bricks with such a ridiculously small quantity of straw."

"He might give us a lot of trouble," said Gregoroff.

"How can he?" demanded Berendosi. "Even granted that he knows everything, which I think is doubtful, what can he do? As I told his large friend only an hour ago, I should have no hesitation, if I deemed it necessary, of cutting short their visit here. In fact, I think I shall anyway do so to-morrow. If your charming daughter is successful, as I am sure she will be, they will be better out of the country. That Mazarin woman is no fool: it will only be a question of time before she suspects we've got young Denver here. And then I don't want Standish to take any diplomatic action. It might complicate things."

He strolled to the window and stared over the country that lay, spread out like a map, before him.

"A fine view you've got from here, Gregoroff," he said thoughtfully.

His face was as impassive as usual, but into his eyes there had come a sudden gleam. For Paul Berendosi was allowing himself a rare luxury: he was day dreaming. After long years he saw his life's ambition within his grasp: so far as he could see nothing could upset his calculations. If it had been a good thing before, the providential arrival of the young man himself now made it a certainty. The thing was fool-proof, and he had said no more than the truth when he had remarked to Gregoroff that he didn't care if Standish knew everything.

Therein lay the beauty of the scheme: the hand could be played with all the cards on the table. The ground was prepared: his spies and underlings had done their work well. Now all that remained was the one culminating thing which would split the country from top to bottom. Bloodshed perhaps: what of it? No man can step suddenly into supreme power without some payment.

With an effort he came out of his reverie: Gregoroff was speaking.

"What of Zavier? Is he coming?"

"As soon as I heard your news I wired him at once. He should be here at any moment."

"What do you make of that man, Berendosi?"

"It is hard to say, my friend. Undoubtedly a gentleman whom I would sooner have for me than against me." He glanced through the window. "And here, unless I am much mistaken, is your daughter."

A big red car had turned off the main road, and was coming up the winding drive to the castle.

"I wonder if she has been successful."

He leaned still further out, as the car stopped by the front door.

"Yes—she has. Our young friend is with her. Now under no circumstances, Gregoroff, must he see me; at any rate until our little play is staged. I am under no delusions as to what Standish will have told him about my poor self. And I am not at all certain that it would not be better for you to keep out of the way also. However, we will wait until we see your daughter, and find out what she has to say."

He swung round as the door opened, and a dark, striking-looking girl came in.

"Bravo! my dear Sonia," he cried. "You have done admirably. How did you manage it?"

She gave a short laugh.

"I sent him a note saying that someone very dear to him was in grave danger, and would he come at once. And he came."

"Yes, but what of the Englishman—Standish. Does he know where he's gone?"

"No, I asked him that in the car. You see the note was given to him when he was alone: I saw to that. Standish was in the bar, waiting for the big man."

"And the note itself?"

"Was in Denver's pocket. It is now torn up."

"Admirable, my dear, admirable," said Berendosi. "But how did you explain to him about the grave danger?"

"I admitted that it was a fib," she laughed, "put in to make sure that he came. And then I pitched him the yarn we arranged. That it was unsafe for him to see her at the Palace, but that I was arranging a meeting for them here. He swallowed it whole."

"And you don't think anyone knows he is here?"

"I'm sure no one does. I took every precaution, and made him sit right back in the car."

"Excellent. Not that it matters very much, but it saves trouble. Did you find out anything of interest from the young man?"

"A lot," she said, lighting a cigarette. "He was simply frantic to know what all the mystery was. Evidently this man Standish has told him that something is in the wind, and that you are at the bottom of it. He talked about a letter written by her to him."

"So he doesn't know the truth," said Berendosi softly. "And apparently Standish doesn't know it either. That is most interesting. Undoubtedly, my dear Gregoroff, Standish and his friend leave this country to-morrow."

"And this man Denver?" asked the girl.

"Remains here—until the end. Though I don't think it is necessary, I have already taken the precaution of closing every frontier to him. But that is only in case he should escape from here, which is an unlikely eventuality. By the way, what is he doing now?"

"Dreaming of the meeting to come," she said with a sneer.

"Well, I think, my dear, that it wouldn't be a bad thing if you went and dreamt with him. I should hate him to dream anywhere near a telephone if he was alone."

"I'll go," she said at once. "And I suppose neither of you will appear till after it's over."

"That's right," answered Berendosi. "Till then we leave him entirely to you."

"A girl in a thousand, my dear fellow," he said, as the door closed behind her. "You are to be congratulated on such a daughter."

"How long are we going to keep him here, Berendosi?" said the other.

"As I said before—until the end," said Berendosi curtly. "Though if it is of any comfort to you, I think that moment is considerably nearer than we at one time anticipated. A lot will depend on what Zavier says."

"Indeed!"

They both swung round: the man was standing in the door, the monkey perched on his shoulder.

"And what is this new development you wired me about?" he asked.

"Come in, Monsieur Zavier," cried Berendosi. "I am delighted to see you. The new development is nothing more nor less than the arrival in the country of the young man himself."

"So." Zavier took a chair, and lit one of his little cigarettes. "That is interesting. And when did he come?"

"A few days ago, whilst I was in England. Gregoroff recognized him."

"And where is he now?"

"In this house. A small trap was laid for him into which he obligingly walked. Yes—he is in this house, and in this house he will remain."

"You propose to keep him as a prisoner, do you? I should have thought that better results might have been obtained by leaving him at large."

"But for one fact you are quite right," agreed Berendosi. "But we have some other English visitors who complicate things somewhat. You may perhaps have heard of Ronald Standish?"

Zavier's eyes half closed.

"So he has arrived too, has he? But surely they didn't come together."

"No. But I cannot help thinking that there is a very close connection between the two things. By some means or other Standish found out that Denver was here. So he at once came himself. And though I have since found out that he doesn't know the truth, he is very near it. That being the case it is obvious that his first idea would be to get Denver out of the country. And though of course that can be prevented it might give rise to unpleasantness with the British Embassy. So taking everything into consideration I thought it best to bring him here."

He held up his hand for silence as footsteps passed the door, and Denver's cheerful laugh rang out.

"He seems in excellent spirits," remarked Zavier in some surprise; and Berendosi smiled.

"He has at present no idea of what the future holds in store for him," he remarked. "In fact he thinks he is going to meet a certain lady here after dinner to-night."

Zavier stared at him for a moment or two in silence.

"And why not?" he said thoughtfully. "Such a meeting might be made use of."

"It was the first idea I had," remarked Berendosi, "but I dismissed it for two reasons. First it gives away his presence here, and secondly I doubt greatly if the lady would come. Gregoroff is not *persona grata* with her. But I have staged what I think you will agree is a most entertaining little performance, and one which will benefit us even more than her Majesty's presence. I don't know if you have met our host's charming daughter?"

"I have not yet had that pleasure," answered the other.

"The same build, the same colouring as our gracious Queen. In fact when dressed in the same way it would be difficult if one could not see their faces to tell which was which."

Zavier nodded appreciatively.

"An understudy. Excellent. And the window wide open."

"Better than that, my friend: far better than that. But—wait and see. It may, of course, not come off. If so, there is no harm done. He will anyway cease to be in good spirits when he discovers he has been trapped. To return to more important matters. This young man's unexpected arrival has rather altered things. And although nothing could have suited our plans better, it has introduced certain difficulties. He can, of course, be kept here, and will be kept here till he is no longer required, but with a man in Standish's position instituting inquiries and pushing them hard, there is bound to be a considerable hue and cry. It will naturally be done through the Embassy. And so I would like to curtail the time before we strike as much as possible. Everything is in train: I was only waiting because for many reasons September is the most suitable time of year. But Denver's presence overrides everything. Therefore I propose to do the thing immediately—that is, say, in a fortnight. Does that suit you?"

"Anything, my dear Signor, suits me," said Zavier languidly, "so long as the money is forthcoming. But I doubt," he continued with a little chuckle, "if it will suit Felton Blake."

Berendosi frowned.

"Is he likely to give trouble?"

"People with whom I deal never give trouble," remarked Zavier. "But, as I think I told you before, one of his conditions was that he should be allowed to further his ridiculous love affair. To return, however, to Standish for the moment. You say he does not know the truth."

"At present—no. How long that state of affairs will continue I can't say—nor does it really matter very much. As a matter of fact I was surprised when I found out he didn't. Countess Mazarin—a lady who has no affection for me—was travelling with his friend Carteret to Paris the day before yesterday, and I fully expected she had told him. But—apparently not. And so, my dear Monsieur Zavier, if you would be good enough to deliver the goods within the next few days I think we shall soon be able to congratulate ourselves on a successfully planned and still more successfully executed coup."

"I shall await the result with interest, Signor," murmured Zavier, glancing at his watch. "And since there would appear to be nothing further to discuss, I think I will return to my hotel. Unless, that is, you could give me a little dinner here?"

"Delighted," said Gregoroff. "We three will feed alone, leaving the stage set for the other two."

He gave an odious chuckle, and Zavier glanced at him thoughtfully. An unpleasant specimen, he reflected: a hanger-on, a cringer. For Berendosi he had the respect that one strong, unscrupulous man feels for another of the same kidney: for Gregoroff he felt nothing but contempt. But his face was expressionless as he spoke.

"I shall be interested to see the play," he said suavely.

"You have fixed everything?" asked Berendosi.

"Everything," answered Gregoroff. "The curtain rises at ten. And in case the leading man becomes annoyed with his part, I have six strong supers in readiness to soothe him down."

"There is the castle you want."

Andrew Mackintosh, correspondent for the *Planet*, halted his ancient Fiat and indicated the place with a large hand.

"I will drive no nearer, for this damned machine makes a noise like a tank. And may God help you on your nefarious undertaking. I will await you here."

"Good for you, Andy," said Standish, getting out of the car. "But we may be the devil of a time."

"Mon—the night is warm, and I have a flask. But dinna forget that I have a wife and bairns, and if trouble arises, as I'm thinking it will, we are perfect strangers. I will turn the car round, and I will wait till dawn. But if you're no here before then, I shall be away back to Dalzburg."

"Stout fellow," said Standish. "Come on, Tiny: it's dark enough to start."

From the back of the car he took out a coil of rope which he slung over his shoulder.

"Got your torch, Tiny? And little Willie? Right—come on."

He had from the first decided against taking fire-arms, and little Willie was the substitute. And no mean substitute either. It consisted of a piece of stout rubber with a lump of lead at the end, which when connected with the base of a man's skull, produced oblivion for as long or short a period as desired. It also produced oblivion in silence, an essential factor if they were to succeed that night.

It was Mackintosh who had suggested the rope, and lent them a coil of his own.

"It may be no use," he had remarked, "but it's no trouble to carry, and maybe it will come in handy. Supposing they mean to keep him there, they will put him in a top room. And perhaps you can find a way of getting it up to him. But it's going to be a difficult and a dangerous business."

A fact of which they were both aware. Not that the danger deterred them: as Standish had pointed out, it was not danger in the accepted sense of the word. But it was essential that they should not be caught because of the consequences. They were putting themselves outside the pale of even Bessonian law: they were doing a thing which rendered them liable to sample the inside of a prison for months. And once there, there they would remain until everything was over.

So strongly did Standish feel it that he again impressed it on Tiny as they moved cautiously forward.

"It's got to be stealth, Tiny," he muttered. "Stealth and cunning all the time. We must only use force as absolutely our last resource."

The ground rose fairly abruptly from the road, which helped them considerably as far as cover was concerned, and a steep bank about six feet high on the edge of the drive allowed them to get to within thirty yards of the castle. Fortunately for them there was no moon, and they could lie against the bank with their heads above it without fear of being seen. A light was filtering out from two rooms, one almost directly in front of them on the ground floor, the other some way to the left on the first. Heavy curtains covered both windows, so that it was impossible to see who was inside, though once a man put his head out of the upper one and stared round.

Suddenly a woman's laugh rang out from the room opposite, and they heard Denver's voice in answer.

"Evidently they haven't aroused his suspicions yet," whispered Standish in Tiny's ear. "Hullo! the other light has gone out."

Once more silence fell, broken only by the low murmur of conversation from across the drive. Five minutes passed—ten, when Tiny gripped Standish's arm.

"Look," he whispered. "Away to the left. Someone smoking."

Sure enough from some distance away there came the even glow of a cigarette. The smoker was standing motionless: they could see the little lines of light as he lifted it to and from his mouth.

"In front of us, Tiny," breathed Standish in his ear. "Between the man smoking and the room where Denver is. There are half a dozen of them."

They peered into the darkness, and at last he picked them up. They were standing bunched together not far from the window, and it seemed to him they were waiting? But, what for?

Boom! From a clock tower above rang out the first note of the hour, and instantly things began to happen. The smoker flung away his cigarette: two shadowy figures detached themselves from the group opposite and moved swiftly towards the window. There they paused, and began adjusting something that looked like a tripod. And when at length the last note of the clock had quivered into silence, all was as before save that the smoker no longer smoked, and the thing that looked like a tripod was in position.

"Standing by for the clock," muttered Standish, "to cover the noise. What's going to happen now?"

They had not long to wait for the answer. Suddenly the curtains parted, and a woman's arm showed for a moment through them. They saw two men spring forward to the tripod: then the curtains swung back revealing the whole room. And for a moment they could hardly believe their eyes. Seated beside the table, a look of stupefied amazement on his face, was Joe Denver. On her knees at his feet, her arms thrown round him, her face buried against his chest was a woman. It might have been a *tableau vivant* representing "The anguish of a woman in love." And even as they watched in astonishment there came the blinding flash of magnesium, and the mystery was solved. A flashlight photograph had been taken.

"Ronald," whispered Tiny, "it's the Queen."

"Rot," said Standish. "It's someone whose back view looks like the Queen. We've got to get that camera. Hullo! things move."

The door of the room opened and Gregoroff stood there, his eyes blazing. And slowly the woman rose from her knees and faced him, trembling.

"So, Madame," he thundered, "I have caught you, have I?"

"Holy Smoke," muttered Ronald, "that wheeze came out of the ark with Noah. But we've got to miss it for a bit, Tiny. The camera man is away to the left. After him."

Like shadows they faded into the darkness. From behind them came the sound of Gregoroff's angry voice, and Joe Denver's stammered answers, but they paid no attention. The camera was their objective, and they caught its owner, a little rat of a man, just as he was turning in at the front door. He gave one squeal like a frightened rabbit; then Tiny's vast hand closed over his mouth.

"Take the camera, Ronald," he said in a low voice. "I've collared the excrescence."

"Right, old boy. I've got it. And here's the plate."

There came the crack of breaking glass—the sound of the pieces being thrown into the bushes. Then—

"What now, Ronald? What are we to do with this thing?"

"We've got to dot him one, Tiny. Otherwise he'll give us away. Hold his head forward."

And with the skill born of practice Ronald Standish laid him out.

"Into the bushes with him. And his camera too. Now we've got to get young Denver out of it."

They reached the cover of the bank again, and crept back to their original point of vantage. Two of the men who had been outside the window were now inside the room, but they could see the other four in readiness close at hand. The girl was no longer there: only Gregoroff, still simulating righteous anger, faced the utterly bewildered youth.

"I assure you, sir, there is some extraordinary mistake," Denver was saying. "I have never met your wife before in my life."

"You expect me to believe that," sneered Gregoroff. "You expect me to believe that my wife asked a perfect stranger to dine with her! Explain why you came, if what you say is true."

"I came to..." Denver paused: then he threw back his head. "Damn you," he shouted, "go to Hell. It doesn't matter why I came. What are you going to do with me?"

"We will decide that later," said Gregoroff icily. "In the meantime you shall be shown your quarters for the night. Take him away."

"Let's rush 'em, Ronald," muttered Tiny, but Standish shook his head.

"Odds too great, old boy. Eight of them, and the betting is they've got guns. We must wait and hope for the best. But, by God! they're a bunch of swine."

The two men rushed Denver out of the room, and Gregoroff leant back in his chair shaking with laughter.

"My dear," he chuckled as the door opened and his daughter came in, "I congratulate you. He doesn't know whether he is on his head or his heels, in fact he has visions of fighting a duel with me. Where are the others?"

"Just coming," she said, lighting a cigarette. "I think it went off very well."

"Capitally: capitally. Ah! my dear Berendosi, the stage has lost a shining light."

He pointed to his daughter, and Berendosi bowed.

"In order that we may enjoy it more fully," he murmured. "So it was successful. You hear that, Zavier?"

And Tiny suddenly found Standish's hand on his arm.

"That man who has just come in, Tiny." His voice was shaking with excitement. "With the monkey on his shoulder. Can it be possible? Damn it! it must be." He relapsed into silence. "Let's listen."

"Admirable," said Zavier. "And where is the young man now?"

"Where he is likely to remain for a time," laughed Berendosi. "Locked in upstairs. Those men needn't wait, Gregoroff. Well," he continued as the group outside the window dispersed, "I think we have every reason to congratulate ourselves. Everything has gone off without a hitch. I would keep up the fiction as long as you can, Gregoroff, though I fear he is bound to suspect sooner or later."

"You intend to produce him at the crucial moment, I presume," said Zavier.

"Exactly. I fear he may have an unpleasant time at the hands of my outraged fellow-countrymen, but it will be in an excellent cause. Well, Zavier—I think we might return to Dalzburg. Good night, dear lady, and a thousand thanks for your assistance."

He bowed over her hand, and the three men left the room. And shortly after the girl followed them.

"It's now or never, Tiny," said Standish. "They've put him up in that tower; you can see the light. Are you on?"

"You bet I'm on," grunted the other. "Let's move."

Keeping in the shadow beyond the light thrown from the window, they darted across the drive and into the now empty room. The door was open and Standish peered out. From one end of the passage came voices, and without hesitation he led the way in the opposite direction till he came to a flight of stairs. And a moment or two later they were both on the first landing.

"Passages too damned well lit," he muttered. "We've got to make the fourth floor at least."

They darted up the next flight: then the third, and there Standish paused. From above them came the sound of voices and the chink of money.

"They will be guarding his door," he whispered to Tiny. "Wade in—but do it silently. My God! look out."

Flattened into a little recess, hardly daring to breathe, they watched Gregoroff himself go past them so close that they could almost have touched him. He went up the next flight, and they heard his voice.

"All right, is he?"

"Fought like a madman," came the answer, "but he's quieter now. He started trying to break the door down, but I guess he hurt himself more than the door."

"You'll be relieved in a couple of hours. Leave him alone unless he starts shouting. Then gag him."

Once again Gregoroff passed close to the recess where Standish and Tiny were crouching, and they waited until his footsteps died away downstairs.

"Now, Tiny," whispered Standish, "we've got to hurry. That camera merchant may come to at any moment. But for Heaven's sake—no noise."

Tiny Carteret

Cautiously—step by step—they crept up the last flight. And this time luck was with them: the passage, save for one light under which two men were playing cards, was in darkness. They were engrossed in their game, and the thing was over in a flash. Two dull thudding blows, and the card players rolled gently off their chairs on to the floor.

"I've got the key," said Standish, "and that must be the door where the light is. By Gad! old boy, I believe we're going to pull it off."

He turned the lock, and they went in to find Joe Denver sitting disconsolately on his bed. He sprang to his feet with a cry of amazement when he saw who they were, but Standish silenced him at once.

"Move, young fellow, and move quickly. Good Lord! what's that?"

Through the open window came an uproar from below, and he looked out.

"Tiny, they've found the camera bloke. It will have to be the rope."

He darted to the door and locked it: already the sound of footsteps could be heard rushing up the stairs.

"Put that wardrobe against the door," he said curtly. "I'll fix this."

He lashed one end of the rope to a leg of the bed, and threw the rest of the coil out of the window.

"Now, Denver, down you go. Don't argue, damn you: move. Go into the main road and get into a car you'll find there. We're after you at once."

Crash after crash was coming from the other side of the door, and it was obvious it could not hold much longer.

"After him, Tiny. Quick, man, quick."

He gave him two seconds: then he too clambered out and started to swarm down. And even as he dropped out of sight, the door above him gave way.

"Drop freely," he shouted; all pretence of concealment was useless now. "They'll cut the rope."

But luck held. The heavy wardrobe delayed their pursuers sufficiently to let Denver and Tiny reach the ground, and when at last they did get to the rope and cut it Standish had only some ten feet to fall.

"Run like hell," he said curtly.

Panting and breathless they reached the car to find Mackintosh had started the engine.

"I thought I observed a slight commotion," he remarked as they fell in. "We'll have to hop it, boys: yon man Gregoroff has a powerful car."

"And, by Jove! Andy," said Standish, when they had covered a couple of miles, "he's let it loose. Give her every ounce you can."

"Hopeless, mon, hopeless. But bide a while: there's a turn a little way ahead."

Suddenly he swung the car right-handed up a narrow lane, and then switched off his lights.

"He has a Hispano," he explained; "I could never have got away from him. What happens if he spots us?"

"We fight," said Standish tersely. "Here they come."

Exhaust open, head-lights flaring, the car roared past them crammed with men, and not until the noise of the engine had died away in the distance did they breathe freely again.

"And now," remarked Mackintosh, "we go back on our tracks. We can make a detour which will bring us into Dalzburg by another road. Otherwise I'm thinking we may meet them coming back."

The castle was blazing with lights as they approached, and suddenly Mackintosh cursed under his breath. Three men were standing across the road holding out their arms.

"Drive at 'em, Andy," cried Standish. "Denver, get down: hide."

And Andy Mackintosh drove at them, all out. Came a thud on the mudguard, a brief vision of jumping, swearing men and the castle was left behind them.

"And me—a respectable married journalist," groaned Andy. "I'm hoping they did not get my number."

"You see the trouble you've caused, young fellah," said Standish to Denver with a laugh. "However, it looks as if the first hurdle was safely over."

"For Heaven's sake tell me what it's all about," cried the youngster. "My brain is in an absolute whirl."

"All in good time," said Standish. "Let's get back first."

"But they'll be watching the hotel," said Denver.

"That's why we're not going there. Or at any rate you're not. You are going to bed down, any way for a time, with the excellent Andy."

"And after that comes the second hurdle," said that worthy gloomily. "Dinna forget that."

"You damned old croaker," laughed Standish, "we'll think of something."

But though he spoke cheerfully, he was far from feeling it. No one realized better than he did that the second hurdle was going to be considerably harder than the first. For it consisted of getting Joe Denver out of the country. Luck, astounding luck, had been with them so far: how long would it last? Obviously every frontier post would be watched, and Denver would simply be arrested on some trumped-up charge and returned to Berendosi. It was true that he might lie hidden for a time with Andy Mackintosh, but that was only postponing the evil. And two things made him unwilling to leave him there longer than absolutely necessary. First, it seemed probable that Berendosi would get him and Tiny out of the country as soon as possible, which would mean leaving Denver on his own. And second, though Andy had not hesitated for a moment to come in with them, he was, as he had said, a respectable married journalist, not too well off at that. And the last thing Standish wanted to do was to get him into trouble.

The devil of it was that the problem seemed almost insoluble. And yet there must be some way of smuggling the youngster out. One trouble was that he did not speak a word of the language. Still, surely there must be some method. But he was still racking his brains for an answer when the car drew up at Mackintosh's house.

It was past one, and the street was deserted. There was no sign of anyone watching the house, so that even if the men they had driven at had got the number of the car, as yet it had not been traced.

"I'll put the car away," said Andy. "You go in."

His wife opened the door to them: a homely, sweet-faced Scotch woman.

"But you've got him," she cried. "Good. Come in, and have a drink."

"You've guessed right there, Mrs. Andy," laughed Standish. "And here's the young blighter who is responsible for all the trouble."

She smiled at Joe Denver, and then led the way upstairs.

"I thought it would be safer above," she explained, "in case they started to watch the house."

"You're a marvel," cried Standish. "We would never have pulled it off without you and Andy. Now, young fellow," he went on, "let's hear how they got you to walk into their parlour so easily."

"They sent me a note to say that ... that ..." He hesitated for a moment and glanced at Mrs. Mackintosh.

"You can speak out freely," said Standish. "Mrs. Andy knows."

"To say that the Queen was in danger, and would I go at once. There would be a car waiting in the square, and I was to tell no one."

"And into that singularly obvious trap," laughed Standish, "you walked with both your great flat feet. Ah! well, perhaps I'd have done the same."

"But what was the meaning of all that damned foolery?" cried Denver. "That flashlight photograph, and the rest of it."

"Young fellah," said Standish gravely, "we're in pretty deep waters—you especially. The whole of this evening's performance was staged with the express purpose of getting a photograph of you with a woman in your arms, who in colouring and size might easily have been the Queen."

"The infernal swine," said Denver savagely. "What are we to do about it?"

"Don't worry about the photograph. Tiny and I attended to that. The point to be decided is what are we to do about you."

"Aye," said Andy, helping himself to whisky. "That's the point."

"We've got to get you out of the country somehow, Denver, and do it damned quick. For if they get you a second time, they'll keep you."

"But if you've smashed the photo what does it matter?" cried Denver. "They won't get another."

"Perhaps not," agreed Standish. "But there's something else behind it all, though at present we don't know what. It's not a letter; Tiny found that out. What is it? Countess Mazarin could tell us..."

"Which reminds me," interrupted Mrs. Andy. "I rang her up as you told me, and promised to ring her up again if all went well."

"Bit late, isn't it, my dear," said her husband doubtfully.

"She told me to ring her whatever time you came back," she said.

"Well, be careful what you say, Mrs. Andy," warned Standish. "Telephones at this hour of the night are dangerous."

"I feel as if I was in a sort of daze," cried Denver as she left the room. "The whole thing seems like some mad nightmare."

"It's going to be madder soon," said Andy gravely. "It's getting mighty near, if I'm any judge."

"What is?" asked Denver.

"Hell let loose. Civil war. Well, my dear, did you get through?"

"I did. And she's coming here."

"The devil she is," said Andy uneasily. He went to the window and peered out. "I don't see anyone at present, but pray the Lord she's not followed."

"Hardly likely, Andy, at this hour," said Standish. "They've got no cause to suspect her."

"Mon, this place is a hot-bed of spies and intrigue," answered the other. "And the Palace is the worst spot of the lot. However, we can but hope for the best."

"And at any rate, Andy, we'll know at last. That's worth running a bit of risk for. Though it's not going to help us over this blighter's immediate future."

"But what's the difficulty?" cried Denver. "I'll go to-morrow, if you want me to."

Standish laughed shortly.

"My dear boy," he said, "every frontier has been closed to you days ago. There are no strings you can pull at all, Andy, I suppose?"

"I've been racking my brains, Ronald, and I'm just phased. It's a fair snorter. He can stop here, of course, but after a time the servants are bound to talk."

"No, no, Andy," said Standish, "if we can't get him away we must find somewhere else. If necessary he must go like the Biblical gentleman, into the mountains with the ravens."

Andy shook his head.

"They'll go through the country with a tooth-comb," he said.

"I seem a damned popular bird," remarked Denver ruefully. "What exactly are they going to do with me when they do get me?"

"Produce you as an exhibit at the psychological moment," said Standish. "Though now that that photograph is destroyed it seems to me you lose a good deal of your value. Unless..."

And at that moment the front-door bell rang.

"It's the Countess," said Andy, peering through the window. "I'll go and let her in."

"Thank Heaven you've got him," she cried a little breathlessly as she entered the room. "I've made all the arrangements for a fast car to get him away."

"Hopeless, Countess," cried Standish. "The frontier will be closed. We should simply play into their hands."

"But we must get him away," she said. "We *must*. What happened to-night?"

He told her briefly, and when he'd finished she opened her bag.

"The only comfort," concluded Standish, "is that the photo was destroyed."

"Comfort," she cried. "Precious little comfort, Mr. Standish. The one they took to-night may have been destroyed, but this one hasn't."

She threw a faded print on the table, and they crowded round.

"Good God!" said Standish. "So that's the trouble. How did you get hold of this?"

"But I don't understand," muttered Denver, scarlet to the roots of his hair. "It's the day I said good-bye to her. What damned ineffable swine took this?"

"Steady, Denver," cried Standish. "Don't tear it up. It's more serious even than I thought, but at any rate we know what we're up against, at last."

"But who took the damned thing?" said Denver between his teeth.

"Immaterial, young fellow," remarked Standish shortly. "Good Lord! you might both have posed specially for it."

Which was no more than the truth. For the photograph showed a little glade in a wood. Two people were standing in it, their arms round one another. Their profiles were towards the camera, and the woman was looking up into the man's face with an expression which caused the warm-hearted Mrs. Andy to wipe her eyes surreptitiously, and whisper, "You poor bairns." For the woman in the photograph was the Queen: the man was the youngster who now stood with his back to them, staring out of the window.

"At any rate," repeated Standish, "we know what we're up against. Now, Countess, we'd very much like to hear your side of the story, because there is a good deal that is still mighty obscure. And incidentally, Denver, come away from that window. Your face is a darned sight too well known in this country."

CHAPTER VII

"There's not much to tell," she began. "I got it about two months ago by sheer luck. I had been out motoring one day, driving my own car, and I ran out of petrol. I was miles from a garage, but as luck would have it I was only about ten minutes' walk from the Castle of Birenden, which is Berendosi's country house. It was a case of needs must, or else nothing would have induced me to ask the brute for anything. But if I was to get home at all I'd have to borrow some petrol from him. It was a pitch dark night, and stiflingly hot, and the house was in darkness save for one room on the ground floor, from which a light shone out through partially drawn curtains. I knew the place fairly well, because Berendosi entertains lavishly, and the room which was lit up was either the dining-room or his study. And acting on the spur of the moment, instead of ringing the bell, I crossed the lawn towards it. I intended to ask him for the petrol, and for a man to carry it to the car.

"When I got close to I heard voices, and I don't quite know why, I hesitated for a moment or two. Somehow I had expected to find him alone and now it looked as if he had a dinner-party. And then I heard one remark of Berendosi's that made me go cold all over.

"'What about that for proof, Gregoroff? Our gracious Majesty herself.'

"Now I give you my word that up to that moment I'd had no intention of spying or listening. I had crossed the lawn quite openly with no pretence at concealment, and in another second I should have appeared in the open window. I'd really forgotten all about everything except that I'd run out of petrol. And to hear a remark like that suddenly when one wasn't in the least expecting it, brought me up with a start.

"My first inclination was to go back and ring the front-door bell, but I soon decided not to. Eavesdropping it might be but I was going to find out all I could. Evidently I had not been seen crossing the lawn, and if anyone came to the window and I was discovered, I should have to put as good a face on the matter as I could. So I crept a little closer until I could just see into the room. There were three of them inside: Berendosi, Gregoroff and a third whom I had never seen before. He was the most strange-looking individual—completely bald with a high, domed forehead. But the most peculiar thing about him was that on his shoulder there sat a little monkey, which he fondled continuously. Did you say anything, Mr. Standish?"

"Go on, Countess. It will keep."

"This man was smoking a cigarette and watching the other two, who were poring over something that was lying on the desk in the centre of the room.

"'Marvellous,' said Gregoroff at length. 'My dear Paul, I congratulate you. And you also, Monsieur.'

"Then he picked the thing up, and I saw what it was—an unmounted photograph. I didn't know what to do. At first I didn't understand what it was all about. I couldn't see what the photograph was, though I guessed from Berendosi's remark that it was a snapshot of the Queen. But as they went on talking I realized that it must be more than that.

"'Do you know who the young man is, Monsieur Zavier?' asked Berendosi of the bald-headed man.

"'I have forgotten,' he answered. 'I was told, but for the moment it has slipped my memory. I can, however, easily find that out, and let you know.'

"They talked on for a while, and then Gregoroff lit a cigarette.

"'A quarter of a million is a lot of money, Monsieur,' he said to this man Zavier.

"'A lot is a relative term,' answered the other. 'My dear sir,' he added contemptuously, 'you don't suppose I deal in children's saving accounts, do you? That is my figure, and you can take it or leave it. I told Signor Berendosi weeks ago that I would deliver the goods as I had promised. There is a proof of it: though to be on the safe side,' he added with a smile, 'it is only an unfixed proof, which will fade. But at the appointed time you shall have the genuine article. And it is for you to arrange that time: it is not my affair.'

"You can imagine, Mr. Standish, that by this time I was nearly crazy. I still had no idea what was in the picture, beyond the fact that there was a man and Olga. But it was pretty clear that if a quarter of a million was the price, there must be something more in it than that. And I stood there racking my brains as to how I could get hold of it and see. They had left it lying on the desk: in two seconds I could have darted in and picked it up. And I very nearly did. After all they couldn't hurt me, and at any rate I should know the worst.

"And then, just as I was nerving myself to do so, the whole sky was lit up by lightning and almost simultaneously came the crash of thunder overhead. It was one of our usual mountain storms, but it was a particularly fierce one. There was no rain, but the wind got up like a tornado. The curtains flapped wildly: the monkey jibbered, but all that I had eyes for was that photograph. For it had blown off the desk, and was lying just inside the window not a yard away from me. And then I had a stroke of luck. There came another terrific gust of wind and the lamp blew over. So I made one grab at the photo and fled. The lightning was almost continuous, so I kept in as close to the house as I could. Two of them had dashed into the garden and were peering round in every direction, leaving the other one, I suppose, to attend to the lamp. But I dodged along as quickly as I could and they neither of them saw me. And at last I got in among the trees bordering the drive, and felt safe."

"Well done, Countess," said Standish. "It was a ticklish situation. And they have never suspected you?"

"I'm sure they don't. They imagine it blew away in the gale. At any rate a car came along as I was standing there, and I borrowed some petrol and drove home in a sort of daze. What was to be done about it? And the more I thought the more hopeless did it appear. I'd got one print it was true, but there must be others in existence. And so beyond making myself half sick with worry I'd really accomplished nothing.

"There was no one I could turn to for help. I didn't say a word, of course, to Olga—that would have been too cruel. She could have done nothing, and if the blow had got to fall it might just as well be unexpected. And it was no good trying to console myself with the idea that the picture was harmless since it had been taken before Olga's wedding. Berendosi is far too clever a man to let a trifle like that bother him. I was distracted until, out of the blue came Mary Ridgeway. She was someone I could confide in, at any rate.

"Judge, then, of my amazement when I found she knew all about it and was dumbfounded to find that I did. It appeared that a man in London—you know, Mr. Carteret, Felton Blake—had written to her begging for an interview. She had met him at some party or another, and since he said it was of vital importance that he should see her she allowed him to call. He apparently went straight to the point and produced a copy of the photo.

"She was as much bowled over as I was when she saw it, and demanded how he came to have such a thing. He told her it had come into his possession by roundabout means."

"More than likely," said Standish dryly.

"So she asked him what he was going to do with it.

"'Why burn it, of course,' he answered, and did so then and there.

"'But then why, Mr. Blake, bother to come and show it to me?' she cried.

"'Because, Lady Mary,' he explained, 'I wanted to show you the intense gravity of the situation. To make a print there must be a film. And I have the best of reasons for believing that that film is in existence.'"

"The very best," said Standish with a short laugh.

"You mean..." she said, staring at him.

"Shall I tell you the rest? Our Mr. Felton Blake, appalled by the vileness of the scoundrel who had taken such a photograph, ranged himself on the side of virtue. He somehow or other would get hold of that film: he somehow or other would see that it was destroyed, and any other prints that might be in existence."

"As a matter of fact, he has found one more print," she said.

"It would be equally easy for him to find a dozen," said Standish grimly. "My dear Countess, I am not a wealthy man, but I would cheerfully wager a thousand pounds to a sixpence that I could lead you to that film now. It is where it has always been—in Felton Blake's safe."

"But if that is so," she cried pathetically, "it's our last hope gone. Or do you think he's only trying to make it seem harder, so as to..."

Her eyes met Tiny's and he laughed savagely.

"So as to ingratiate himself with Mary?" he said.

"More than likely," said Standish. "But don't delude yourself into thinking that when the ingratiating period can no longer be prolonged he is going to hand over the film. Unless, of course... Do you really think, Tiny, that the swine is in love with Lady Mary?"

Tiny waved his hand at the Countess.

"There is my informant," he said shortly.

"Yes, Mr. Standish, I do," she answered.

"Then it is possible that Felton Blake might drive the bargain. It's quite in keeping with the man's character. If she will marry him, then she gets the film as a wedding present."

"The ineffable swine," muttered Tiny.

"Agreed, old lad," said Standish. "But we've got to take the facts as they are. And I'm bound to say they look just about as grim as they can."

"But, good God!" exploded Joe Denver, "we can put the police on to him."

"What for?" asked Standish quietly. "What are you going to charge him with? Having that photograph in his possession doesn't constitute a crime. That's the devil of it, young fellah. As I see the matter at present, they are absolutely within the law."

He relapsed into silence, tapping his teeth with the stem of his pipe.

"Let's try and get things in order," he remarked at length. "Somehow or other Blake has got hold of an incriminating photograph. As the Countess quite rightly observed, the fact that it was taken before a certain marriage is of no account. Berendosi, as she says, is far too clever a man to let that worry him. So little in fact does it do so that he is prepared to pay a quarter of a million for it to this man Zavier... And Zavier is a very interesting gentleman."

"I gathered you had seen him before to-night," said Tiny.

"He did me the honour of being somewhat curious over my movements when I was staying in Territet. I don't think he realized I had spotted his interest, but it is a game which two can play. Then he vanished, and I dismissed him from my mind. But now we hear from the Countess that he was the actual man who offered the photo to Berendosi months ago. Very interesting."

Tiny Carteret

"Why particularly?" demanded Tiny.

"Do you suppose that Felton Blake would have given away the handling of a show involving a quarter of a million unless he had to? That he would have passed it over to one of the smaller fry—one of his own equals? Not he. He would have negotiated himself, and pocketed the whole of the boodle. Don't you see what that means, Tiny? It means, unless I am vastly mistaken, that at last we have found our bird. Zavier is the big man. However, that will all keep for the moment. Let us concentrate on the immediate issue. Andy, you are more in touch with things here than we are. What is your candid opinion of the situation?"

The journalist puffed thoughtfully at his pipe.

"With that film in his possession," he said at length, "Berendosi has the game in his hands. It's fool proof. Things are on the edge of a precipice now: with that photograph comes the landslide."

"But why?" cried Denver. "All he can do is to show it to his friends."

"Laddie," answered Andy gravely, "he can show it to the whole country. What is to prevent him having thousands of copies made, till your face is as familiar as Charlie Chaplin's? He can distribute them broadcast through the land. And had Ronald not smashed the plate to-night there would have been a pair. The plot is as clear as the nose on your face. And your arrival here has given it the finishing touch. Not only will they distribute the photograph, but they will produce the original."

"I agree with you, Andy," said Standish. "It's incredibly simple, and incredibly sure. *And it must not be.* But how the devil we're going to prevent it, I, at the moment, do not see. By the way, Countess, how did you know Mr. Denver was here?"

"I told my very greatest friend, Mr. Standish, about the photograph and showed it to her. And she by chance saw Mr. Denver here in the hotel. She thought she recognized him, and when she saw the name in the book she knew at once. So she wired me in Paris and I wired Mr. Carteret. I hoped he would be able to persuade him to go at once, if I couldn't. And now it's too late..."

"Don't be too sure of that. There must be some way."

"Look here," said Denver quietly, "don't go ahead too fast. If that entrancing exhibition of beastliness Berendosi is going to flood the country with copies of that photograph, I'm going to be here."

"Very understandable, old lad," said Standish, "but it won't do. Any man would feel the same. But it's one of those cases where not only could you do no good, but you'd do an enormous amount of harm. It would at once appear as proof that the affair was still going on. No; I sympathize with you. But if we can manage it you have got to be removed from here. And it's easier said than done."

"Well, if you've all quite finished talking," said Mrs. Andy quietly, "I'll tell you how to do it."

"Good for you, Maggie," said her husband, reaching for the whisky. "Come into the office, boys, for you can bet it is all settled."

And when twenty minutes later Standish and Tiny strolled back to their hotel, it seemed to them that there was at least a sixty per cent chance of her scheme succeeding. Denver had remained with the Mackintoshs: the Countess had gone home, and the most searching examination had failed to reveal any sign of men watching the house. In fact, up to date everything seemed to have gone splendidly, and yet Standish seemed gloomy and depressed.

"It's worse—far worse than I thought, Tiny. It's fool-proof, as Andy said—once they get that photo, even if young Denver isn't in the country. A letter would have been bad enough, but that photo—why, good Lord! it's a cinch. And we don't want a change of regime here."

"I wonder how they got it," said Tiny.

"That we shall probably never know. She was well known by sight, of course, and someone must have followed them that day. But all that is only of academic interest. The only thing that matters is that they *have* got it, or rather Felton Blake has."

"I suppose that is certain, Ronald. You don't think that possibly that man Zavier has taken it over by now. Or even Berendosi himself."

"I've thought of that, and it is undoubtedly a possibility. But I'll tell you my reasons for thinking Blake still has it. He got it in the first place, otherwise he would never have come into the game at all. Now from every point of view it is to his advantage to hang on to it as long as he can. The more time he gets with Lady Mary, the better for him. And once that film is out of his possession, the show here might be sprung under his feet at any moment."

"It seems sound," said Tiny. "Gad! I'd like to wring the swine's neck. Ronald, we've damned well got to do these blighters down."

"And so say all of us, laddie," answered the other with a short laugh. "Honestly, Tiny, I don't see how we're going to do it. But there's one thing that is intriguing me at the moment. What line is our friend Berendosi going to adopt when he sees us? Because he must know that it was we who did the trick."

They turned into the hotel, and Standish gave a short chuckle.

"Obvious police spy the first," he muttered, "lurking in corner of lounge. And behold! he moves at speed. Come into my room, Tiny, for a night-cap. I'm thinking we may have a visitor, and I wouldn't like you to miss the fun."

And sure enough a few minutes later there came a knock on the door.

"My dear Signor," cried Standish, as he opened it, "this is indeed an unexpected surprise. And—er—pleasure. Will you join us in a little whisky?"

Berendosi, still fully dressed save that he had substituted a dressing-gown for his coat, came into the room and shut the door.

"Mr. Standish," he said shortly, "do we put the cards on the table, or not?"

"Surely in lives as blameless as ours, there should never be anything to conceal," remarked the other. "What about a *deoch-an-dorriss*?"

Berendosi waved away the proffered drink.

"It isn't poisoned," said Tiny mildly. "We still maintain our English habits even in this country."

"Will you kindly be silent?" snapped Berendosi. "When I wish you to speak I will tell you."

"Indeed," said Tiny ominously. "And when I wish you to speak to me like that, I will tell you. But if you do it again, you rat-faced swab, I'll take you by the scruff of the neck and hang you out of the window."

"Steady, Tiny," said Standish with a grin, as Berendosi recoiled against the wall. "But you really must remember, Signor, that my friend is very large, and choose your words accordingly. Now what can we do for you?"

With an effort the other recovered his composure.

"I would prefer to discuss the matter alone with you, Mr. Standish. Your very large friend is, I should imagine, more suited to the football field than to a matter of this sort."

"The interview is not of my seeking," said Standish curtly. "And I know of nothing that I wish to discuss with you alone."

"So be it," remarked Berendosi, with a shrug of his shoulders. "I gather then, from the tone of your remarks, that you do not propose to put your cards down. It seems a waste of time, but have it your own way. A few hours ago, Mr. Standish, you and your friend here forcibly entered the house of a colleague of mine, and removed a young man whom I require. Where is he?"

"Am I to understand that this young man whom we are reputed to have removed was being detained against his will?" asked Standish.

"Come, come, Mr. Standish," said Berendosi irritably, "what is the use of this pretence? We are alone together: we all know the facts of the case. As a clever man, don't you think it would be as well to have a perfectly straight discussion, and then we can all go to bed?"

"I am waiting," remarked Standish quietly.

"You are a man whose knowledge of the political situation in Europe is profound. I am well aware that England does not desire any change of government here: nevertheless, that change is coming. You know that as well as I do: hence your presence here. You also know that by one of those strange turns of Fate, this young man Denver is a very important person in that change. Therefore you remove him. Good! I admire you for it. But, Mr. Standish, I require him back. Where is he?"

Standish laughed gently.

"Your ideas of argument are rather crude, Signor. Even supposing for a moment that this extraordinary assertion of yours is right, and that we removed Denver, we must have done it because we wished to hide him. Why then should we completely negate what we've done by telling you where we have hidden him? I don't quite see what we get out of it."

"Then I will explain," said the other. "And I am relieved to see that we both know where we stand. The point you raise is a perfectly fair one: the answer, however, is simple. As you will doubtless have guessed, every frontier post has already been closed to Mr. Denver. He can leave the country neither by car, by rail, nor by air. As a further precaution, his passport is being temporarily taken care of for him. In fact, Mr. Standish, you will not believe the activity that took place on his utterly unexpected arrival. I mention these points merely to show that we are in earnest. Very well then: I will come to the point. For how long do you think it would be possible for this young man, whose description has been widely circulated and who cannot speak a word of the language, to remain hidden?"

"I was never much good at riddles," murmured Standish.

"Sooner or later he is bound to be found. And," continued the other slowly, "it is for you to decide whether it shall be sooner or later."

"I may be dense," said Standish, "but I still fail to see the *quid pro quo*."

"Mr. Standish—as a lover of law and order, I know you will be grieved to hear that a dastardly crime has been committed to-night. At a house belonging to a high state official two miscreants nearly killed an inoffensive photographer, forced their way in, stunned two of the old family retainers and then decamped—for all I know with large quantities of valuables. Justice cries aloud for the names of these criminals, in order that they may be punished. Do you see now where the *quid pro quo* comes in? Should you decide on it's being sooner, I don't think the names of the criminals are ever likely to be disclosed. Should you decide on it being later—well, one of the criminals was a thick-set man of medium height, the other was a very large friend of his. Do I make myself clear?"

"Perfectly," answered Standish. "There is, however, one point that strikes me, Signor. When these two villains are haled before the law to answer for their sins, they will naturally give a reason for their scandalous behaviour. They will say what the photographer was doing, and people will wonder why. They will say who was there and all sorts of embarrassing and awkward things, which will doubtless get into the papers."

"My dear Mr. Standish, can you possibly believe for an instant that a man in my responsible position, knowing as I do the unsettled state of the country, would allow such a thing as that to get into the papers? You quite pain me. Think of the terrible example to the youth of the land. No, I fear that the two miscreants would have no chance of stating their case until later—considerably later. And I may further say that amongst other reforms which are urgently needed here the state of our prisons leaves much to be desired."

"So that's it, is it?" said Standish, lighting a cigarette.

"That is it, Mr. Standish. I do not think I can make it any clearer. As I said before, sooner or later Mr. Denver will be found. For reasons into which we need not enter I would prefer it to be sooner. I therefore offer you the two alternatives. If you make it sooner there is a most comfortable train de luxe which leaves for Paris to-morrow night: if the other, well, as I said, our gaols are not all they might be."

"And what do you propose to do with Denver when you get him?"

"I can assure you that he will be treated with the utmost consideration," answered the other. "Be reasonable," he continued as Standish said nothing. "As a clever man you know that I hold the top trumps: I've got a winning hand. And clever men cut their losses under those circumstances. Hand over the young man to me and clear out. And when things are more settled, believe me we shall be only too delighted to welcome you back to our country."

"Sooner and later are relative terms, Signor," remarked Standish abruptly. "By when is this decision to be made?"

For an instant a gleam of triumph showed in Berendosi's eyes, but his voice was quite casual as he answered.

"Shall we say lunch-time to-morrow, or rather to-day? I have a most boring function to attend in a few hours at the aerodrome—the inauguration of the new service between here and Le Bourget. So lunch will suit me admirably."

"All right," said Standish, opening the door. "I will tell you then."

"But let there be no misunderstanding, Mr. Standish," remarked the other. "I must have proof."

"You shall have proof," said Standish coldly, ignoring Berendosi's outstretched hand.

"Strange men—you English." The Bessonian's hand fell to his side. "I thought you were always reputed to take a beating like a sportsman."

"Only if that beating comes from a sportsman. Signor Berendosi, it would be idle to pretend that I don't know your game. But it would be equally idle to pretend that I do not consider you a cad of the first order. A man who deliberately sets out to obtain his ends by blackening the reputation of a perfectly innocent woman in the eyes of the whole world, is not a man whose hand I would ever shake."

He turned to Tiny as the door closed, and gave a short laugh.

"I feel a little better for that, Tiny. Lucky he suggested lunch: we shall know by then."

"But if it doesn't come off—are you going to tell the swine?"

"That he's at Andy's? Yes. It's not fair to them. What Berendosi said is right—they're bound to find him in a place like this. The servants would give it away. And don't be under any delusions as to what he said about our going to jug. That was no bluff. And though we may be precious little use out of prison, we'd be even less inside. So one way or the other we'll tell him at lunch. And I'll go round to the Embassy in the morning and get Bunny Rogers to feed, for I'm thinking that if we do pull it off Berendosi will be as sore as if he'd sat in a hornets' nest. So a little diplomatic flavouring at the meal may be helpful. Well, good night, old lad. We'd better get a few hours' sleep."

But though he undressed and got into bed sleep would not come. Round and round in his brain the problem twisted and turned, and when the broad light of day was streaming through the window it was still unsolved. How was the negative of that photo to be procured? And mixed up with it was another even more important factor. How was he to get a line on Zavier and hold it?

He felt that his reasoning was correct with regard to that gentleman. Even if he was not the biggest man of all, he was considerably nearer that position than Felton Blake. And though he had made no effort to trace him from Territet—his suspicions then had not been aroused—he was under no delusions as to what would in all probability have happened if he had. Time and again had he and others got on the trail of men who they knew belonged to the gang, in the hope of tracking them to their headquarters: time and again had those men vanished as completely as if the earth had swallowed them up. True they had only been underlings, but if underlings could shake skilled men off their heels, how much more easily could a man in Zavier's position.

He recalled a case where a man who was known to be a forger in the employ of the gang was purposely allowed his freedom in the hopes that he would lead them to their quarry. That man had got on the boat train at Victoria: he had not got off at Dover. At least Inspector Mead had been prepared to swear he hadn't. And yet the run had been non-stop. That it was a disguise of some sort was obvious, since no man can disappear into thin air. But what was this disguise that— not in one isolated case but in several—could completely hoodwink some of the shrewdest men living?

At last he gave up any attempt at sleep and, lighting a cigarette, he pulled up a chair to the open window. For the moment he had to dismiss the bigger problem from his mind and concentrate on the smaller—how to obtain the negative from Felton Blake. And after a while he began to laugh gently to himself: there was only one possible method. Clearly Blake would not hand it over voluntarily: therefore, there was no good asking for it. Equally clearly there was no good attempting to obtain it by force: Blake was a powerful man who would certainly be armed, and who also had an alarm on his desk which sounded in the rooms of two large men-servants. He remembered that fact from a previous interview he had had with him when tempers had become a little frayed. And since those two methods were both ruled out, there remained only one other—the negative must be stolen.

He began to pace thoughtfully up and down the room: was it feasible? It was a risk—a very grave risk: on that point he was under no delusions. If he was caught he would be treated exactly the same as any ordinary burglar: therefore he must not be caught. But burglary was a skilled profession and up to date he had not served an apprenticeship at it. And yet it was worth taking a big chance— the issues at stake were so big. Moreover, it was quite possible that once he got inside Blake's safe other things would come to light— things that might lead him to the headquarters of the gang.

He argued it out in his mind, weighing up the chances. Given favourable conditions he could deal with the safe, but it was not going to be an easy matter to get those conditions. Gentlemen of Felton Blake's mode of living took considerable precautions over their houses. Still, there was no device yet invented by human brain, that could not be circumvented by the same agency, and the more he thought of it the more did it seem to him the only way. In fact, when he went downstairs after his coffee and rolls his mind was made up: he was going to try and steal the negative.

Berendosi was in the lounge, and greeted him affably. He apparently bore no ill feeling over Standish's final remark of a few hours previously: garbed in a frock-coat and top-hat he oozed complacency.

"A tedious performance," he remarked, "but *pro bono publico*."

"A most apt quotation," said Standish politely. "You are making a speech?"

"A few words only. Well—at lunch then, we will resume our talk."

"Precisely," answered the other with a faint smile. "At lunch."

Thinking over the bigger problems had almost driven the immediate point at issue from his mind. And now as he watched Berendosi enter his car he began to feel doubtful. Would the thing come off? Its principal hope of success lay in the calm audacity of the scheme, but now that the actual moment had arrived he didn't feel quite so confident as he had done the previous night. Right under Berendosi's nose as Andy had gleefully exclaimed, but was the nose big enough to hide it? And at that moment Tiny hove in sight.

"Go off, old man, to the aerodrome," he said, "and see what happens. I'm going to the Embassy."

He found George Potter pretending to work, and was at once taken in to the Ambassador.

"Hullo! Standish," cried the latter. "Delighted to see you. What brings you here, though it isn't hard to guess?"

He listened in silence while Standish told him the whole story, and his face grew graver and graver.

"Mackintosh is right," he said at the conclusion. "It means the end. And probably a lot of bloodshed. What on earth induced the boy to come here?"

"That is the least part of it, sir," remarked Standish. "It is this damned photograph."

"Well, don't get yourself into trouble, my dear fellow. And take George along with you to lunch. Gad! I'd give something to see friend Berendosi's face if you pull it off. And if the blighter gets gay with you and your pal, George can put it on to me. In fact, he'd better stop with you till you go."

It was midday when they got back to the hotel, and a quarter of an hour later Tiny came in grinning all over his face, with Andy Mackintosh.

"Thumbs up, Ronald," he cried. "Went without a hitch."

"A verra impressive spectacle," said Andy gravely. "In fact I lapsed into journalese. Like a giant dragon-fly with gossamer wings outstretched the flying bird lay motionless, gleaming silver in the sunshine. Soon it would spring to life, and soaring into the blue empyrean, bear its living cargo over the snow-capped peaks towards the smiling fields of France, gliding smoothly under the master hand of the keen-eyed bird-man in control. And then the great Berendosi himself drew nigh. In a few well-chosen words he painted a dazzling picture of the future, with Dalzburg not the least important link in the world flying route. And what of the men who made such things possible: the intrepid pilot: the clearbrained, efficient mechanic...."

"For the love of Allah, Andy, shut your mouth on a drink," laughed Standish. "For here, if I mistake not, is the bird himself. George, my boy, we're going to have some fun. Have you ever seen a finer example of *'l'État, c'est moi'*?"

And undoubtedly at the moment Paul Berendosi was feeling that life was good. The ceremony had gone off swimmingly: the cheers of the onlookers still rang in his ears. And to crown everything, a plain-clothes officer had told him as he alighted at the hotel that the young Englishman he wanted had returned to his room. Evidently Standish had seen wisdom: now all that remained was to get him and his boring friend out of the country as soon as possible. He glanced into the bar, and for a moment a slight feeling of uneasiness assailed him. The party in there seemed very hilarious considering they had been beaten all along the line. Someone from the Embassy, he reflected, and the correspondent of one of the English papers. And at that moment Standish hailed him.

"I trust everything went well, Signor?"

"Admirably, thank you."

He moved on, his uneasiness increasing. Why on earth were the four of them looking so pleased? Standish must know that Denver had returned to the hotel. And just then the police officer came up to him.

"May I have a word with you, your Excellency?" he said in a low voice. "There is some mistake. The young man upstairs is in possession of his passport, and it is in perfect order. And he is not even an Englishman: he is French."

"What's that?" snarled the other. "Are you certain?"

"But of course, Excellency. I have just been speaking to him."

"Who is he, you fool? Go and find out."

So Standish was trying the funny stuff, was he? And a sudden burst of laughter from the bar seemed to bear out the fact. He moved a few steps to one side so that he could see in: the four men were examining something intently.

"Come and have a look, Signor," called out Standish. "It's an excellent one of you, and I know your interest in photography."

Without a word he joined them: an advance press proof of the morning's proceedings lay on the table. There was the aeroplane, the passengers, himself, the crowd, but what the devil was the jest?

"Quite good," he said indifferently.

"Particularly of the mechanic," murmured Standish blandly. "And I hear you said some very nice things about clear-brained, efficient mechanics."

Berendosi stood very still: a sudden ghastly suspicion had assailed him.

"It was verra lucky that such an able substitute could be found at the last moment," said Andy gravely. "It would have been terrible, Signor, if your impassioned eloquence had been wasted."

"May I ask exactly what you are talking about?" said Berendosi quietly.

"Didn't you hear?" boomed Tiny cheerfully. "That's too bad. Just as everything was ready, what should occur but that the mechanic felt the urge for a drink upon him. So back he trotted to the hangar with his tongue hanging out. And there who should he find but another man ready, aye ready! to take his place."

"And the lucky thing was that he had already gone through the necessary formalities," said Standish. "Because this noble fellow who was prepared to sacrifice himself that another man should not thirst, had in some extraordinary manner lost his passport. But since most people look more or less alike in goggles and a crash-helmet, the point escaped the notice of the aerodrome authorities."

For perhaps ten seconds Berendosi stared at Standish with a look of smouldering fury in his eyes. What had happened was clear. The man upstairs was the real mechanic, for whom they had substituted Denver at the last moment. And now Denver was gone beyond recall. How they had fixed it mattered not: the one salient fact remained that he had been completely outwitted. Moreover, in the presence of the others it was impossible to show the furious rage that was seething in him.

"How very interesting," he said at length.

"I was sure you would find it so," remarked Standish affably. "Will you join us in a little lunch?"

"I thank you—no," answered the other. "You leave to-night?"

"I do."

"Then I will say good-bye."

Tiny Carteret

"Au revoir is more suitable, Signor Berendosi. I shall return."

And once again the eyes of the two men met.

CHAPTER VIII

That, up to date, luck had been with them all along the line Ronald Standish was the first to admit. The comparative similarity of build between Denver and the mechanic: the fact that Denver held a pilot's ticket and so was fully capable of taking over the job: above all, the sportsmanship of Laval the French pilot in agreeing to the change, was a combination of circumstances they could hardly hope to strike again. But it was a good omen: the first hurdle, even if it was the least formidable, had been cleared. Joe Denver was out of the country. Now they were faced with the second. And it was after dinner was over that Standish broached the subject to Tiny.

"Are you prepared to take a pretty useful risk, old lad?" he said quietly.

The restaurant car was empty save for the staff having a meal behind the partition at the end.

"We've run one or two already," laughed the other, "so a few more won't hurt."

"After you went to bed last night I got thinking," went on Standish. "Thinking about this damned negative. Tiny — there is only one way to get it, and that is to steal it."

Tiny raised his eyebrows.

"Not too bally easy, old man, is it? I should imagine a man of Blake's type takes fairly good precautions against burglary."

"Undoubtedly he does. Hence the risk. But there is no other way. He won't give it to us: we can't take it by force, so we've got to get it by stealth if we get it at all."

"Seems sound enough reasoning," agreed Tiny. "How do you propose to set about it?"

"I know his house, and I know the room in which he keeps his safe. It is a ground-floor room looking out on to the garden, and as far as I can recollect there are some trees fairly close to the window. The first thing we've got to do is to get him out of the way. And there, Tiny, Lady Mary comes in. She must contrive to keep him clear of the house for at least two hours round about midnight. Then we'll have a dip at it. I can manage the safe if I've got the time. And if by any chance we are heard—he keeps a couple of tame bruisers about the place, disguised as footmen—we'll wade into 'em, or cut and run."

"Sounds easy: too easy. Still, it's worth chancing."

"The chief risk is if some zealous Hampstead policeman catches us in the act. If we are just seen by some of his staff, however good a description of us is circulated, I don't think we shall be implicated. There are times," he added with a wink, "when Scotland Yard can be very dense."

"And when do you suggest we should do it?"

"On the first possible occasion," said Standish. "Time is becoming one of the most vital factors in this matter. And I propose we should try to-morrow night. Always provided, that is, that we can get hold of Lady Mary."

"Shouldn't be much difficulty about that. I know she will be in Town, and she'll cancel any engagement to help us. Incidentally, what do we do about young Joe?"

Standish shrugged his shoulders.

"There's nothing much to be done. I'm damned sorry for the boy, but other people have been in love before and got over it. We'll go round to Laval's flat when we get to Paris, pick him up and take him over to England. I can probably help to square matters over his passport."

He lit a cigarette and leaned back in his seat.

"Gad! Tiny, it would be great if we could pull it off. Just great, with..."

He paused suddenly, eyes narrowed, staring over Tiny's head. Then he went on—

"all the odds against us."

"What's stung you, Ronald?"

"One of the biggest of those odds, who for the moment had slipped my mind. Our friend Zavier is on the train, though I certainly never noticed him get on at Dalzburg. And he's watching us, Tiny!"

"How do you know?"

"He was standing in the corridor of the next coach, and for a moment our eyes met."

He called for the bill, and a few minutes later they returned to their carriage. Sleeping berths had been impossible, and they had a first-class compartment to themselves.

"Be careful, old man," he said abruptly, as Tiny prepared to throw his coat, which he had left to mark his place, into the rack. "Don't touch anything. Apparently nothing has been moved, but..."

His eyes were searching every corner of the carriage, and after awhile he drew on a pair of gloves.

"We may be several kinds of ass, Tiny, but I don't trust railway trains when members of this fraternity are about. We've been in the restaurant car for a good two hours, and this carriage has been empty."

He ran his fingers gently over the upholstery, while the train rocked and swayed through the darkness. And not until he had explored every corner did he at length sit down.

"False alarm this time," he said. "But it alters things a little for tonight. We mustn't both sleep at the same time: that's obvious. We'll shut the door into the corridor, and we'll open the window. But for the love of Pete if it's your watch don't forget to shut it whenever we stop at a station."

But nothing happened throughout the night. Once, when they had stopped at some comparatively small and ill-lit place, it had seemed to Tiny that something had hit the window, but the blow was so soft that he couldn't have sworn to it. And peering out he could see nothing, so he dismissed it as imagination. Once also during another period when he was on duty a peculiar-shaped shadow showed for a moment in the corridor—a shadow so indefinite that it might have been thrown by a sack. But it disappeared as abruptly as it had come, and when he glanced out the corridor was empty. And so without event they arrived in Paris.

"You deal with the kit, Tiny," said Standish, as the train ran into the Gare de Lyon. "I'm sprinting like a hare for the barrier to see if I can spot our friend."

But when Tiny joined him there, he shook his head a little ruefully.

"I didn't," he said. "And I saw every soul who came off that train."

"If your idea over the headquarters being in Switzerland is right," remarked Tiny, "he may have got off there."

"Possibly," agreed Standish. "And yet I have a sort of hunch that his goal is the same as ours—Felton Blake."

He gave Laval's address to the taxi-driver.

"I may be wrong, but I don't think they would trust a thing so important as that negative to the post. Moreover, a man of Blake's type trusts no one. He will want to see the colour of his money before he parts. Still, it's guesswork. The only thing we know is that Zavier has disappeared for the time as far as we are concerned."

They found Laval having his breakfast and introduced themselves.

"It was to me a great pleasure," he remarked when Standish began to thank him for what he had done. "When the so charming Madame Mackintosh tell me her scheme and I realize zat the honour of a lady is at stake—*que voulez vous*? It was so easy. And I arrange the affair of the passport here. I say my mechanic he is ill, and zat this gentleman—a qualified pilot—he take his place at ze last moment so as not to disappoint ze passengers."

"Splendid, Monsieur Laval," cried Standish. "A thousand thanks. And where is he now?"

"He sleep late, I think, in zat room."

He crossed the passage, and knocked on the door of a room opposite. And then, receiving no answer, he flung it open.

"He is not here. *Probablement* he is gone out. Ah! but here is a note. Let us see what he say.

"DEAR MONSIEUR LAVAL,—

"My warmest thanks for all that you have done. I looked into your room but you were sleeping so I did not awaken you. Tell Standish when you see him that I have gone to London. I'll square the passport business somehow. And tell him I'll get what we want. Again many thanks."

He laid the letter down on the table, and Standish re-read it, frowning thoughtfully.

"A nuisance—that," he said. "You don't know his address in London, Tiny, I suppose? Or his club?"

"Not a notion. Why?"

"My dear old lad, Joe Denver is an excellent youngster. But the last thing I want is to have him blundering round Felton Blake. And that's what he evidently means to do. It's going to completely queer our pitch. He'll do no good: and he'll put Blake on his guard."

"I should think it is more than likely he will go and see Mary," said Tiny. "What about getting her on the 'phone?"

"That's a good idea. May we put through a London call, Monsieur Laval?"

"But assuredly. It is in the hall."

"Tell her, Tiny, that if ever she sees Denver she must tell him from us to do absolutely nothing until he sees us. Tell him to come to the club at six to-night."

"And what about Felton Blake to-night?" said Tiny, hanging up the receiver.

"Tell her what we want to do. But be guarded."

The call went through quickly, and in less than three minutes Tiny heard Simmonds' voice from the other end.

"Speaking from Paris, Simmonds. Mr. Carteret. I want Lady Mary urgently."

"Her ladyship is out of London, sir. Not returning until lunch-time."

"Give him the message about Denver," said Standish, as Tiny repeated it. "Not Felton Blake."

"Simmonds," went on Tiny, "you remember Mr. Denver. Tall, fair gentleman with curly hair. You do. Good. If he comes to call on Lady Mary to-day tell him that he is to do nothing until he sees Mr. Standish. Got that? And tell him to be at my club at six."

He listened while the butler repeated the message, and then rang off.

"So far, so good," said Standish. "We couldn't have passed a message through him about Felton Blake. We must wire."

He sat down and pulled a telegraph form towards him.

"How's this?" he said a few moments later. "We want F.B. out of his house to-night from eleven till one. Please arrange. Urgent and vital. Tiny."

"That ought to do it," said Tiny. "And she'll pull it off if it is humanly possible."

"My man can take it for you at once," said Laval. "The bureau is just around the corner. And first he shall get you some hot water for a shave."

"Excellent," cried Standish. "And then we must catch the ten o'clock boat train."

"*Pour les pauvres, Messieurs.*"

Two nuns were standing in the passage, and the speaker, as if to account for their unexpected appearance, added almost apologetically—"*La porte était ouverte.*"

The three men each handed over a note, and then, while one of the nuns carefully entered the amounts in a little book, Laval led the way to the bathroom. And for a moment the nuns were alone. So that there was no one to see the sudden quick movement with which the top telegraph form of the pad was detached, carefully folded, and put away in a bag. And when Laval returned they were standing meekly waiting for his signature in their book before leaving as silently as they had arrived. Nor was there anyone to see that instead of continuing their house to house visitation the two nuns walked swiftly away to where a large car was waiting, and paused by it just long enough to say *"Dix heures"*—and to place the piece of paper in a hand extended through the window—the hand of a man on whose shoulders sat a small monkey.

The car rolled off, and Boris Zavier studied the telegraph form. He saw at once the imprint of the pencil, which had been made when the wire had been written, but realizing the impossibility of deciphering it in a moving car he re-folded it and placed it in his pocket book. Then he lay back and began to think. For the events of the last few days had shaken his nerve badly.

The first had been the Demeroff affair. That the Russian had been coming to Lausanne with the express purpose of meeting Standish he now knew, and though he had acted in time it had been a very close shave. But the disquieting part of the thing was that it proved that what he had said to Felton Blake was wrong. It was not only the Bessonian affair that had brought Standish to Switzerland: it was something much bigger. That the existence of his organization was known to the authorities was obvious: activities on such a scale as he had carried them out could only be inspired by one controlling brain. And it struck him with a sort of cynical humour that it would be amusing if this—one of the least of his schemes—should prove to be the one that revealed to whom the brain belonged.

It was the abduction of this boy Denver that worried him. Not that he really cared in the slightest whether Berendosi succeeded or failed: save for the money involved the whole thing bored him. But what did matter was the fact that Standish and his friend must have seen him at Gregoroff's place.

He cursed himself now for ever having attended such an absurd farce, but at the time he did not know Standish was in Dalzburg. Had he had an inkling of the fact nothing would have induced him to go. For he was under no delusions with regard to the Englishman: he was not a man to be trifled with. Once let him suspect and he would pass his suspicions on. And it seemed to him more than likely that he suspected already.

It had been a pure accident, that momentary glimpse in the restaurant *wagon*, but the result of that accident had alarmed him more than he cared to admit even to himself. Was it merely coincidence that one or the other of them had been awake all through the night? Was it merely coincidence that the door into the corridor had been closed, and the windows shut whenever he had alighted from the train? And finally, was it merely coincidence that Standish should have been standing by the barrier watching the passengers intently as they left the station? The fact that he had passed within two feet of him in safety was beside the point: all that mattered was whether these precautions had been due to that accidental glimpse in the train. And being a man who never believed in underrating the odds on the other side, he came quite definitely to the conclusion that it would be better to assume it was not a coincidence, and make his plans accordingly. Standish and his friend Carteret suspected him: therefore, they must be dealt with, and at once.

The car pulled up at the door of a luxurious flat, and Zavier alighted. They were going by the ten o'clock train: he would go by the one at midday. And that would leave him comfortable time to see if the wire contained information of any importance. It proved unexpectedly easy to decipher: the writer had evidently pressed hard with his pencil. And when the complete message lay before him on his desk, for awhile he stared thoughtfully out of the window. Then a faint smile curled round his lips, and he rubbed his hands gently together.

"Excellent," he murmured: "Excellent."

And with the smile still on his face he went into his dressing-room.

At half-past five Tiny rang the bell of Lady Mary's house, and the door was opened by Simmonds.

"Her ladyship is not at home, sir," he said. "She left a note for you."

"Did she get my wire?" asked Tiny.

"She got a wire, sir, when she returned at lunch-time."

"Has Mr. Denver been here?"

"No, sir: no sign of him. Will you come in, sir, and read the note: you might like to write an answer."

Tiny went into the boudoir and as he glanced round the familiar room he gave a short laugh. Only four days since he had last been there: only four days since he had felt her lips on his for the first time—but what a lot of water had flowed under the bridge since then.

"A whisky and soda, sir?" suggested the butler.

"Thank you, Simmonds," he said, sitting down and opening the note.

MY DEAR,—[it ran]

I have done what you asked in your wire. But what on earth is the idea? I gather from your telephone message to Simmonds that Joe Denver must be safely out of Dalzburg. Nada Mazarin wrote me from Paris to say he was there, and that she had travelled with you. It's distracting that I can't see you to-day, but I've got an engagement I simply cannot break. I'm dying to hear all your news: come round and see me first thing to-morrow.

MARY.

P.S.—There has been no sign of Joe here.

He crossed to her desk as the butler came in with the drink.

"If I may say so, sir," he said with the familiarity of an old servant, "her ladyship seems to have been very worried lately. Not at all her usual self."

"You are quite right, Simmonds. She has been. By the way, has a gentleman called Blake been here at all?"

"Once or twice, sir," he said. "Might I ask, sir, if he is—er—a friend of yours?"

"A friend of mine!" cried Tiny. "Emphatically he is not."

"I am not surprised, sir," said Simmonds quietly. "Will you ring if you require another drink, sir?"

So even the servants had noticed it, reflected Tiny savagely as the door closed. And any lingering doubts he might have had about the night's work ahead vanished. That negative had *got* to be obtained.

He pulled a sheet of paper towards him.

MARY DEAR,—[he wrote]

Well done. I'll come round and see you to-morrow and maybe—though I don't promise—it will see the end of all our troubles. I've got lots to tell you.

TINY.

He sealed the envelope and finished his drink. Then he rang the bell.

"Give this to Lady Mary, Simmonds, will you? And if by any chance Mr. Denver does arrive, my telephone message to you still holds. Send him round to my club without fail."

Ronald Standish was waiting for him in the smoking-room.

"Fortunately it is the more important of the two things that has come off," was his comment when he heard Tiny's news. "And we can only hope that young Denver postpones his visit till to-morrow. I put through a call to the Folkestone passport people, and he'd arrived all right by the one o'clock boat. And after they had satisfied themselves he was British they let him go on. He was very insistent apparently on getting to London as soon as possible—strangely insistent was the phrase they used. However, we can only hope for the best."

"Did you find out anything at the Yard?" asked Tiny.

"Not a thing. I described Zavier in detail, and clearly he is a new one on them. Which proves just nothing at all. Then I went along and saw Gillson, and gave him a résumé of our doings. In fact I whispered to him of our expedition to-night. At first he tried to dissuade me: said the risk was too great. But after awhile he agreed that it was the only possible solution. Not that he can do much if we're caught," he added with a short laugh. "We're definitely putting ourselves outside the pale of the law. And, 'pon my soul, Tiny, I don't know if it is fair to you. You are only a volunteer, so to speak: it's not your palaver."

"Go to blazes, you ass," cried Tiny. "Unless you want a rough house here and now."

"Right ho!" grinned the other. "I'm not denying you won't be damned useful, but it's only fair to warn you that there is going to be the devil of a risk."

"How are you going to open the safe if we do get in?" said Tiny.

"One of my little secrets that you don't know," answered Standish. "You shall after dinner."

"And since it will probably be our last," laughed Tiny, "we'd better make it a good one."

It was nine o'clock when they left the club, and there was still no sign of Joe Denver. During the meal they had both been unusually silent: as the time drew nearer the bald fact that, if they were caught, it would without a shadow of doubt mean a term of imprisonment, began to obtrude itself with increasing clearness. But neither of them had the slightest intention of drawing back.

They drove to Standish's flat. There was at least an hour to put through before they dared start, but there were several preparations to be made. First he went to the safe in the corner of the room, and from it he extracted a rolled-up green wallet of the type used for motoring tools. Then he drew the blinds, before opening it out on the table.

"This room is overlooked," he said with a grin. "And I'd hate anyone to think that this represented my normal method of livelihood."

Inside was a complete set of safe-opening tools. Braces, bits—all the paraphernalia of the professional cracksman lay gleaming in the electric light.

"Good Lord! old man," cried Tiny. "Where did you get that lot?"

"I got them in the States from a professional user of them," laughed the other, "as a small token of gratitude for something I did for him. According to him they weren't quite up to his form, and he was getting some others. Moreover, he showed me how to use 'em."

He rolled up the wallet again and put it in his pocket.

"Now—two masks." He rummaged in a drawer. "Here are two that will do."

"Are we taking any weapons?" asked Tiny.

"I think not, old lad. Certainly not guns. Burglary is one thing: shooting is another. No: we'll stick to the perfectly efficient fist, if we're caught in the act, and then run like stags. For the trouble is that we daren't go in my car. We'd have to leave it some distance from the house, and a car untended for two hours or so would have the police on it at once. We'll just take a taxi to somewhere near the house and then walk."

It was half-past ten when they decided they could start, and a quarter of an hour later they dismissed their machine at Swiss Cottage. If Blake was meeting Lady Mary at eleven, he would have left his house already and the coast would be clear.

They walked along Eton Avenue, comparatively dimly lit after the glare of Finchley Road behind them. And after about a quarter of a mile Standish turned left-handed up an even quieter road. They were in the centre of one of the wealthy residential quarters of Hampstead, and the houses on each side of them proclaimed the fact. Solid, comfortable and above all eminently respectable, they seemed to personify their solid, comfortable and eminently respectable owners.

"There is the spot we want," said Standish. "Number 12."

They paused opposite it on the other side of the road. It was in darkness save for a light from one of the top windows. To the right of it as they looked lay the garage, and over the top of it they could see some trees.

"Up and at it, Tiny," chuckled Standish. "Take your last look at London as a free man. My God! what's that?"

For suddenly there had come a ghastly strident shriek of agony, and it had seemed to proceed from the house they were watching. A window was flung up behind them, and a man peered out. With a quick pressure on his arm Standish indicated to Tiny that they should walk on. But the scream was not repeated, and after strolling a few yards, they retraced their steps.

"Was that from Blake's house?" said Tiny.

"Sounded like it. We must wait now for a bit: it's probably alarmed the neighbourhood. Hullo! what's this?"

Once again he gripped Tiny's arm and the pair stood motionless under a tree. A man had come out of the gate of Number 12, and keeping in the shadow of the trees was walking rapidly towards Eton Avenue. It was quite impossible to recognize him: a hat pulled well down over his forehead obscured his features even if they had been visible at the distance. But not till the sound of his steps had died away did they move.

"Our friend would seem to have other visitors to-night," said Standish thoughtfully. "Things grow interesting."

"Well, the alarm doesn't seem to have spread," remarked Tiny. "And the place is deserted. What about it?"

They crossed the road some fifty yards from Blake's house, and strolled gently towards it. The man who had looked out had shut the window again: the moment was propitious. And with one quick glance round Standish turned in at the gate, and moved swiftly towards the garage.

There was a space of nearly a yard between the garage and the wall that divided Number 12 from the next house, and in a second they were both standing in it. It afforded perfect cover, and gave them a direct approach to the garden without the slightest chance of being seen. A certain amount of old rubbish had collected in it, and Standish picked his way carefully: it was not the time to play football with old oil cans. But nothing untoward occurred, and they reached the shadow of the trees without mishap.

To their right lay the garden: in front of them and a little to the left was the back of the house. It, too, was in complete darkness, and after a while they began to creep cautiously towards it.

"It's the room with the big French windows," whispered Standish. "The second one we come to."

They were close to it when he paused suddenly, and Tiny, glancing at him, could just see that he was frowning.

"Why are the windows open, Tiny?" he breathed, "when there is no light in the room? There is something damned funny about this show."

They could see the curtains moving gently in the slight breeze. No sound came from inside: the place seemed ominously quiet. And then they both shrank against the wall: a telephone bell was ringing in the room.

"Back to the trees," said Standish urgently. "Someone will probably answer it."

But no one did, and after a few more abortive attempts the operator gave it up. Silence settled once again save for the faint rustle of the leaves above their heads. They allowed five minutes: then for the second time they crept towards the window. There was no good delaying: every moment of time was valuable.

"I'll get on to the safe at once, Tiny," whispered Standish. "You lock the door, and then stand by the window. Great Scott! look there."

He had parted the curtains, and was crouching down staring at the floor. The wood was of a light colour inside the window, and stretching out from the edge of the carpet a dark stain was visible. And even as they looked at it, it altered its shape.

With a sudden exclamation he switched on a small electric torch: then his eyes dilated.

"My God!" he muttered. "It's blood. For Heaven's sake be careful where you tread."

Holding his torch in front of him he stepped into the room. And there they stood, motionless: the failure to answer the telephone was explained.

Lying on his back, with legs and arms sprawling, was Felton Blake, and driven up to the hilt in his heart was a dagger. The blood had welled out, soaking into the carpet and finally reaching the woodwork, though now it had ceased to flow.

"That scream we heard," muttered Tiny. "It must have been his."

But Standish shook his head.

"No man killed like that would scream. It was instantaneous."

He bent and felt one of the dead man's hands. "He's been dead some time. Hold those curtains together: I'm going to get some light on the scene."

He crept noiselessly away and in a moment there came the click of a switch. And once again they stood motionless, too stunned to speak. For the door of the big safe was open, and the contents were flung in wild confusion all over the carpet. But it was not empty. Lying half inside it, his head wedged in a corner, with teeth bared and only the whites of his eyes showing, was Joe Denver. No need to ask the cause of his death: both of them recognized it only too well. Somewhere on him they would find the death scratch: he had been murdered even as Demeroff and the others had been murdered. And it was his dying scream they had heard from the other side of the road.

"So that's what he meant when he said he'd get the negative somehow," said Standish gravely. "Poor young devil! And I don't know that I blame him."

"You think he killed Blake?" said Tiny.

Standish pointed to the key which was in the safe door.

"I think that he killed Blake, and then took the key from him. Blake has been dead for more than an hour: Denver for less than a quarter."

"And the man we saw leaving killed Joe?"

"Possibly, though we have no proof. Possibly there is some infernal device in the safe itself." He was drawing on his gloves as he spoke. "But now we've got to get a move on. We don't want to be discovered here if we can avoid it. The first point is—did he find the negative?"

Gently they pulled the twisted body on to the carpet, and then swiftly and methodically Standish went through his pockets.

"No sign of it," he muttered.

"If he'd found it he would have destroyed it," said Tiny, but though they searched every corner of the room, the paper basket and the fire-place, they could find no traces of it anywhere.

"Useless, Tiny. He'd surely have destroyed it here by the safe, if he destroyed it at all."

He was peering at the carpet with his torch held close.

"Nothing: nothing at all. And even a film leaves some residue if it is burnt."

At length he straightened up.

"He didn't get it, Tiny, and that means it isn't here."

"Then what do we do now?"

"We collect these papers," said Standish quietly. "Every one of them probably means some poor devil's happiness. Our burglary shall have some result, anyway."

He crammed them into his pockets till they bulged, while Tiny stood by him. Some result perhaps—but it was only a side issue. As far as they were concerned it had all been wasted; the negative was still in existence. And a damned good man had been killed. Of Felton Blake he gave no thought: men such as he deserved to die. But in his imagination he could see the youngster going feverishly through the safe: he could feel the despair that must have gripped him as he drew blank. And then—the end—the ghastly agonizing end.

"Tiny."

He glanced up at the sharp whisper: Standish was by the window looking at the floor.

"What is it?"

"You didn't tread in the blood here, did you?"

"No." He crossed the room and joined the other.

"Look there," said Standish.

In the crimson patch, clear and distinct was a footmark.

"Someone has been watching us," he continued gravely. "The waters grow deeper."

CHAPTER IX

"So it's hopeless, Tiny: they've beaten us."

"I must say, Mary dear, that at the moment it looks rather like it."

It was eleven o'clock the following morning, and the two of them were in her boudoir. He had told her the whole story of what had happened since they last met, and she in her turn had filled in one or two blanks.

"You see, Tiny," she said, "I knew the man was a sweep, and I can't pretend that in one way the news of his death isn't a profound relief. At the same time I did think he was genuinely trying to get it."

"But how dared such an excrescence fall in love with you?" he demanded.

"My dear man," she said with a short laugh, "I don't know about love. But he was received in a lot of places, and I think he thought that marrying a Duke's daughter would enable him to be received in more."

"Would you really have married him," he said curiously, "if he had produced the negative?"

"Heaven knows," she answered. "Anyway, the point does not arise. It's the thought of Joe that upsets me so much. They must have been both lying there when I telephoned."

"It was you, was it? We were just outside the window, and it startled us some."

"My dear, I was getting wild with anxiety. I'd arranged for him to meet me here at ten-thirty. And when eleven came with no sign of him I rang up. Tiny—what *are* we to do?"

She rose restlessly and stood by the fireplace.

"Dunno, Mary dear," he said. "I'm absolutely beat."

"Can't Mr. Standish suggest something?"

"I haven't seen him to-day," said Tiny. "He was going round to see Gillson, and I told him I was coming here."

"I wish she had seen him once. Olga and Joe," she added with a faint smile as she saw the puzzled look on his face. "I'm jumping a bit this morning: nerves all on edge."

"It was impossible, my dear," he answered gravely. "Every other person you meet there is a spy."

"And to think he did it for nothing: that is the wicked part of it. Oh! Tiny, we can't let it be in vain: we *can't*."

"The Lord knows, dear, that those are my sentiments too. And Ronald's as well. But it's the devil and all of a proposition."

"And it will be the end of all things if that photo is published?"

It was a question, but he could see she was clutching at a straw of hope.

"My dear," he said, "as you know, my acquaintance with Bessonian politics is microscopic. All I can tell you is that both Ronald and that fellow Andy Mackintosh, who I was telling you about, view the case as hopeless if Berendosi gets hold of that negative. And now that we've drawn blank in Blake's safe it might be anywhere."

Simmonds opened the door, and entered with a card on a salver.

"Tiny," cried the girl, "it's your pal—Mr. Standish. Show him in at once, Simmonds. Do you think he's thought of something new?"

"We'll soon hear if he has."

He turned as Ronald Standish came in, and it seemed to him as if there was a certain suppressed excitement in the other's face.

"Something fresh," he cried. "Oh! by the way, you two haven't met, have you? My fellow-criminal, Mary ..."

"Mr. Standish," she said eagerly, "you look as if there was a new development."

"I won't go so far as to say that, Lady Mary," answered Standish, "but we have just obtained a piece of information which *might* lead us somewhere. May I smoke?"

"Please do."

He lit a cigarette, while the others waited breathlessly.

"Tiny, of course, will have told you everything that happened last night. How young Denver went to interview Blake in order to get the negative, and when Blake refused to part he killed him. He took the keys, opened the safe, and later was murdered himself. So much is clear. From now it becomes a question of surmise, with only one fact standing out as certain. And that fact is that the man we saw leaving Blake's house shortly after we heard Denver's scream was either the murderer or knew that he had been murdered."

"Now that action on his part is understandable: he would naturally clear off for fear the scream should attract people to the place. But what is not so understandable is why they should have murdered Denver at all."

"Perhaps Joe had found it," said Tiny, "and he murdered him to get it back."

"The first thought that occurred to me, but there is one insuperable difficulty. We know that poison and its method of working. Take

Demeroff: take other cases. It requires at least a quarter of an hour to act. During that quarter of an hour if Denver had found the negative, he might and probably would have destroyed it. Would the murderer, then, dare to have risked it? The film was far more important to him than killing Denver. In fact, the last thing he wanted to do was to kill Denver: he is much more value to the other side alive than dead."

"Anyway he *did* kill him, Ronald—so there is no more to be said."

"But did he *mean* to, Tiny?"

"You mean it was an accident."

"Yes and no. He meant to kill someone—but not Denver. He killed the wrong man."

"But, good Heavens! old man, it's impossible. And anyway, who did he mean to kill?"

"Me," said Standish quietly. "And possibly you."

"But do you mean to say he didn't know he was killing Denver?"

"That is what I mean to say. I admit it sounds wild—almost fantastic. Nevertheless, can you give me any reason whatsoever why the other side should commit such a suicidal act from their point of view as to kill a man who was vitally important to them?"

"I can't. But neither can I give you any reason why they should have imagined we were going to be there at all."

"Let's go on with our surmise, and put ourselves in the other bloke's place—in Zavier's place. Zavier knows that we are fully aware of the existence of that negative: he knows we connect Blake with it: he knows we are in London. Surely his first assumption would be that we would seek an interview with Blake and do our best to get it. He may not have thought we would go as far as burglary, but he must assume on our trying to obtain it. He therefore lays his plans accordingly. He instructs a subordinate—or possibly that was Zavier himself last night—and proceeds, in some mysterious way, which I frankly admit I cannot explain, to lie up for us. First he removes the negative to avoid any possibility of danger to it: then probably in conjunction with Blake he sets the scene. He obviously cannot be present—that would give the whole thing away. And if the plan comes off Blake is safe, because my death would appear as all the other deaths have appeared to be, due to heart trouble.

"Then comes the one thing he had not anticipated. Instead of us appearing, Joe Denver turns up.. He, as I say, was not there: he was probably hanging about somewhere to see what happened. Nothing at all might have occurred, in which case he would try again next night. Suddenly he hears the scream, and goes in. To his horror he finds Blake murdered and the wrong man dead in the safe. He waits only to remove whatever there was in that room to cause death to Denver, and bolts."

"But, Mr. Standish," cried the girl, "I don't quite see how all this helps. Even if you are right, this man Zavier has the negative. And that's all that matters."

"Sorry to be so long: I'm coming to that now. As you say, that is all that counts, but I wanted to start from the beginning. As I said, he then bolts: we know that—we saw him. Which brings us to the second very peculiar incident, as peculiar in its own way as the killing of Denver. What brought him back again? As Tiny has probably told you, Lady Mary, we saw his footprints in the blood by the window. Why did he return?"

"How do we know it was the same man?" said Tiny.

"Well, it can't have been a policeman or any ordinary outsider: in either of those cases the alarm would have been raised at once. Therefore if it wasn't the same man it was at any rate someone who knew what had happened and so must have been one of the gang. And since the film was safe as far as they were concerned, what object was served by his coming back? This morning I got a possible answer.

"You remember, Tiny, that I took away all the papers from Blake's safe. This morning I went through them with Gillson. Ye gods! the half of that man's vileness has not been thought of. There were letters in his possession belonging to people whose names are household words, and who he has been bleeding to death. Needless to say we burned the lot, with the exception of one most interesting one."

He took from his pocket a legal-looking document.

"This is the lease of 11 Gregory Street. The landlord is, or rather was, Felton Blake: the tenants are three in number. A bookmaker has an office on the first floor: there is a branch of some wholesale hardware store on the second. But the basement is let to an organization with a somewhat strange name—the Universal Benevolent Society.

"At first sight admittedly there is nothing very peculiar about it, but when we studied it a little closer an interesting point emerged. The first two 'lets' are drawn up in the orthodox legal fashion with rent and all the usual conditions stated, but for the Universal Benevolent Society the document is simply worthless. From a business point of view it has no value whatever. In fact it is not a lease.

"Knowing Felton Blake's characteristics, this seemed strange. He was not the type of man to let the Universal or any other benevolent society have an office without paying for it. And when Gillson's secretary, who was in the room at the time, happened to remember where Gregory Street was, the matter began to take shape. To cut it short, this house abuts on to the back of the Fifty-Nine Club, and the basement therefore is on the level of the dance floor.

"Now you know, Tiny, that for some time past the police have had that club under close supervision. And there have been two or three strange incidents there. The other night, for instance, a man who was well known as a trafficker in drugs came to the club and was spotted by one of our men there, who tipped the wink to his companion upstairs. There was no question of arresting the man—he was only one of the smaller fry: but as a matter of interest they kept an eye on him. Our fellow downstairs was acting as a waiter, and so was not in the room the whole time. And it so happened that he did not actually see this man leave his table. But at some period during the evening he did so, and he did not return. Moreover, he did not go out by the front entrance."

"Your point is, then," said Tiny, "that there is some form of communication between the club and this house in Gregory Street?"

"Exactly. And my further point is that it was to obtain this document, which he had forgotten in the excitement of the moment, that our friend of last night returned. He knew the police would spot it as soon as they came to go through it carefully: and he knew that in a few hours the police must discover the murders and take possession of all the papers. And so he came back to get it, only to find us in occupation."

"But where is all this leading us to, Mr. Standish?" cried the girl, a little impatiently.

"It does seem a bit beside the mark, I agree, Lady Mary," said Standish with a smile, "but I've very nearly finished. You see it has put the gentleman in an awkward quandary. Assuming—and one must make assumptions in a case like this—assuming he has the negative in his possession, his first instinct, realizing we are on the trail, would be to take it direct to Berendosi and pocket the money. But he now knows that we are in possession of this information about 11 Gregory Street. He knows that the Universal Benevolent Society has served its turn and must close down. Dare he therefore leave the country until he has closed it down? Which is not likely to be a matter that can be done in two or three hours.

"And so, if you want some fun, go to the Fifty-Nine to-night. Anyway, Tiny, you must go even if Lady Mary doesn't, and you must get a table from which you can command a view of the staircase. At one o'clock the club will be raided, though I promise you that your names shall not appear. At a little before one there will be a certain activity round the office of the Universal Benevolent Society, which I hope may bolt the badger. And even though a raid is on in the club he can only bolt that way. If, as I hope and believe, our badger is Zavier himself, you will recognize him. Then tip the wink to the Inspector in charge of the raid: we'll do the rest."

"But is he likely to have the negative on him, Mr. Standish?" said the girl.

"More than likely. What safer place could there be from his point of view? There is nothing criminal about it. But if by chance we pull it off, I fear that an accident will happen to it."

"By Jove! it sounds possible, old man," cried Tiny. "I'll be there."

"So will I," said the girl excitedly.

"Easy does it," warned Standish. "Don't for Heaven's sake let's build on it. It may come off: there's a bare chance of it's coming off—but that's all."

"Anyway there is a chance," she said. "Which is more than we thought a little while ago."

"What is your part in the show, Ronald?" asked Tiny.

"I shall be with the Number 11 party. It is essential that you should mark one exit while I take the other, because we are the only people who know him."

"Always provided it is Zavier."

"Always provided it is Zavier," agreed Standish, getting up to go. "And somehow, Tiny, I believe we shall find that it is. This whole business is too big for a subordinate. Well—I must be off. And if I don't see you again, be at the Fifty-Nine from midnight onwards. And—*don't* build on it."

But it was well-nigh impossible not to. All through luncheon they fluctuated between hope and despair, and the afternoon seemed to drag on leaden wheels. There was an account of the previous night's tragedy in all the midday papers, but somehow naturally it told them nothing they did not know already. The police, as usual, were in possession of a valuable clue, and further developments were expected at any moment.

At four o'clock Standish rang up.

"Developments, Tiny," he said, "and hopeful ones. There is considerable activity round Number 11. Two car loads of suit-cases and packages of various sorts have been removed, and have been followed to their new destination, where we can lay our hands on them at any time."

"Can't you raid the place now?" asked Tiny.

"Got no warrant. And no magistrate would issue one on our present knowledge. Cheer up, old lad: I'm feeling more confident."

At last midnight came. Their table was almost next to the foot of the stairs leading to the street, which they had insisted on having much to the amazement of the head waiter, who pointed out that it was the worst in the room. The cabaret show was just starting, and having ordered kippers and a bottle they tried to watch it, without, however, much success. Apart from the fact that they had both seen it before, they were far too keyed up to pay any attention.

"What happens in a raid, Tiny?" asked the girl.

"My dear, it's a perfectly harmless proceeding. Some large men will appear on the stairs, and other large men will walk gracefully round the room taking our names and addresses. Hullo! do you see that waiter over there—the one attending to the woman with magenta hair? He is police—one Dexter by name."

And at that moment the man turned and caught Tiny's eye. It was the flicker of an eyelid that he gave, rather than a wink, before he resumed his job, but it was vaguely comforting. It seemed to establish a sort of liaison with the imperturbable Gillson and the powers that be generally.

"Is it my imagination, Mary," said Tiny after awhile, "or is there an air of tension about the place? Giuseppi has been in twice talking to the head waiter, and it strikes me the staff seems uneasy."

He glanced at his watch.

"Quarter of an hour to go. Gad! I wish I knew what was happening next door."

The show was over: dancing had started again. And now there was no mistaking it: something was in the air. Giuseppi had come in again and was gesticulating in a corner with his second in command, while the waiters in their vicinity listened eagerly. Then abruptly the band stopped.

The head waiter issued rapid orders to his underlings: Giuseppi stepped into the middle of the floor.

"Ladies and gentlemens," he called out, "ze police..."

"Quite so," came a deep genial voice from the stairs, "the police."

A dead silence settled on the room.

"I must ask you, ladies and gentlemen, please to keep your seats. You will not be put to any inconvenience. I shall require your names and addresses, and I may say that I shall view any Mr. Smith of Birmingham with grave suspicion. In the last raid I undertook there were six."

There was a general laugh as he came down the stairs, leaving two men in uniform standing at the top. And the first table he stopped at was Tiny's.

"I need hardly ask your name, sir," he said with a twinkle in his eye. "I've watched you too often at Twickenham. If you see your man, wait till I am talking to him, and then come up to me and ask if you can go."

The whole sentence was spoken without the faintest change of inflection, while the Inspector was apparently writing in his book.

"I get you," said Tiny, in the same tone of voice, and the Inspector passed on.

A general buzz of conversation had broken out: the Inspector's jovial manner had put everyone in a good temper except Giuseppi whose agitation was obvious. In fact, it seemed to Tiny that it was out of all proportion to what might have been expected from the anticipation of a hundred-pound fine. He watched him closely, and soon he noticed that he was shooting continual little bird-like glances at a far corner of the room. There was a small alcove there containing a table where he had sometimes sat himself, and beyond it was a door with frosted glass marked "Private." He had always assumed it was Giuseppi's office, but now he began to wonder. He made a quick calculation: Gregory Street lay beyond that side of the room. And at that moment he noticed a man with a small pointed beard sitting at a table by himself not far from the alcove.

To Zavier he bore not the slightest resemblance as far as he could see. This man's hair was plentiful while Zavier was bald: moreover Zavier was clean shaven. But those were trifles: wigs were easy to obtain. What did count was, that whether this man was Zavier or not, he had not been at that table ten minutes previously. Of that fact Tiny was certain. He had happened to notice on glancing round the room earlier that the table next to the one this man now occupied contained a well-known actress in the party, and it had momentarily attracted his attention in that direction. And he was convinced he would have noticed this bearded man if he had been there.

It was the wildest guesswork: he realized that. The man might have been away for a moment, or dancing. But no: he couldn't have been dancing. The cabaret show had been on most of the time. And suddenly he made up his mind.

"Mary—I'm going to chance it," he said. "It may be the most ungodly bloomer, but I can't help that."

"Do you think you've spotted him, Tiny?" she cried eagerly.

"It's that bloke over there with a beaver, sitting next the table where Paula Rayne is. I swear he has only just sat down there."

"Go on, Tiny: it's worth it every time."

He waited until the Inspector was about to reach him: then he rose and crossed the room.

"I say, Inspector," he remarked, "is there any jolly old reason why one shouldn't push off?"

He glanced at the man, who was staring at him with unwinking blue eyes.

"Are you quite certain you want to go, sir?" said the Inspector quietly.

"I'm never quite certain about anything, dear old lad," laughed Tiny, and at that moment it happened. He had one glimpse of a face distorted with fury glaring into his: then both he and the Inspector were on their backs on the floor with the table on top of them and the cloth round their heads.

They scrambled up swearing: the man had disappeared. And after a pause of stupefied silence, everyone near them began talking at once.

"Up there."

"That's where he went."

"Towards the private room."

One of the constables had come running down the stairs, but it was Tiny who headed the pursuit, closely followed by the Inspector. They darted along the passage to find a frightened waiter cowering up against the wall.

"Where did he go?" shouted Tiny.

"In there, sir," stammered the man.

And even as he threw himself against the door he noticed it was Number 7.

"Locked," cried Tiny. "All together, boys."

Which proved an admirable prophecy. For at the precise moment they charged the door, it was opened from the inside. And once again the Inspector and Tiny found themselves on the floor, with the addition this time of a large constable. They picked themselves up: confronting them was a vacuous-looking youth with an eye-glass, while at the table there sat an extremely frightened girl.

"I say," he bleated, "has the whole place gone bug house? First of all there comes a man with a beard, who locks the door and vanishes through the wall..."

"What part of the wall?" snapped the Inspector.

"Just there: by the fire-place..."

In a couple of strides the Inspector reached the spot and hit it with his fist.

"Hollow," he cried. "Once again, sir: all together."

They felt it crack under their weight, and with the third charge it gave way, revealing a narrow brick passage.

"Careful, sir," said the Inspector warningly, as Tiny started along it. "He's probably a dangerous customer."

He turned to the constable. "Get everyone out of the room, except the two who were in there first. Now, sir."

Cautiously they moved forward. The room behind gave them some light to begin with, but after awhile the passage bent left-handed, and almost at once they felt cooler air on their faces. With a grunt the Inspector hurried forward: in front of them was a chink of light.

"The damned fellow has done us, sir," he said. "There was a third bolt-hole."

They had emerged into a deserted mews. An old lean-to shed concealed the entrance to the passage: a solitary gas lamp supplied the illumination. Not a soul was in sight, though there was a certain amount of traffic in the street at the end. The spot where they stood formed a cul-de-sac, and once again the Inspector swore under his breath.

"Staffordale Street," he said. "And we've lost him right enough. Haven't got anyone posted there at all. How did you spot him, sir?" he added curiously.

"I took a chance," said Tiny. "I knew he had not been long at that table: in fact he suddenly arrived."

"Well, he was our bird evidently. Come on, sir: we'd best be getting back. Useless going along the mews: he's got clean away."

They retraced their steps along the passage. The vacuous youth was still declaiming loudly against life in general, and even Tiny, sore though he was at being baulked, couldn't help smiling. To bring a girl out to supper in a private room and then have dozens of people playing leap-frog through it is a trifle disconcerting, to say the least of it.

"Got away, Mary," he said gloomily as he joined her. "There was a secret door in Number 7—the room where you fed with Blake. And he did a bolt through it. Of course that beard was false, and the wig too."

"You'd better wait, sir," said the Inspector, coming up to their table. "I'll soon have finished with the rest of these people, and then we'll clear the place. Mr. Standish is here: I've told him about it."

And at that moment they saw him threading his way through the tables towards them.

"Pretty sickening," he said. "Especially after you'd spotted him, Tiny. Evidently Zavier right enough: the Inspector mentioned those light-blue eyes of his."

"What are you going to do now, Mr. Standish?" asked the girl.

"Keep a watch at every port for a man with eyes like that," he answered. "Nothing else to be done."

"How went things with you, Ronald," said Tiny. "Did you find out anything?"

"Enough to jug the whole lot," said the other grimly. "We've got one of them under lock and key now. The Universal Benevolent Society still retained on its premises enough drugs to dope an army. The rest they had got rid of this afternoon, as I told you, by taxi. In addition we found the remains of what was obviously a forger's plant in a cellar off the basement. Damn it!" he continued, thumping his fist on the table, "if we'd been one minute earlier we'd have caught him. Or if the police hadn't had to appear to act legally we'd have done it. You see you can't force an entrance to a place without either a

Tiny Carteret

warrant or some very good excuse. So as we couldn't get the first, we had to fall back on the second. A little straw was lit and thrown down outside the basement, and that gave us the pretext of fire. It also gave the alarm inside.

"We forced a window, and rushed below. A pale-faced youth was sitting at a table, who rose and demanded what we wanted. We told him we thought the house was on fire, and at that moment I noticed the butt of one of those tiny cigarettes Zavier always smokes. Moreover, it was still smouldering, while the youth had a Gold Flake in his mouth.

"'Where is the man who was here with you?' I cried.

"He denied it, and I pointed to the butt end in front of him. He turned a bit green about the gills when he saw it, but he still continued to stick to his story. In fact he began to bluster, and demanded by what right we dared to intrude.

"'Look at this, sir,' sang out the sergeant to me, and our friend turned greener still.

"'This' was a mass of charred paper in the grate, in which quite a number of fragments were unburned. And anyone could tell at a glance that it was the paper used for counterfeiting bank notes.

"'How came this paper in your possession?' I said, but he merely shook his head. He was only a paid clerk, and knew nothing about it.

"All this time I was wandering round the room trying to find the second exit. That Zavier had been there just before we came, I knew. He couldn't have got out by the stairs, therefore there must be another door. And after a few moments I found it. There was a bookshelf in one corner, and on closer inspection it proved to be a blind. It swung back, revealing a cellar beyond leading out of a passage. The music from here was plainly audible, and while the police searched the cellar I tried to find the communicating door. But it was concealed too well."

"I'll bet it is behind that door marked 'Private,'" said Tiny.

"Probably. Anyway we'll get it from this side, once they've emptied the place. They've had months, you see, to make a good job of things."

"What chance is there of catching Zavier, now?" asked the girl.

"Not so good as half an hour ago, I'm afraid," he admitted. "No good blinding ourselves to the facts. From one point of view this raid has been a brilliant success: but from the point of view that concerns us most it's been a failure. He's slipped through our fingers once again. And the only ray of comfort that I see is that he is bound to try and leave the country sooner or later with the negative on him. He would never dare risk sending it by post to Berendosi. He'll want to see the colour of his money before he hands it over."

The Inspector approached the table.

"I've interviewed Giuseppi, sir," he said, "and he either can't or won't say a thing. He is terrified out of his life. Swears he knows nothing about the house next door."

"That's a lie," said Tiny. "You bring him down here, Inspector, and ask him what's behind that glass door over there."

"I'm going to explore that now," said the other.

He signalled to one of his men to fetch the Italian.

"Now, Giuseppi," he remarked curtly, as the proprietor appeared, "we're going to have a little further exploration. Where does that door lead to?"

"To my private room," wailed the other. "I give you my word, sare, ze word of an Italian, zat zere is noddings zere."

"I'd sooner have the key, thank you," laughed the Inspector. "Come on, Giuseppi," he added sternly. "Get a move on. If you don't open that door at once I'll break it down."

Protesting volubly the little man produced a bunch of keys and led the way across the room, with the others behind him. And after much fumbling he at length got the door open. It was a small plainly furnished room. Against one wall stood an ordinary roll-top desk: for the rest a couple of easy chairs completed the contents, except for some overcoats which hung on pegs from the wall. And Tiny, happening to glance at Giuseppi, saw that it was at these he was staring.

"What the devil is this?" said Standish suddenly.

He was bending over the paper basket, from which he proceeded to pull out a number of pieces of torn brown cloth. Some of them had been ruthlessly slashed with scissors: others had been ripped by hand. And in a corner of the room was another heap of similar fragments.

They all stared at the Italian, who shrugged his shoulders deprecatingly.

"Signors," he said, "it is an old dressing-gown of mine. There are times, you understand, when I take off ze coat and ze waistcoat..."

"Why have you ripped it to pieces?" said Standish curtly.

"It is old, sare. Besides zis afternoon suddenly he annoy me. I like not his colour. I snatch him off: I tear him up."

"You're a pretty bad liar, my lad," said Standish. "Though I frankly admit I can't quite spot where it comes into the general scheme. However, that may come later. Where is the communicating door, Giuseppi?"

"Zere is no such sing, sare," he protested. "Zat is all brick wall behind."

"Get out of the light," snapped the Inspector, and pushing the Italian on one side he proceeded to make a minute inspection. And at last he gave a cry of triumph.

"Here we are, Mr. Standish. You can see the crack in the woodwork. Now, see here, Giuseppi—we've wasted enough time already. Get that open, and do it at once. Very well, if you won't—I'll send for a pickaxe."

"Wait a moment, Inspector," said Standish. "Here is a small keyhole."

It was barely visible in the pattern of the wood: anyone not looking for it would never have found it.

"And here's the key that fits it," remarked the Inspector quietly, as he examined Giuseppi's bunch. "Do you still pretend you know nothing about it?"

He inserted it in the lock, and gave a heave with his shoulder. Without a sound a part of the wall swung outwards, revealing a passage on the other side.

"Who's there?" came a stern voice, and into the light there stepped a police sergeant in uniform, who saluted as soon as he saw the Inspector.

"Number 11 Gregory Street," said Standish. "And what is that I see on the floor?"

He bent and picked up a long brown cord with a tassel at each end.

"This would seem to belong to your dressing-gown, Giuseppi," he said quietly. "One wonders why it should be this side of the door."

CHAPTER X

"Well, sir," said the Inspector half an hour later, "I don't know that there is anything more to be done here. It's been a magnificent round up."

"Except for the one big fish," answered Standish a little bitterly.

"We'll get him, sir. With those blue eyes of his it's only a question of time."

"And that's the one thing we can't afford at the moment," said the other. "However, as you say it's been very successful as far as it goes. Go through all those books and papers, will you, and let me know anything you may find."

"I will, sir. Good night. Good night, your ladyship."

The four of them were standing on the pavement outside the entrance to the club. Giuseppi, still protesting volubly, and the youth from Number 11, had both been removed to the police station: the street was empty save for one belated taxi, which Standish inspected carefully before entering.

"I'm taking no risks this trip," he remarked, after giving Lady Mary's address to the driver. "Zavier must be mad as a civet cat with you and me, Tiny. We've completely smashed his organization here in England, to say nothing of collaring thousands of pounds' worth of dope."

"I wonder if that little sweep Giuseppi is really as ignorant of things as he pretended to be," said Tiny.

"Of course he wasn't ignorant of the fact that those two places have been run in conjunction for months. But I'm not at all sure he wasn't speaking the truth when he said he knew nothing about Zavier. I tried him suddenly with the name, as you heard, and though I watched him closely I believe his ignorance there was genuine. It's a damned interesting business, and if it wasn't for the other affair I should be loving life."

"It's that that is worrying me so frightfully," said the girl. "We don't seem to be any better off there."

The taxi had stopped outside her house.

"Cheer up, Lady Mary," he cried. "We haven't lost yet by a long chalk."

But his face was grave and preoccupied as they drove back to Tiny's rooms.

"What do you think his next move will be, Ronald?"

"He will either try and leave the country at once, or he'll have a dip at you and me. My own candid opinion is the latter. You and I are the only two people who have seen him, and who know him for what he is. All the other people who have had dealings with him—Berendosi and the rest of them—have no idea whatever that he is a cold-blooded murderer. We do, and as long as we are alive he's not safe. We've broken up his show here, so the probability is that once he is out of the country it will be some time before he returns. And that is why I think he will try and do us in before he goes. He's desperate, and he'll run a big risk to get us out of the way. So for the love of Allah, old man, keep your eyes skinned."

"I'll do that all right. It's this cursed negative I'm thinking of."

"I agree. But the two things march together. If he gets us good-bye to any chance of ever seeing it."

The taxi pulled up, and Tiny got out. He cast a searching look up and down the street: as far as he could see there wasn't a soul in sight.

"Good night, old lad," said Standish. "Inspect your room with a microscope: sleep with your window shut: and meet me at Gillson's office at eleven to-morrow. We may hear something fresh about to-night's raid."

But though Tiny undressed he could not sleep. It was already dawn: his thoughts kept whirling chaotically. Round and round in a vicious circle they went, always finishing up with the negative. Had it all been in vain? Was this swine Zavier going to do them after all?

He went over the events of the night once more, Surely somewhere amongst the mass of papers they had obtained, they would find something which would put them on his trail. And then those bits of torn brown cloth. He had noticed that Ronald Standish had seemed strangely interested over them. Again and again his eyes had returned to the basket with a thoughtful look in them, as if he felt some clue lay there. And yet what could it be? That Giuseppi had lied over the dressing-gown was obvious, but beyond that it did not seem to advance them much.

In a way it was Mary he felt most sorry for. She had done so much—striven so hard, and though she had said very little, he knew how bitterly she had felt the disappointment. What a darling she was! He rose and began to pace up and down the room. Once or twice the previous day words had been trembling on the tip of his tongue—words he had bitten back. Instinctively he had felt that until this matter was settled one way or the other she would resent anything at all personal. Afterwards it would be different, and somehow he felt distinctly hopeful. There had been a moment in the taxi coming home, and another at supper before the raid, when he thought he had read the unmistakable message in her eyes. But for the time being all that must be in abeyance: to get on with the job was the order of the day.

At last he heard Murdoch moving about, and ringing the bell he ordered some breakfast. He wanted exercise: for the past week he seemed to have been permanently sitting in trains. And a brisk four miles finishing up with a bathe at the R.A.C. made life seem distinctly better.

It was still some time before he was to meet Standish at the Home Office, and going into the smoking-room he glanced over the morning papers. "The Hampstead Mystery," as it was called, occupied a prominent place in them all, and he picked up the *Daily Leader*.

"There is no doubt," ran the paragraph, "that Mr. Felton Blake was first stabbed by the young man who was found dead by the safe. The fingerprints on the handle of the dagger proves this conclusively. So that over his death there is no mystery. The strange part of the affair is the death of the murderer, who is at present unidentified. What happened in that room while the owner of the house lay dead on the floor? The safe was empty. What happened to the papers in the safe? Above all, who was the third man whose footprint was found in the blood by the window, a footprint which could not have been made by either of the dead men?"

He laid down the paper, and lit a cigarette. Precisely: what had happened to him? It was a question they all wanted answered. And then his thoughts turned to Standish's theory. Could it be correct, could it be that Joe Denver's death was an error, and unintentional? If so, what was this diabolical contrivance they were up against that murdered blindly?

It seemed almost incredible, and yet he was forced to admit that there was some force in Standish's argument. Once granted the negative had first been removed, why kill Denver? What possible object could it serve? No one but a madman murders needlessly.

At length he rose: he would go round and see Ronald. Then they could go together to meet Gillson. The more he thought over things the more hopelessly befogged did he feel: sitting still was an impossibility. He walked quickly, hardly noticing the greetings of two or three men he knew who passed him. And it was not until he turned into the street where Standish lived that he paused, his eyes narrowed, a sudden dreadful presentiment clutching at him. For outside his friend's house a crowd had gathered, and two policemen were standing in the door.

He elbowed his way through the people, heedless of angry remarks, and approached one of the constables.

"What has happened?" he said. "I was just coming round to see the gentleman who lives here."

"Well, sir," answered the man gravely, "I'm afraid you won't be able to. He's dead: burned to death."

"What!" shouted Tiny. "Good God! man, it's impossible. Why, I only left him three or four hours ago."

"Sorry, sir, but it's the truth. Fire engine's been gone some time."

"Can I go in?" said Tiny dazedly.

"No admittance, sir, unless the Inspector gives permission," said the constable firmly.

"Where is the Inspector? Ah! there he is."

It was the same officer who had raided the Fifty-Nine, and the instant he saw Tiny he beckoned him in.

"This is a bad business, sir," he said gravely.

"But it's unbelievable," cried Tiny. "Mr. Standish—burned to death."

The Inspector looked at him queerly.

"There's a bit more in this than meets the eye, sir. It's the rummiest fire I've ever seen."

"Damn the fire. Is he dead?"

"Yes, sir: he's dead, I'm sorry to say. Do you want to see him? It's not a pretty sight."

He followed the officer dazedly: the thing was so utterly unexpected that he felt stunned. It was inconceivable, a fantastic nightmare: he'd wake up soon, and find he'd been dreaming.

"There, sir." The Inspector opened the door of the room from which Ronald and he had started for their expedition to Felton Blake, and it was a moment or two before he could force himself to enter. The smell of smouldering wood was heavy in the air: the charred and blackened desk, dripping with water from the fire engine, was still smoking. But it was not on that that his eyes were riveted: it was on the twisted figure lying by the hearth-rug. The knees were drawn up almost to the chin, and by one blistered hand there lay the remnant of the cloth which had covered the little table standing by the arm-chair—the table on which his reading-lamp had always stood. It had been a fad of Ronald's—an oil lamp to read by, and now it lay smashed to pieces on the floor beside the body.

Here too everything was sopping wet: the rug, the chair, the body itself had all come under the hose. And at last with an effort he took a few steps forward and looked at the face. It was burned beyond recognition: a gruesome, terrible sight.

"My God! Inspector," he muttered, "it's awful. When did it happen?"

"Early this morning, sir," said the other.

"We went back with Lady Mary, and then he dropped me, and came on here."

"That would be about it, sir. It was dawn when the man on duty on this beat, saw smoke coming out of the window. He rang up the fire station at once, and they had no difficulty in putting it out. Apparently the oil was concentrated in a pool by his head, and was already nearly burned out. Then in the ordinary course of events the

Yard was notified. Now I was still working on the papers we got tonight, but as soon as I heard where the fire was I made a point of coming round myself. As you see, the features are unrecognizable. But that's the suit he was wearing: and that's the tie and tiepin he had on last night."

"Moreover," said Tiny, stooping down and looking at one of the hands, "that is his signet ring."

"It's Mr. Standish, sir, right enough," went on the other gravely. "But it's a mighty queer thing. I'd very much like to know what happened. The doctor suggests that he tried to beat out the flames with his hands: but it won't do, sir — it doesn't hold together."

"Why do you say that, Inspector?" said Tiny slowly.

"Try and reconstruct it, sir, and you'll see for yourself. Mr. Standish wasn't an invalid, or a cripple. He wasn't a man who suffered from heart trouble or fainting fits. There is that cloth by his hand, so it's clear that it was pulling it off the table that upset the lamp. But why should he pull the cloth off the table?"

"He might have fainted," suggested Tiny, "and clutched at the table to save himself."

"Even then, sir, a faint is a faint. That" — he pointed to the blackened face — "didn't take place in a minute, nor yet in two. Do you mean to tell me, that the agony which must have been caused by a burn like that wouldn't have brought him to. And then he wouldn't have gone on lying there. He'd have dashed about the room: he'd have shouted, put his coat over his head — done something, at any rate."

"What do you suggest, then?" said Tiny.

"He was dead before he fell, sir. It's another of the same cases. We know all about them at the Yard, and if Mr. Standish was right, and it's that man that gave us the slip who is at the bottom of them, it's he who was responsible for this. We know that poison acts suddenly at the last moment, and I believe that as he died he, as you said, clutched at the table, pulled off the cloth as he fell, and upset the lamp. But he was dead before he was burned."

"I believe you are right, Inspector," said Tiny slowly.

A cold, over-mastering rage was getting hold of him, the more dangerous because he was a man who was slow to anger. First Denver: then Ronald—his greatest friend.

"By the living God above," he went on quietly, "I'll get even with the fiend who did this thing. If it's Zavier, then Zavier shall pay to the uttermost farthing. If it's someone else, I'll get him if it takes me years."

The Inspector shook his head gravely.

"Be careful, sir. For unless I'm much mistaken, you are the next on the list."

"So much the better," said Tiny, his jaw set like a steel trap. "And even if I swing for it, Inspector, I'll kill the man who did this, so that his screams will be heard at the other end of London."

He turned on his heel abruptly, and left the room. Through the crowd outside he passed as if they were non-existent, and hailed a taxi. He would see Mary first, then he would put his affairs in order. And after that...

"I must see her ladyship, Simmonds. I can't help it if she is still in bed. Ask her to put on a wrap and come down to the boudoir."

Something in his face precluded further argument, and the butler went off to find Lady Mary's maid. And a few minutes later she came downstairs.

"What is it, Tiny?" she cried anxiously. "What's happened?"

"They've got Ronald," he said grimly. "Murdered him last night after he got back to his rooms."

Slowly the colour ebbed from her face, as she stared at him speechlessly.

"I've just been round there, and seen the dear old chap's body," he went on in the same ominous voice.

She listened in silence while he told her what had happened: then she went up to him and put her hands on his shoulders.

"I'm dreadfully sorry," she said gravely. "Sorry for him, and sorry for you too, old Tiny, for I know what pals you were. But it's not going to alter our plans, is it?"

"How do you mean, Mary?" he said.

"I mean that we—you and I—go on just the same," she cried. "We won't give up hope till the end."

"You bet your life we won't," he answered savagely. "There are several items now on Mister Zavier's account which have got to be settled. But there's just one thing, Mary dear, I'd like to say."

He hesitated a moment, and she didn't hurry him: only looked steadily into his eyes.

"I'm under no delusions," he went on quietly, "as to my capabilities. I'm a pretty average damned fool, and if this swine can catch a man like Ronald napping, the chances are that he will catch me as well."

Her hands tightened on his shoulders, but she still said nothing.

"I hadn't meant to say anything at present," he continued, "but this has altered things. You see, dear, as Ronald said last night after we left you, he and I were bound to be the object of Zavier's attentions, and now that he has been got it's my turn next. And in case he succeeds again I'd like you to know that what I said the other day wasn't a jest. I meant it with every fibre of my being. I love you."

"Same here, Tiny," she answered quietly. "In fact I've done so for a considerable time," she added with a little laugh.

"Mary, my dear."

His arms went round her, and for a moment or two she let him hold her with his lips on hers. Then very gently she pushed him away.

"For we'd never look each other straight in the face again," she said, "if we didn't do our damndest to beat this brute. So this is dangerous, old man—too dangerous altogether. It makes one want to ease up."

"My dear," he said, "believe me there was no thought of that in my mind."

"There was in mine, Tiny. Do you suppose, dear man, that I don't realize the danger you are running. And the mere thought of it makes me sick. So I want you to realize that I'm in it with you. Two heads are better than one, and it's more than likely I can help."

He looked at her doubtfully.

"I don't like it, my dear," he said slowly. "It's an infernal risk."

"Dry up," she laughed. "I don't know that I'll be able to do anything, but I'm going to have a shot at it. Now first of all let's try and see exactly where we stand."

"Not much difficulty about that, dear," he said shortly. "Zavier is after me, and I'm after Zavier. And if I was making a book I know which of the two would start favourite. I'm no match for the swine in cunning. Moreover, the devil of it is that as far as I can see it's a question of sitting down and waiting for him to strike. One can't go wandering through the streets of London looking for a man with light-blue eyes."

"If he strikes, Tiny," she said thoughtfully, "he's going to strike soon. He's not going to stop in this country a day longer than he can help. So we've just got to sit in one another's pockets for the next few days. Perhaps he'll make a slip: that's all we can hope for. You go round now to the Home Office and see this pal of yours there. Find out if anything fresh has materialized, and then come back here for lunch."

"Right you are, my dear." He caught her in his arms once again. "You adorable person," he muttered, and was gone.

He glanced up and down the street as he left, though he realized the futility of the precaution. If skilled men had failed to spot the enemy, he was hardly likely to succeed. Then he chartered a taxi and drove to the Home Office. He found Gillson as quiet and impassive as ever, studying the documents obtained in last night's raid.

"By God! Colonel," he burst out, "this is a foul business. I still simply can't believe it."

"Pretty grim, Carteret," said the other gravely. "I heard you'd been round."

"Do you agree with the Inspector that he was murdered?" asked Tiny.

"Looks remarkably like it," answered Gillson. "Well—that is the end of it."

"End of it be damned," cried Tiny. "You don't imagine I'm going to let this drop now, do you? Zavier may get that negative through to Berendosi—that I'm afraid he's bound to do now. But he's killed my best pal, and either he or I are going to follow Ronald."

"Good for you, Carteret." A gleam of approval showed in Gillson's eyes. "But I'm afraid you will find the dice loaded pretty heavily against you."

"No one realizes that more than I do," said the other doggedly. "But it just can't be helped. Have you found out anything from those?"

He pointed to the papers on the table.

"A lot," answered Gillson. "Enough to put half a dozen of them in prison for a long stretch, But of the one vital thing we wanted—not a word. There is nothing that gives us a clue to Zavier, or his main headquarters."

A clerk entered with a type-written sheet of paper.

"Will that do, sir?" he said handing it to Gillson, who read it.

"That is all right," he answered. And then, on a sudden impulse he passed it to Tiny.

"A shocking tragedy occurred in the early hours of this morning," it ran, "which but for the prompt action of the Fire Brigade might have ended in a disastrous fire. Smoke was seen issuing from one of the rooms of 10 Hooper Street by a constable on duty. He gave the alarm at once, and the outbreak was soon extinguished. Unfortunately the owner of the rooms, Mr. Ronald Standish, perished in the flames. His body was discovered afterwards so badly burned as to be practically unrecognizable. Identification was only possible through the deceased man's clothes and his signet ring. The accident appears to have been caused by an oil reading-lamp upsetting."

Without a word Tiny handed it back, and not until the clerk left the room did he speak.

"For the Press, I suppose," he said. "Why no word about the murder?"

"What's the good?" answered the other. "There is enough hue and cry already without adding to it."

He rose and stood by the window, hands deep in his trouser pockets, and Tiny contemplated his back with rising anger.

"Damn it! Colonel," he exploded at length, "you seem to take the old chap's murder pretty calmly."

"How else is one to take it, Carteret?" said Gillson. "There is no good running round in small circles biting the blotting paper. They've got Ronald, and there is no more to be said."

"Isn't there, by Jove," cried the other. "Do you imagine I'm going to let the matter drop?"

"Well—what do you propose to do?"

"Find this man Zavier if it takes me the rest of my life."

"How are you going to set about it? Look here, my dear fellow," went on Gillson kindly, "I know what you are feeling: I know you are mad with rage. But don't let that distort your vision. As I've told you, the dice are loaded far too heavily against you. And for any chance of success we have got to get them a bit more evenly balanced."

"How do you suggest we should do it?" demanded Tiny.

"Ever done any big-game shooting, Carteret?"

Tiny stared at him in amazement.

"No—never."

"First you get a nice tree, and in that tree you build yourself a place where you can sit. Then you get a goat and you put it on the ground not far from the tree. Then you wait for the tiger to come and feed. And then you shoot the tiger—perhaps."

He swung round and faced Tiny, with the glint of a smile in his eyes.

"See the point?"

"Can't say I do."

"You are the goat. Only I'd prefer that you come out of the performance alive."

"Deuced considerate of you, Colonel," said Tiny with a grin.

"The flying fellers did it in the war," went on the other. "Sent slow machines over the Boche lines fairly low to attract the wily Hun. Then when Fritz was engaged in what looked like a soft job our fast fighters, who had been up much higher, came down on top of him. Bait, young Carteret—that is what you have got to be. Provided, of course, you feel like going on with it."

"You can take that for granted," answered Tiny quietly.

"Good for you. Though I tell you quite candidly that I don't think the decision lies in your hands. Whether you want to or not, you'll have to go through with it: the other bloke is going to see to that. He wants your head on a charger, and he won't feel safe until he's got it."

"Quite a number of people seem to share your opinion," remarked Tiny resignedly. "But there's one point, since we are on the subject, that might be a bit clearer. The goat we know, and the tiger, but who is the bird who is going to sit in the tree?"

"I'll see to that, Carteret," said the other. "You'll have to trust me there implicitly. All I propose to tell you is that he's the best man available, and if it is humanly possible he won't let you down."

"Well, if that's all you can tell me, I suppose I'll have to be content with it. What do you want me to do?"

"Nothing," answered the other. "Just live your ordinary life as if this affair had never been. Of what to warn you against, I know no more than you. We're still as much in the dark as ever as to how he commits these murders. So take every precaution you can, and we can only hope for the best. If he thinks you've dropped the thing, he may get careless."

He rose and held out his hand.

"Good luck, Carteret. It's not a pleasant job: in fact it's damned unpleasant. But I'd like to feel we'd got a bit of our own back over Ronald."

"By Gad! you're right, sir," cried Tiny. "So the motto is, Business as usual."

"That's it," said the other, and Tiny turning at the door saw that Gillson was already immersed again in the documents in front of him.

He walked slowly along the passage and out into the street. That Gillson was right, he realized. Since the chances of his finding Zavier in London were infinitesimal, the only thing to do was to wait until Zavier found him. And that was a simple matter, especially if he lived his normal life. His rooms were known: his club was known: there was no secrecy about his movements. In fact it all seemed delightfully simple—a feeling doubtless shared by the goat.

He paused in the Park, and looked behind him. Was one of that hurrying crowd the man with the gun who was sitting in the tree? And was another of them the tiger? And then he realized suddenly that he was doing a foolish thing. When it is business as usual, one does not stop and peer into the faces of passers-by. If he was going to play the part he would play it properly. He would blot out the events of the last few days from his mind as Gillson had said. Was it not beer time, and there was at least an hour before he was due to lunch with Mary.

He strolled along Pall Mall, and turned into his club. Already the news about Ronald seemed to have got round, and he was immediately besieged by members clamouring for details. Mindful of the official statement he had been shown he made no mention of the word murder, and as soon as he could he shook them off and buried himself behind a paper. Here at any rate he could relax: Zavier couldn't get him in his own club.

And that brought him back to the question of Mary. When they had decided to join forces, he had not seen Gillson. The whole thing had been vague and indefinite. Now a very different complexion had been put on the matter. In the rôle of goat which he now had to fill, the one place of all others where she must not be was anywhere near him. The danger was far too great.

He hesitated for awhile as to whether he would ring her up and say he was not coming to lunch, but thinking it over he decided to go after all. There was a lot to explain to her, and it could not be done over the telephone. But lunch was going to be positively their last appearance together until things were settled one way or the other. She would make a fuss about it, he knew, but her objections would have to be got over. It would cramp his style and spoil his nerve far too much if he felt there was any risk for her. The game had got to be played as a lone hand, with the man in the tree a shadowy figure in the background.

At a quarter to one he left the club, wondering what was the best way to persuade her. If he stressed the danger side of it it was quite sufficient to make a girl like her all the more determined to face it with him. And if he did not there was no valid reason why she should back out. And he was still undecided when he pressed the bell. He would have to stress the point that it would make it more difficult for him.

Tiny Carteret

Mechanically he handed his hat and stick to Simmonds, and walked towards the boudoir, suddenly to become aware that the butler was delivering himself of startled noises.

"What's the matter?" he said turning round. "Her ladyship is expecting me to lunch, isn't she?"

"But, sir," stammered the man, "Her ladyship went with you to Paris by the midday boat train."

Tiny stood very still. The statement was so staggeringly unexpected, that for a moment or two his brain refused to act. All that he was conscious of was the monotonous ticking of the hall clock.

"What in Heaven's name are you talking about?" he got out at length. "To Paris—with me?"

"Well, sir, I'll tell you what happened. And Janet here can bear me out."

Tiny looked round to see that the maid had appeared, and was looking at him in amazement.

"About half an hour after you left this morning, sir," went on the butler, "a lady called. She wanted to see her ladyship and she told me to say that she was a friend of a Countess Mazarin. Also that it was urgent, and that she had just come from you. She held a letter in her hand, sir, which however, she did not give to me. I at once told Janet, and as her ladyship was dressed she came down immediately. She took the letter, and read it through standing here in the hall. And then, sir, though it didn't strike me at the time, not thinking that anything could be wrong, a most extraordinary expression came on her face. She had half turned her back on the other lady, and only I could see it. It was—how shall I say, sir—sort of half puzzled and amazed. And then it changed. Her frown went away, and she got that look, sir, that I remember when she was a kiddy, and was told not to do a thing she wanted to do. She'd made up her mind.

"'There's only just time to catch the train,' she said, turning to the other lady. 'Will you walk into my parlour?' she went on, and it was such a funny thing for her to say, that I stared at her—'Will you walk into my parlour while I throw a few things into a bag?'

"She went upstairs, sir, and for some reason Janet wasn't there. Anyway she was down again in a minute carrying her little dressing-case. Then she went into the boudoir, and the two of them came out together.

"'I hadn't expected to go to Paris at quite such short notice,' she said as she passed me, 'I do hope Mr. Carteret will catch the train.'

"And that's all I know, sir. But you will understand how surprised I was to see you."

"What on earth can it all mean?" said Tiny dazedly. "I never had the slightest intention of going to Paris."

Mechanically he had opened the door of the boudoir, and now he stood staring round the room. A letter was lying on the writing-table, and as his eyes fell on it they slowly dilated in amazement. Then, heedless of the two servants, he darted across the room and picked it up.

"A scrawl, dear," it ran, "to say that the most extraordinary development has taken place. The bearer of this note is a pal of Nada Mazarin, who is in Paris now. She wants us both to go over there by the eleven o'clock boat train. Hotel Majestic. Will catch it if I possibly can. Tiny."

He stood by the table as if carved out of stone while the two servants watched him anxiously.

"Is this the note that woman brought?" he asked at length.

"From the glimpse I got of the envelope, sir," said Simmonds, "it looks the same writing."

"I suppose we are not all mad," remarked Tiny.

He read through the note once again: then with a hopeless gesture he threw it back on the desk. *For the writing was the writing of Ronald Standish.*

"For the love of Allah, Simmonds, give me a drink. I've got to try and think this thing out."

He threw himself into a chair. What on earth did the thing mean? Why should Ronald write a letter to her and sign it "Tiny" after he was dead? For a time a wild hope surged up in him. Did it mean that Ronald was alive: that the scorched and blackened body had belonged to someone else? But he soon dismissed the possibility, principally because he failed to see, even with the wildest stretch of imagination, what possible object could have been served by sending such a note if it was Ronald who had done it. He would have known that Mary would spot it at once as a forgery.

A forgery: the thing was a forgery. That was obvious. Someone had written her a note purporting to come from him, and had committed the trifling error of employing the wrong writing. How it had happened was beside the point: even the fact that it was Ronald's writing was not the main issue—as far as he knew Mary had never seen it. But she had sampled his own often enough. Therefore, she had realized it was a forgery. Why, then, had she gone to Paris?

And gradually light dawned on him. Deliberately, and with her eyes open she had walked into the trap. Her remark to the woman which had stuck in Simmonds' mind came back to him.

"Will you walk into my parlour?"

He supplied the end without difficulty. With complete disregard of danger she had elected to play the rôle of the fly, in an endeavour to locate the spider. He could see it all: the puzzled frown as she first read the letter: the sudden set of that small jaw as she came to a decision. And then the calm carrying through of the thing so that the woman should not suspect that she suspected.

"You priceless kid," he muttered ecstatically.

She had left the letter there on the desk on purpose that he should see it. She knew that the instant he did, he would realize the error, and act accordingly. And she had been careful not even to telephone him, for fear of rousing the woman's suspicions. All the information he required was given by the note.

Exactly: and the fact started another train of thought. What was their object in getting Mary to Paris. Obviously as bait for him. It was Gillson's plan over again, only this time he was to be the tiger and Mary the goat. And suddenly he began to laugh: they did not lack audacity.

He grew grave again. Astoundingly plucky though she was, this was no show for a girl to be in alone. It was time he got a move on. The Hotel Majestic was his destination, and at once. Gillson's instructions must go by the board: this development altered everything. Mary was first, second and last. The two o'clock service would not get him there until ten, which was too late. A special aeroplane was the only thing.

"Get me a car, Simmonds," he cried. "At once. Then ring up the Home Office."

He would speak to Gillson, explaining what had happened. But when he got through Gillson was not to be found, nor had he arrived at his club. And so he scribbled a note, and gave it to Simmonds to send round. Then, the car having arrived, he started for Croydon, nearly knocking down a man from the Telephone Exchange as he ran down the steps.

"Bloke seems in a bit of an 'urry," said the man. "Is this 'ere the habode of Lady Mary Ridgeway?"

"It is," said Simmonds. "And what might you be wanting?"

"She's put in a complaint about the hextension of 'er telephone. Lead me to it, Gussie."

"In there," remarked Simmonds coldly. "And kindly reserve your funny business for them that appreciate it."

"Try sitting on a drawing pin, Adolphus," laughed the other. "You look dead from the neck down. This room, is it?"

He went to the instrument, and for a few moments Simmonds watched him from the door. Then he stalked majestically to his own quarters.

And with his departure the interest of the telephone operator in his job faded rapidly. His eyes darted round the room, to rivet themselves on the note Tiny had thrown down on the desk. And if Tiny had been amazed, this man seemed literally dumbfounded as he read the letter.

A door opened somewhere, and he returned to the instrument.

"Seems all right now, Clarence," he said as Simmonds reappeared. "Only I won't guarantee it if you breathe down it. So long, matey."

Two hours later the second private aeroplane of the day rose from Croydon. Moreover, its occupant bore a striking resemblance to a certain very temporary member of the London telephone staff.

CHAPTER XI

It was seven o'clock that night that Tiny realized how completely he had blundered. Since five he had been sitting in the entrance-hall of the Majestic, watching the door. A consignment of Americans from London had arrived by the Golden Arrow: a few more people had come by the ordinary boat train, but of Mary there had been no sign. And at last he saw what a fool he had been. The other side had never had any intention of her going to the Majestic at all.

He marvelled that such an obvious point could have escaped him. How could they let Mary meet him in a crowded hotel lounge? Believing as they did that the letter they had forged to her was in his writing, they would assume that she was quite unsuspicious. But at the first word she spoke to Tiny she would realize the whole trap. That, naturally, was the way they must look at it.

So it boiled down to the fact that he had come at maximum speed to the one spot in the whole of Europe where there was not the slightest chance of finding her. And the point now arose as to what would be the next move on their part. That Zavier would know by this time that he had come to the Majestic was practically a certainty. Any one of the men—or women—sitting round him might be a spy. So what was going to happen now?

He could do nothing himself except sit and wait. It was the rôle of the goat to perfection, and had it not been for the maddening anxiety over Mary he could have obtained a certain amount of cynical amusement out of it. But what were they doing with her? Common sense told him that it was unlikely she would come to any physical harm: from Zavier's point of view such a thing would be foolish, because it was unnecessary. And as long as she continued to act her part of suspecting nothing she would, at any rate, be safe. Nevertheless, the mere thought of her playing a lone hand drove him nearly crazy with worry. She might be literally anywhere: she might not even be in Paris. If he could even know that it would be something.

And it was at that stage in his reflections that happening to look up he saw one of Cook's couriers standing by the concierge's desk. The man caught his eye at the same moment, and after a momentary hesitation saluted. And it suddenly dawned on Tiny that not only was he from the Gare du Nord, but that he was the identical man who had on one occasion looked after Mary and a pal of hers who was ill, when they were going to Nice. Tiny had gone as far as Paris with them himself, and he recognized the man perfectly. He was evidently fixing up some luggage question, and acting on a sudden impulse Tiny crossed and spoke to him. Only a hundred-to-one chance? but still a chance. Had he seen Mary?

"Lady Mary Ridgeway, sir? Why, funnily enough—I did. I was standing outside, where you get a taxi, and I saw her plain."

"Was anyone with her?"

"Another lady, sir. They got into a car and drove off."

"What sort of a car?"

"A big private one, sir. One of the large Renaults."

"You didn't hear where they went?"

"No, sir: I didn't. They just got in and the car went straight away."

The man hesitated a moment, and looked at Tiny curiously.

"Seemed to me, sir, as if her ladyship was expecting someone. She kept looking round over her shoulder, and peering into the crowd."

Tiny thanked him and resumed his seat. Of course, she'd been looking for him. He should have met the train, not sat doing nothing in the hotel. And yet as things panned out he couldn't have done much good. Following a Renault is somewhat beyond the powers of a Paris taxi. For all that he cursed himself for not having been there: he would have stopped the whole thing then and there.

In an overwhelming wave all his fears had come back to him. There was something ominous about that big car driving straight away, without a word to the driver. Just one more link in the skilfully constructed chain that seemed to be tightening round them. And there was a ruthless efficiency about it all that made him feel helpless. If only he could do something, and not merely have to sit and wait.

At length he went in to dinner. Either there would be a further development soon, or they were going to try and get him in the hotel: anyway food was indicated. He had had nothing to eat since breakfast, and hunger is a bad preparation for a crisis. And he felt instinctively that one was approaching: Zavier would not delay an instant longer than necessary. He glanced round the room wondering if any of his fellow-diners were even shadowing him. Most of them were in evening clothes, and it was at the others that he principally directed his attention. But after a while the futility of the proceeding struck him, and he concentrated on his meal. They could recognize him, and he couldn't recognize them; at that it had to be left.

Suddenly he became aware that a new-comer had sat down at the next table. He was a thin, sandy haired little man, and his clothes—although scrupulously neat—showed signs of wear. The elbow he lifted as he studied the menu shone suspiciously in the light, and Tiny shrewdly suspected that the seat of his trousers would reveal the same story. In short, not the type of customer one would expect at the Majestic, and for that reason Tiny studied him covertly.

After a while he realized the man was shooting quick little bird-like glances at him, and instantly all his suspicions were aroused. Was the next move about to start? He continued his dinner calmly, only moving his chair just sufficiently to enable him to watch the man more easily. A feeling of relief had come over him: anything was better than inaction. And he felt certain the new-comer was one of the players.

It was ten minutes, however, before the game started, and then the opening gambit was so unexpected that he almost decided he had been mistaken.

"I suppose, sir, you can't tell me what has happened in the Yorkshire and Middlesex match?"

Tiny stared at him blankly: so the man was English.

"I'm afraid I can't," he said at length. "You are interested in cricket?" he added perfunctorily.

"Very. I play for my bank here."

A bank clerk, was he? And bank clerks do not generally dine at the Majestic.

"Am I right, sir, in supposing that you are Mr. Carteret, the Rugby player?"

Getting down to it, reflected Tiny, but what the deuce was coming next?

"My name is Carteret," he answered briefly.

"I thought so," said the other. "It was lucky I'd seen your photograph so often in the papers, otherwise I might not have been able to help the lady."

"What's that; you're saying?" said Tiny tensely.

"There's danger, sir, danger. Finish your dinner quickly and come to the bar. I daren't talk here."

"I've finished," said Tiny. "I'll wait for you there."

He settled his bill, and left the room. Then he went to the bar where the other joined him almost immediately.

"Now, sir," he said, after a cautious glance round. "I'll tell you all I know. I'd been on my bicycle to see some friends outside Paris, and I came back through the Porte de la Gare. That would be about half-past six. Drawn up by the side of the road was one of the big Renaults, and inside it were two ladies. Something had evidently gone wrong, because the bonnet was up and the chauffeur and another man were bending over the engine. Just as I got alongside, one of the ladies got out and went and stood by the two men. She seemed to be talking to them earnestly.

"Well, I don't know why, but I happened to look at the other one who was still inside the car, and it fairly gave me a shock. She was staring at me fixedly, and suddenly she deliberately opened the window and dropped her vanity bag on the road. Deliberately, sir: no question of an accident. Of course, that attracted my attention still more. I was pushing my machine at the time, and I stopped at once and handed back the bag.

"She took it, and at the same instant, I felt a twisted note pushed into my hand.

"'Merci,' she said.

"'Not at all,' I answered.

"'Thank God! you're English,' she muttered. 'Give that to Mr. Carteret—Majestic Hotel. There's danger. It's urgent.'

"'The football player?' I asked.

"'That's the one,' she answered, and then she gave a smile. 'Thank you so much for picking it up.'

"For a moment I couldn't understand: then I saw the other lady was watching us. So I took off my hat, and mounted my bike."

"Have you got the note?" interrupted Tiny.

"Here it is, sir."

He handed the slip of paper to Tiny, who unrolled it eagerly. Inside, in a hurried scrawl which, however, was obviously Mary's, was the one word "Brig."

"What the devil does it mean?" he muttered.

"Well, Mr. Carteret," said the other a little apologetically, "I have to admit that I took a liberty. The whole thing was so strange that when I got out of sight I dismounted and opened the note. 'Brig,' I said to myself, 'that's a funny message.' And after a time I turned my machine and rode back again, to find that the car had gone. Now I happen to know one of the men at that gate very well—I use it a lot—and acting on an impulse I decided to have a talk with him. Quite casually I turned the conversation round to the big car.

"It appeared that the chauffeur had been cursing like blazes at the breakdown, because he had such a long drive in front of him. My pal had said that there was a second driver, and the chauffeur had remarked that they wanted three on such a trip.

'Four hundred and fifty kilometres to the frontier,' he had grumbled, 'and another two hundred on.'

"Well, that was all I could get out of him, so I got on my bike again and went back to my rooms. Now it so happens that I'm a bit of a map fiend, and what with this curious message and the chauffeur's remarks, I got down some of my maps and had a look. And I can't help thinking I've solved it: in fact I'm sure I have."

"What do you make of it?" said Tiny eagerly.

"First of all, Mr. Carteret, take the gate they were leaving by—the Porte de la Gare. That's the gate you leave by for Dijon, and after that Switzerland."

He paused impressively, while Tiny possessed his soul in patience.

"Secondly," went on the little man, "the Swiss frontier is just about four hundred and fifty kilometres from Paris."

"By Jove!" said Tiny, as Ronald's words in Lausanne came back to him. "I believe you're right."

"Well, if I'm right so far, sir, I have solved it. Brigue, which is the Swiss end of the Simplon tunnel, is another two hundred or so kilometres farther on. They spell it both ways—Brigue and Brig."

He glanced at his watch.

"Just half-past eight, Mr. Carteret. There's a train at 9.10. If you hurry you can catch it."

For a moment Tiny hesitated. Was it genuine, or was it all part of some elaborate trap? And then with a shrug of his shoulders he made up his mind. Anything was better than staying on in the Majestic.

"I'm much obliged to you," he said, holding out his hand. "I'll go at once."

He hurried over to the concierge's desk to confirm the time of the train, and countermanded his room. A Frenchman with a small pointed, black beard was having an excited argument over something, but he politely stood on one side as Tiny approached.

"9.10, Monsieur. That is correct. Shall I get you a taxi?" He gave an order to a chausseur. "Will you be wanting a sleeper?"

He paused as the Frenchman made some remark.

"Because, if so, sir," he went on, "this gentleman suggests that you might perhaps care to share one with him."

"Thank you," said Tiny grimly. "I shall not be wanting a sleeper."

No more sleepers for him, he reflected, unless he knew his fellow-traveller. And a Frenchman with a beard struck him quite definitely as being a suspicious character under existing circumstances. Not that he could be, of course: he had been talking to the concierge before Tiny came up. But the principle held. No unknown men: certainly no unknown beavers.

"The taxi is here, sir," said the concierge, and the last words Tiny heard as he left the hotel were—"*Un autre, pour Monsieur.*"

The train was not full, and he had no difficulty in getting a first-class corner seat. On purpose he chose a compartment that was not empty: though he had no intention of sleeping he was not neglecting any precaution. And by no stretch of imagination could anyone already seated in one particular carriage selected at random, be involved in the matter: the coincidence would be too extraordinary.

He selected a corner next to the corridor, and it was just as the train started that he got a bit of a shock. Standing in the door of the next compartment was Black Beard. True—if looked at from one point of view there was nothing very surprising in the fact. From what the concierge had said the man was going to travel by this train, and probably he had been unable to get a sleeper. That was all there was to it, and yet...

Zavier, when the Fifty-Nine Club had been raided, had worn a beard. Was it possible that this man was Zavier himself? As far as he remembered his eyes were not blue, but he had taken very little notice of him at the Majestic. Anyway, that was a point which could easily be settled. He went into the corridor, and looked into the next compartment. The man had put on a pair of tinted glasses, and was reading a newspaper.

Tiny returned to his seat and shut the door. Was it Zavier? could it be? If so, was he going to strike on the train? His jaw set grimly. Ass he might be, but at any rate on this occasion he was forewarned. And he proposed to give the gentleman a run for his money. If only he was not in such an agonizing condition of uncertainty over Mary....

Came Laroche, and his mind went back to the last time he had done this same journey. It was there, according to Ronald, they had got the Russian, and instinctively he kept his eyes glued on the small expanse of open window opposite him. Would some strange mysterious thing come through and strike him? Then he happened to glance into the corridor: the bearded man was standing outside his compartment watching him intently. For an instant he had a wild idea of tackling him then and there: but he dismissed it. So long as he kept his door shut nothing could get at him from that side at any rate, and his job was to get to Brigue.

At last the train started again and Tiny relaxed. Strong as his nerves were the strain was beginning to tell on him, and he found himself longing for the daylight. And then, to keep his mind occupied he tried to work out a plan of campaign for what he should do when he arrived at Brigue. He remembered the place hazily—a small typical Swiss town at the east end of the Rhone valley. It seemed the last place in the world where one would expect to meet with adventure, and yet the little clerk's solution appeared correct. Moreover, Ronald had said that the headquarters were somewhere in Switzerland.

But what to do when he got there was the problem. Presumably there would be no difficulty in tracing such a conspicuous car as a big Renault if it had already reached the place: and if the train got there first he could keep a look-out for it. After that events would have to shape themselves.

Dawn came at length and he stretched himself wearily. The bearded man had not appeared again: the halts at Dijon and the subsequent station had passed without incident. At Lausanne his fellow-travellers alighted, and from then on he had the carriage to himself. An attendant announced breakfast, and Tiny, after a moment's hesitation, rose and stepped into the corridor. After all, nothing much could happen in broad daylight. And the next instant he laughed softly to himself. The next compartment was empty: the bearded man was no longer there.

"Might have had an easier night, if I'd known that," he reflected. "The wretched fellow was probably a harmless commercial traveller."

At eleven o'clock they reached Brigue, and for a while he stood undecided on the platform. He had vaguely thought of the possibility of some message awaiting him, but there was no one who looked in the least like a messenger. He would have to make for the town and ask there. The local *gendarme*, however, proved the first difficulty. Doubtless the worthy man did his best, but at the end of five minutes all he could do was gravely to indicate the church. Then, with a hoarse grunt of satisfaction at having at last interpreted Tiny's question, he relapsed into his habitual stupor.

It was an hotel proprietor who stepped into the breach.

"Can I be of any assistance, sir?" he asked in perfect English.

Tiny heaved a sigh of relief.

"I'm trying to find out," he explained, "if a big Renault car has passed through here this morning? It would have come from Paris, with two ladies on board and two chauffeurs."

The other shook his head.

"Not that I'm aware of, sir. But I will make inquiries, and if you would care to come into the hotel, I can put you in an excellent position."

He led the way to a small beer garden fronting the main street.

"Now, sir," he said, "anyone coming from Paris must pass you here. The road forks down there to the left—one branch over the Simplon, the other over the Furka. So whichever pass they are going to take, they must come by here."

"Splendid fellow," cried Tiny. "Send out a magnum of ale."

Tiny Carteret

And even as he spoke his eyes narrowed. A man had crossed the street some thirty yards away, and he could have sworn it was the bearded Frenchman of the Majestic. He half rose, then sank back again in his chair: the man had disappeared. It was useless to try and follow him, if not dangerous, but it gave Tiny a jolt. Why had he changed his carriage in the train, and what was he doing in Brigue?

The beer came and, with great rapidity, was gone. And after awhile Tiny began to feel drowsy. Periodically a car passed along the hot, airless street, but of the big Renault there was no sign. And with increasing frequency his head fell forward as he dozed. Which perhaps was just as well for his peace of mind. For had he been his usual alert self he might have noticed a strange phenomenon in the window of a house some thirty yards away. For curtains do not move suddenly when there is no wind unless someone is there touching them. And had that elementary fact penetrated Tiny's brain, he might have seen a small object which lay on the sill — circular and black: an object which bore a strange resemblance to the muzzle of a gun when pointed at the observer. And had he got as far as that he might have looked even more closely. In which case he might have caught a glimpse through the opening of the curtains of a black-bearded face peering motionless and patiently over the sights of a rifle. And the analogy of the tiger and the goat might have struck him unpleasantly. But none of these things happened: he dozed.

A hand on his shoulder awoke him with a start: the hotel proprietor was standing at his side.

"Monsieur," he said gravely, "I fear I have some bad news for you. Is your name Carteret?"

"It is," said Tiny, getting up. "What's the matter?"

And then he noticed that behind the speaker a monk was standing.

"There has been an accident, sir — a bad accident."

With a gesture he indicated the monk.

"My son," said the latter in a deep voice, "you must prepare for a shock. Early this morning there were brought to the monastery two men and two women. One of the men was dead, and one of the women: the others were badly injured. It appeared that their car had overturned at a dangerous corner, and fallen some thirty feet into a ravine. Two hours ago the injured lady recovered consciousness. She could barely speak, but she kept saying—'Monsieur Carteret—Brigue. Monsieur Carteret—Brigue.' So the Brother in charge sent me to see if I could find you."

"Get a car quick," said Tiny curtly.

"My son," answered the monk, "we have a car at the monastery. It is outside now."

"What about a doctor?"

"A doctor is with her now."

"Is there no hope?"

The monk crossed himself.

"It is in the hands of *le bon Dieu*. Come: the car is on the other side of the hotel."

Almost stunned by the unexpectedness of it, Tiny followed the monk. Mary dying: the thing was impossible.

"But how did it happen?" he cried distractedly.

Laboriously the monk wound up an ancient Fiat, and climbed in.

"On the road to Gletsch, my son, are many dangerous turnings. Moreover, in places it is very narrow. Last night in the mountains there was rain, and one stretch in particular became greasy. It was there that it happened. The car must have skidded: that is all we can think."

"Can't you get some more speed out of this cursed machine?" muttered Tiny.

"My son," said the other gently, "we are only a poor order. What little we have is given to *les pauvres*—not used in buying a new car."

"Sorry," grunted Tiny. "Only, you see I happen to be engaged to the lady. Do we pass the place where the accident occurred?"

"No. It is a mile beyond our doors. The villagers carried the bodies to us."

They drove in silence, till they came to a place like the side of a cliff, up which the road zigzagged. And it was when they were half way up that, looking down, Tiny saw below them another car with a solitary man in it. The driver's face was hidden by his hat, but a glance told him that the car was a Lancia, and therefore capable of some three times the speed of his present conveyance.

"There's a man behind us in a fast car," he said. "Do you mind if I ask him for a lift when he overtakes us?"

"Certainly," answered the monk. "I understand what you must be feeling. We will stop him when he passes us."

But though Tiny, glancing back from time to time, could see the other car it never appeared to get any nearer. The driver seemed to be deliberately regulating his speed by the Fiat, and after a while he resigned himself to his present conveyance. And then, at last, when he felt he could bear it no longer, his companion spoke.

"Nearly there," he said. "That building on the left is the monastery."

Tiny took a deep breath: in a few moments now he would know the worst. Was she still alive? Was there any hope? With a creaking of brakes the car pulled up, and he dashed to the door.

"Patience, my son," said the deep voice behind him. "We have rules in our fraternity which must be obeyed."

Chafing with impatience Tiny waited while the monk knocked three times on the door. And so completely impervious was he to everything save the thought of Mary, that he did not even notice that the Lancia had pulled up some twenty yards away, while the driver peered under the bonnet as if to discover some defect.

At length a small panel slid back and he saw a pair of eyes looking at him. Then his companion said something in a language he did not know, and the door was opened.

"Is the lady dead?" he cried in an agony of apprehension.

Once again there was a remark in an unknown tongue, and then the monk who had driven him turned to him with a smile.

"No, my son: she is not. And the doctor is most hopeful. Follow me."

He led the way along a stone corridor, with Tiny at his heels, until he came to a large vaulted room—a room which was divided into two parts by a steel grille.

"Wait here," he said. "I will find the doctor, and bring him to you."

His footsteps echoed on the stone flags till they died away in the distance. And Tiny, fuming at the delay strode up and down the room. Suddenly he paused. From the direction of the front door had come a short stifled groan. He listened intently: it was not repeated. And then, for the first time, he became aware of the deathly silence of the place. Not a sound of a voice: not a sound of any sort. The building was like a tomb. He walked over to the steel grille and examined it: it was let into the stone-work on each side, and reached right up to the ceiling. In each half of the room were a table and chair, and he concluded that it must be the place where the monks interviewed callers.

He turned round: would the doctor never come? A grille similar to the one he had been examining was slowly closing across the entrance to the room. For a moment he stood rigid—too amazed to move: then, with a shout, he dashed at it. And even as he reached it, it clanged home.

He tugged at it desperately: it was as immovable as the one in the centre of the room. And suddenly he realized the truth: the whole thing was a trap into which he had not only walked, but had galloped at full speed. Instinctively his hand went to his pocket, and he cursed savagely. His revolver was in his bag at the hotel.

"That simplifies matters, doesn't it, Mr. Carteret," came a suave voice, and he swung round.

Standing on the other side of the central grille was another monk—a monk with pale-blue, unwinking eyes. He was face to face with Zavier himself.

"Had you had your revolver I might have had to forgo the pleasure of a little chat with you," continued Zavier genially. "Dodging bullets in a room like this with nasty stone walls is not a pastime I care about."

"Damn you," said Tiny between his teeth. "How is Lady Mary?"

"As far as I know, in the very best of health," answered the other. "But whether she is still in Paris, or has returned to London I can't tell you."

"So the whole thing has been a lie from beginning to end."

A futile rage had seized him, which even the knowledge that Mary was safe did little to calm.

"Naturally," laughed Zavier. "But really, Mr. Carteret, you were a little too easy. I mean one does like a certain amount of run for one's money."

"What the devil are you going to do with me? Murder me, I suppose, like the others, you damned swine."

"I fear that that is your ultimate end undoubtedly," agreed Zavier. "You see, my dear Mr. Carteret, I have the gravest objection to people being at large who know me: or rather, I might put it, who associate me with my activities."

"Get it over, for God's sake," shouted Tiny. "You can play me like a sitting hen if you want to."

"True: very true. But at the moment I don't want to. As I said before, I should like a little chat. It is so rare, Mr. Carteret, that one has the chance of discussing things with one's adversaries in safety. And I have a little pardonable vanity, you know. Now the first time I met you was in the sleeper just after that foolish fellow Demeroff had paid the just penalty for his offence."

"So you were the monk, were you?" said Tiny, interested in spite of himself.

"I was the monk. And my object in visiting your compartment, my dear fellow, was not, believe me, to breathe a prayer over the dear departed, but to make quite sure that the right one of you had departed. By the way, that reminds me. From information I have received I am given to understand that considerable doubt exists in the minds of the authorities as to how these regrettable accidents take place. Am I right?"

"Go to hell," grunted Tiny.

"Well, if you won't answer, you won't. Still, my information is generally reliable. To turn to another subject. What do you think of this idea of mine for disguise purposes? You have no idea how free from suspicion a monk or a nun remains. If one twiddles a few beads, and mutters hoarsely under one's breath, the police of two continents hold up the traffic for you. Besides, on occasions, when the attentions of those who one wishes to avoid become too pressing, and ports are being watched and things like that, I have found but little difficulty in prevailing upon the master of some small tramp to smuggle me on board. I plead extreme poverty and thereby touch his heart. However, I fear I shall have to adopt something new in the future."

He sighed, and lit one of his little cigarettes.

"Yes, I shall have to think of something fresh. I could not destroy that cassock at the Fifty-Nine Club, and it can't be long before your admirable police appreciate its significance. In fact, I wouldn't be surprised if your friend Mr. Standish hadn't spotted the truth before his regrettable end. Burned to death. Poor fellow!"

"You nauseating hypocrite," snarled Tiny. "You know perfectly well he was not burned to death. You murdered him, as you murdered young Denver."

"Come, come, Mr. Carteret, believe me you are wrong there. True, the young man died, but I can assure you that it was the last thing I intended. You see, I happened to know that you and Standish proposed to pay Blake a visit, and it was for you that the scene was laid. And then your young friend Denver went and butted in in front of you."

"How did you know Standish and I were going there?"

"My dear sir, you under-estimate my resources. For what other reason would you wire Lady Mary to get Blake out of his house from eleven to one. Useful, that wire—very useful. It gave me a specimen of your writing, which came in very handy for my little note to Lady Mary."

"Well, you're damned well wrong there, Zavier. Standish wrote that wire, and signed it with my name."

"Dear me! You don't say so." He seemed genuinely upset. "You can't believe how I dislike anything that savours of a blunder. So that letter to Lady Mary was in Standish's writing. You surprise me. Why then did she go to Paris?"

"To try and run you to earth," said Tiny savagely. "She knew it was a trap..."

"And she deliberately walked into it," said the other with an amused smile. "Plucky, but foolish. And I fear rather useless. Well, what message shall I give Signor Berendosi from you? Strange, isn't it, what a lot of trouble has been caused by such a small thing as that."

With a mocking laugh he held up the negative, and Tiny looked at it moodily. Heavens! what a consummate fool he had been. Looking back now he marvelled how he could ever have believed the so-called clerk's story in Paris for a second. And yet, at the time, it had seemed to ring true. And then the next one about the accident.

"Cheer up, Mr. Carteret," cried Zavier. "Admittedly you haven't been very bright, but though I say it myself I am a little bit above your form. And you have had a charming trip to a very delightful part of the country. I shall be leaving you shortly, and I don't quite know when anyone will find your ... er ... body. You see this place has served its purpose. From information I have received Mr. Standish was not the only person who had located my little home as being in Switzerland. And even as near as that, my dear fellow, is too near for my liking. So you will soon have the place entirely to yourself."

"So you definitely mean to kill me," said Tiny quietly.

"For what other reason do you suppose I have gone to the trouble and worry of bringing you out here," answered Zavier. "Had I had the time I should have done it in London. But I didn't: things were getting a little too hot. So it became necessary to devise some other method, though I frankly admit I never dreamed it would come off quite so successfully as it has. Well, au revoir, Mr. Carteret. You made me run very fast at the Fifty-Nine Club, but I bear you no ill-will."

With a wave of the hand he passed through a door which up till then Tiny had not noticed. He left it ajar, and Tiny stared at the aperture fascinated. It commanded the whole of his half of the room, and it was through there, he felt certain, that death would come. But how: in what form?

Suddenly an overmastering rage gripped him: he would not be butchered like a rat in a trap. He went to the grille that blocked the door, and hauled on it with all his great strength. Useless: the thing was a fixture, and he cursed savagely. Then he pulled himself together: there was no good losing his head. Surely something could be done, but his only hope lay in keeping cool. His eyes fell on the table. It was a big one with a stout top. Supposing he was to use it as a shield. True—it wouldn't keep out a bullet, but if Zavier had intended to shoot him surely he would have done so already. He turned it on its end, and placed it so that it shielded him from the aperture. Then getting the chair he sat down and lit a cigarette. Now at any rate he only had one opening to watch—the door in his half of the room.

The minutes dragged on: the silence seemed to grow more intense. And after a time a very natural psychological reaction set in. He fought against it, but it became stronger and stronger till he knew that shortly he would be unable to resist it. What was happening on the other side of the table in that part of the room he could not see? The thought became a craving: he must know.

He stood up, and moved cautiously back from his shield, thereby bringing more of the room into view. But there was still a large area that was hidden: to see that he would have to put his head round the table. After all, if it had to come, it had to—and the sooner the better. He could not go on for the rest of time in his present position. And he had just made up his mind to chance it, when he heard a peculiar scratching noise. It came from the other half of the room, and for a moment or two he listened intently.

Suddenly there came a grating sound, such as the leg of a chair might make when moved slightly on a stone floor. And with a pricking in his scalp Tiny realized that the crisis was at hand. Somebody or something was in the room.

Cautiously he approached his table: to know what it was had now become an imperative necessity. He would thrust his head out quickly, and have a snap look. Then back again under cover to form his plan. He did so, only to remain staring at what he saw.

"Well, I'm damned," he remarked: then he began to laugh. Seated on the back of the chair with its head cocked on one side was a small monkey, solemnly waving a toy Swiss flag, and dressed in a tiny coat.

"You funny little beast," he said. "Where in blazes have you sprung from?"

Like most men of his type he adored animals, and the ridiculous aspect of the situation struck him. There had he been sheltering behind heavy barricades, and the foe turned out to be a diminutive grey monkey!

"Come on, you little blighter," he cried, holding out his hand, and suddenly it put the end of the flagpole in a pocket of the coat so that its hands were free, ran down the chair and came sidling across the floor towards him. It got through the grille with ease, chattering hard. And he was on the point of stroking it when there came a frenzied shout from behind him.

"Don't touch it. For God's sake—don't touch the monkey. Kick it away."

And the voice was the voice of Ronald Standish.

Startled—the monkey paused, and as if in a dream Tiny aimed a blow at it with his shoe. With a shrill squeak of anger it scuttled away, back through the grille, and still half dazed with the sudden development, Tiny saw that Zavier, his face suffused with rage, had returned. And then things happened quickly: so quickly that looking back on it later Tiny was hard put to it to remember their exact order. The monkey darted to Zavier, who had removed his monk's disguise, and swarmed up one of his legs. Then it seemed to wave the flag. And the next instant Zavier was staring at one of his hands, with terror in his eyes. On it was a long red scratch.

"Come home to roost at last, Zavier, has it?" came Ronald's quiet voice. "The reward is just."

Tiny forced himself to turn round. Standing in the doorway behind the grille, in the garb of a monk, was the man he had believed dead and buried.

And then from the other half of the room came a shout of maddened rage.

"Behind the table, Tiny," roared Standish, and with a splintering crash a bullet imbedded itself in the wood. Almost simultaneously came a crack from the door, and a howl of pain from Zavier, followed by the noise of his revolver falling on the stone floor.

"If you bend to pick it up, Zavier, I'll plug your other hand," said Ronald quietly.

"For God's sake do," cried the other hoarsely, "before the poison has time to work."

And Standish laughed grimly.

"As I said before—the reward is just," he said. "Ah! would you?"

The two cracks rang out almost as one and then Ronald Standish lowered his gun.

"You can come out, Tiny," he said quietly. "The swine has cheated us after all."

And Tiny, stepping out from behind the table, understood. The monkey was chattering angrily on the chair, and beside it lay stretched the body of her master, a smoking revolver still clutched in his hand. Zavier had blown out his brains.

CHAPTER XII

"Touch and go, old lad," said Standish gravely. "I can't think what maggot atrophied my brain."

"For the love of Pete, explain, Ronald," cried Tiny. "At the moment my own is in the same condition."

They were back in the hotel at Brigue, and on the table between them was the toy Swiss flag. At first sight it looked harmless enough and the sort of thing to be expected on a birthday cake or a Christmas tree. But a closer examination dispelled the illusion. The little pole was about the length of an ordinary pencil, and half the thickness. It was hollow and made of the finest steel, and a small chain with a little band on the end—a band that was fitted to the monkey's arm—ensured that it could never be left behind.

A special grip like a tiny trigger guard had been made for the monkey's paw an inch from the end, and this grip was connected by a microscopic bar passing up the centre of the tube to a little plunger, on exactly the same principle as a bicycle pump. A slot rather more than two inches long allowed the grip to slide forward that amount towards the sharp end, thereby ejecting any fluid on the other side of the plunger. And at the sharp end there stuck out for the sixteenth of an inch a needle point.

"Damned neat," said Standish, a note of genuine admiration in his voice. "Look how beautifully the thing is made. It is nothing more nor less than a perfectly disguised hypodermic syringe. Who would ever suspect a monkey waving a flag? You'd merely think it was an accidental scratch."

"He must have spent months training the little brute."

"Probably. Though those small ones pick up tricks very quickly."

"I wonder what the poison is," said Tiny.

"They'll find that out at home fast enough," answered the other. "Probably some native concoction, such as they use on their poisoned darts."

He replaced it on the table and picked up a metal bar some three feet long. One end was curved to make it look like a walking-stick, but there the resemblance ceased.

"Exhibit Number two for Gillson's museum. Pull on that end, Tiny."

The thing was telescopic, each new length fitting inside the previous one. Its full length when extended was five yards, and it formed a bar quite sufficiently rigid to bear the weight of a little monkey.

"To introduce the beast into a room he could not reach otherwise," said Standish. "Ingenious: very. But I ought to have spotted it, Tiny."

"I'm blowed if I see how," cried the other.

"Go back a bit, old boy. I admit we had nothing to go on over Jebson: nor did we have anything that helped us over Demeroff. It was when we came to Felton Blake—or rather Joe Denver—that we weren't as clever as we ought to have been. You see, I was right when I said that that was an accident, and that he had meant to get us. Well, having got as far as that I should have pursued it to the logical end. And I didn't. I actually said to you, if you remember, that he had set the scene in Blake's room, and I oughtn't to have been so dense. He merely left the monkey in the room pending our arrival."

"Awkward for Blake," said Tiny.

"Why? He had a perfect alibi with Lady Mary if things had worked out according to plan. It was leaving young Denver out of the calculations that upset the whole arrangement."

"I still don't see why you should have suspected the monkey."

"Perky is probably the finest pen-and-ink draughtsman alive to-day, but unfortunately for himself the medium he prefers is not acceptable to the powers that be. The police have a rooted objection to dud fivers, and as a matter of fact I didn't know Perky was out of prison till I saw him soaking you good and hearty in the bar."

"I thought the little swab was a bank clerk," laughed Tiny. "He told me he was."

"He looks rather like it, doesn't he? Well, clearly, the last round had begun. I didn't dare go into the bar myself—the place was so empty—but I'd made all the necessary arrangements. A man was outside the door to note any address you gave to a taxi driver: I was there in case you consulted the concierge. Which you did, and I must confess surprised me considerably. I had not expected Brigue to be your destination."

"But, good Lord!" cried Tiny, "you weren't that damned Frenchman with a beard, were you?"

"Guilty, old boy," laughed the other. "And your distaste for sharing a sleeper with me came as no surprise. However, if you were going to Brigue, obviously I'd have to go too. Whether they were going to try and do you in in the train, remained to be seen. Anyway I got into the next compartment."

"I know you did," said Tiny with a grin. "And to start with I thought you were Zavier himself."

"Now you've got to remember that I had no idea what particular yarn Perky had put across you," went on Standish. "But what I did know was that you were sitting in a position of considerable danger. So I went to ground in that hotel opposite and during the two hours you were here I had this veranda covered the whole time. Then the monk arrived, and with him came the first flood of light.

"I don't wonder you didn't spot it: you had no suspicion then of any trap. Whereas I knew the entire thing was a plant. I saw, at once, the significance of that heap of torn-up cloth we found at the Fifty-Nine, and the cord on the other side of the door. And so, later on, Zavier's remarks to you came as no surprise. Ingenious, you know, Tiny: he was perfectly right. It is the easiest of all disguises to assume and the least suspicious.

"You have probably guessed by now that it was I in the car following you, and so you have got most of the rest. As soon as you had gone into the so-called monastery I knocked in the same way, and though he was a bit suspicious at first he let me in. And then it was a question of move, and move quickly. I went for him, but before I outed him he gave tongue once."

"I heard him," said Tiny. "Just before the grille over the door shut."

"I put on his rig, and all through your interview with Zavier I was just outside in the passage. Perhaps it was an unfair risk to expose you to, but I was so desperately keen to find out his secret. Then he left, and you very wisely went to ground behind the table. Now from where I was I could watch the door by which he had left, and I saw that darned little monkey come in. And still my brain didn't click. Which is why I said, Tiny, it was touch and go. Gad! I'd never have forgiven myself if he had got you."

"What did make it click at the end?" said Tiny curiously.

"For some unaccountable reason there flashed through my mind the last word that man Demeroff had said in the sleeper. You remember you told me he called out what sounded like 'Bazana.' And it suddenly dawned on me. What he had really shouted was 'Obezïana,' which is the Russian for monkey. Whether in his half-drunken stupor he had seen the little brute come through the window at Laroche, or whether he knew Zavier's secret before, we shall never know. In view of his determination to have the window shut I should think the latter."

He got up and stretched himself, and a look of surprise dawned on his face.

"Bless my soul, if it isn't Lady Mary herself."

Tiny sprang to his feet.

"Where? It is, by Jove! Mary, dear," he called out, "what under the sun brings you here?"

She was in the street below, and turned at the sound of his voice.

"Tiny," she cried, "is it really you? My dear, I've been sick with anxiety. And Mr. Standish there too!"

"Oh! I'm not dead," he grinned. "Come right up and take a pew. We've been having a topping time."

She came up the steps towards them.

"You see, I went off with that woman to a house on the outskirts of Paris, where I had dinner. And after dinner she left me to go to the telephone. I waited and waited and she never returned, so after awhile I had a look round. My dear—the house was empty: there wasn't a soul in it. So I left, and met two men outside, who spoke to me. They were in the police, and I asked them what I should do. Their advice was to go back to Paris, and one of them got me a taxi. I drove straight to the Majestic, and found you'd come here. What was the idea?"

"To keep you out of the way, Lady Mary, sufficiently long to decoy Tiny here," said Standish. "Our friend the late Mr. Zavier was no slouch."

"Late?" She stared at him incredulously, and he nodded.

"He died unpleasantly a couple of hours ago, and left you this."

With a grave smile he produced the film from his pocket.

"I can't believe it," she said very low. "So we've won after all."

"Thanks entirely to you," he answered. "If you hadn't deliberately walked into the trap with your eyes open we shouldn't have this. What shall I do with it?"

"Burn it," she cried. "Burn the beastly thing at once."

In silence they watched it flare up and sizzle away: then Standish began to laugh.

"I've got an idea," he said. "It just breaks my heart to disappoint Berendosi. Supposing you two posed in a similar attitude, and we sent him the film of that."

"Men have died for less infamous suggestions," grinned Tiny. "However, we have no objection to you joining us at lunch provided you pay for it."

CPSIA information can be obtained
at www.ICGtesting.com
Printed in the USA
BVHW050930251122
652759BV00005B/128